REBEL'S CREED

Book 2

DANIEL B. GREENE

Edited by Adam Segaller & Sarah Hansen
Cover art by Felix Ortiz
Book design by Jay S. Kennedy

❧ I ❧
FALLOUT

PROLOGUE

Something tickled Khlid's left wrist. It was an odd sensation, one she had never felt before, like a deep itch. Groggy and wanting to remain asleep, Khlid tried to lift her right hand to scratch it. Yet something held her in place. Through blurry eyes she saw a leather strap pinning her arm down.

Her mind lurched at the realization.

Was something wrong? Was she in the hospital? A buzzing electric light above her made opening her eyes painful.

The city hospitals don't have electric lights.

Memories flashed through her: Gunfire. A figure in black. The horrid sound of Sam's flesh torn by a clawed hand. Something that had once been

Chapman standing over her. Running terrified in the rain. Captain Williams giving his life to protect her.

Sam. *Oh God, Sam!*

Pain swelled in her chest. Tears welled as a sob shook her. The emotion was too much. Khlid let out a wail, but the sound was muffled. Her lips refused to part, though a sharp sting pulsed through her mouth. She tried to raise a hand to feel what was wrong, but— the restraints.

Her eyesight clearing, Khlid looked down. She was sprawled naked on a cold metal table. Her left hand and right foot were gone. She stared at the empty space where they should have been. There was no pain, just an intense itch, burrowing into the empty space where her appendages had been.

Panic cut through her disorientation. She tried to scream again.

As the itch became a burn, Khlid focused on the stump where her hand should be. What looked like black slugs danced in a roiling mass, burrowing into — no, *out from*— her flesh. She watched in horror as a tiny maw ate its way into the light, ripping through desiccated skin. The slug wrenched itself from her body and plopped onto the metal surface, dancing spastically in the light, trying to inch its way into her shadow.

A muffled shriek was all she managed, tears

spilling from her eyes. She crushed it reflexively, smashing not only the creature on the table, but dozens more within her — they were now spilling from her amputation wounds in droves. The intense burning in her arm grew. Khlid smashed her arm down again and again, causing the vile liquid mixing with her blood to splash onto her face.

She felt the worms in her entire body now; not just her arm. Within her legs, chest, groin, she could feel them crawling; even behind her eyes.

Her thrashing seemed to awaken the creatures within her. They moved with greater intensity. A crescendo building within her.

Trying to scream, Khlid finally registered the pain in her lips. Her mouth was sewn shut. The taste of fresh blood played on her tongue.

A tickling inside her ear nearly drove her mad. As fear consumed her last shred of rationality, Khlid managed to scream, partially tearing her lips on the cruel metal wire that bound them.

The squeal of a door opening barely registered to her ears.

"Hush." The voice came closer. "Take a deep breath, Inspector."

That voice seared into Khlid's soul. It was the voice of the monster. The Anointed hunter who had killed Sam.

Still convulsing on the table, Khlid attempted to control her thrashing. She wanted to beg; to grovel; to promise whatever the woman wanted. Anything to end the boiling agony under her skin.

"Inspec— no, that no longer applies. Khlid." The voice's owner emerged from the shadows: Gray eyes set in a pale angular face; a braid of midnight black hair. "You should be proud. You're our first true success."

Khlid kicked against the restraints with new purpose.

I will kill you. I will rip your fucking heart out.

"You've taken to the Drip beautifully, my love." The Anointed walked to the table, unfazed by her prisoner's attempts at violence, and rested a hand on her forehead. Her voice sank into Khlid's ear like a seducing knife: "You're transcending so remarkably well."

Khlid arched her back, lifting herself as far off the table as she could, and spat blood at her tormentor through partially torn stitches. Most of it dribbled pathetically to her chin.

The Anointed's face twisted in revulsion at the sight, but a grin quickly slid back into place. "You do have a lot of fight in you, Whitter. Unlike your husband."

Khlid wasn't sure if it was blood loss or something worse, but her body was trying to return to the void. The world swayed nauseatingly around her.

The squeal of a heavy door filled the room once again."Ah, yes. I brought you a present."

Khlid's vision began to blur. Exhaustion tried to drag her mind under.

A hand roughly grabbed her chin. The Anointed made her meet her eyes. "Not yet, Whitter. I have something to show you."

I will kill you. I will make you hurt.

The thought was fleeting —her last attempt at holding oblivion at bay with rage.

She faintly heard the sound of a metal chest being opened.

"You will want to say your goodbyes, I believe. You certainly were rushed last night."

The rough hand turned Khlid's head to one side. Her eyes focused on a new blur. Before her, Samuel's severed head hung from the Chosen's grip.

Khlid broke through the stitches as she screamed.

A TALL TALE

"That's not true!" Holden's eyes darted from one cold face to another, but neither Minister sitting across the table reacted. "Sam and Khlid are both utterly loyal! They—" He glanced at the reports splayed on the table. "They aren't...."

The gaunt Minister sitting to Holden's left leaned forward, placing his elbows on the table. "Mr. Sanders—"

"It's Officer," Holden cut him off. His emotions were nearing something akin to panic.

"My apologies," he replied in a faux-soothing voice, the tone you took with a petulant child. It singed Holden's nerves. "We have absolute proof of the fact. Your mentors were traitors. The M.O.T. has produced several in-depth reports on the Seventh's unfortunate demise. You are welcome to—"

"Shut the fuck up. Just shut up." Holden leaned forward, hands gripping the end of the table. He stared past the Ministers at the wall, trying to process the situation. "Oh, god."

Khlid is dead. Samuel is dead. Smits is dead. Chapman...

The taller Minister on the right spoke for the first time. "You and two other officers who were in hospital at the time are all that remain."

"How?" Holden barked.

"'How?'" The gaunt man repeated.

"How could the entirety of the Seventh be drawn into a trap? Half of us wouldn't even be on duty— it doesn't make— Sam and Khlid wouldn't set them up. They are loyalists! They love us as family. Chapman was a cunt, but— it's impossible!" Holden realized too late he was yelling. His heart raced in his chest and tears began to appear in his eyes. "I need a glass of water."

The Minister to the left raised a cautious hand. "Officer, we understand you were close—"

"What of the Captain?"

The dark, long-haired Minister on the right proclaimed, "He was killed as well."

A sharp pain gripped Holden's chest. His chair

clattered to the floor behind him as he stood, pressing shaking hands to his forehead. Wet stains streaked his cheeks. "I can't— no. No. Stop, please stop."

The taller Minister stood and moved towards Holden. To comfort or restrain, Holden did not wait to see. He shoved past the smaller man to the door. It rattled as Holden tried to force it open.

"Let me out!" He punched the door. "I need air. Let me out!"

"Officer—"

Blood pumped in his ears. Tears came so quickly, they obscured his vision.

This can't be true. Sam wouldn't. Khlid loved the Captain. Chapman— it must have been Chapman. It had to be him. I'll make him pay!

A logical part of him knew this was impossible. That Chapman was said to be already dead.

A hand firmly clasped Holden's shoulder.

Both Ministers now flanked him, as if approaching a dangerous animal. Big as he was, Holden was used to that, but this was different. Anger and grief roiled in him. Instinctively, his hand went to the empty holster at his hip.

The Ministers noted the gesture.

Holden wanted violence. He wanted to hurt them for what they had told him. Standing over two meters tall, he knew he could break them.

Holden's fist clenched.

"Take a breath, Inspector." The treacle voice suffocated Holden's panic like black honey.

Suddenly, the Ministers both dropped to one knee. Holden turned at the sound of the opening door.

Beautiful gray eyes met his own. He could not look away from the woman's face.

"Leave us." The woman pushed past Holden as the Ministers, gazes averted, took their leave. The large one spared Holden a pitying look as he went

Holden's mind felt both frozen and in revolt. Everything was surreal.

Am I dreaming?

The door closed. The gray-eyed woman sat at the metal table and gestured for Holden to do the same.

He did not move. "Who are you?"

"I am the one who failed you and your precinct. I've come to apologize to you, Mr. Sanders. Please sit." She did not sound angry or impatient, but something told Holden that was an order. Her delicate voice was somehow firmer than seemed possible.

Keeping his back to the wall, Holden picked up the chair he had vacated and sat. With a congested sniff, he wiped tears from his cheeks. He tried to slow his heart rate, but a pulse of pain caused him to sob.

For several beats, they sat in silence. The woman looked him over, judging far more than his physical appearance. It felt as if his soul was being measured for a uniform.

Holden didn't dare look at her with the same frankness, but he did take in her appearance, trying to force his mind off what he had been told. Her face was, in spite of its air of absolute authority, gorgeous; every angle sharp yet delicate. Her black hair was tied tight into a braid that lay flat over her shoulder; she was not only beautiful but carried herself with an aura of great physical power. Every movement was certain.

Her appearance notwithstanding, something about her put his hackles up. He felt in danger. Funny enough, it provided some relief from the other emotions he was fighting to suppress. Holden did tend to find attractive anyone who carried themself with authority; but her mesmerizing quality was something more: He was afraid of her.

His eyes finally took in the symbol of a golden hand clutching a crescent moon upon her robes.

"Oh— you—" Holden sat back in his chair so abruptly the front legs lifted. He overcorrected, causing the chair to loudly groan under his weight. "Anointed."

A grin flicked across her lips. "Most bow when

they notice. Though, I think I prefer your reaction."

"What—"

She cut him off. "I failed you, Inspector Sanders. I failed your whole precinct."

Holden blinked, breaking from a trance. Grief returned in a painful torrent.

"I tried, Inspector," she continued. "Believe me, I tried. As soon as word of what your Captain was doing reached the M.O.D., I ran. I ran to that fucking warehouse. I spent the whole night looking for those responsible, but the rain, it—" the Anointed stopped. She took a breath, suddenly appearing much older. "I failed you. I failed the city."

He felt a surprising emotion: empathy for this demigod.

How can she look so uncertain?

Holden struggled to keep his composure. "Please tell me what happened. I can't read some report. I need to hear it."

She met his gaze. "That night, a messenger from the Seventh came to the M.O.D. He told us you were being sent out to catch the Rebels, who were attempting to destroy evidence."

"Destroy evidence?" Holden blinked at the Anointed. He tried to will his mind to calm and consider what he was being told. It was something Inspectors were trained to do. He had never been as good at it as Sam or Khlid, but Almighty damn it, he would think this through. "Why would the entire precinct be put on such a task? You dump it in the river and move on."

"Not this evidence." She gestured to the papers on the table. Her other hand played with the end of her braid. "They wanted to catch the Rebels. Something has been left off of the official report."

Holden leaned forward. His voice was dry, an angry, smoldering whisper. "What happened to my people?"

The Anointed took another long breath and gave him another calculated look. "The Rebels are developing something. A disease, it seems."

"You can't manufacture a disease." The words felt stupid as they left his mouth. He sat across from a woman who could survive a bullet to the head. By comparison, creating a disease was well within the realm of possibility.

"We thought so too, but what we have found..." She trailed off, as if shaking some disturbing memory. "It was used on the Pruit family."

What under the two moons could rattle her?

"The royals who were killed?" His mind raced, trying to put together a puzzle before he had all the pieces.

"Exactly. Inspector Sanders, that family was

used as test subjects. Chapman, he seems to have been the main responsible party. Apparently there was an altercation between him and Inspector Khlid just prior."

"I knew it." Holden shook from relief; his knees nearly buckled. "Listen, Khlid and Sam, they can't have done this. They're good people."

New tears sprang to his eyes. Holden was worried his excited tone would offend the Anointed, but she just leaned forward. "I don't know why, but I believe you"

The affirming words simultaneously hurt and brought joy.

I can clear their names.

Holden sat back down. "Chapman, he never sat right with me— with anyone. He was always on the outside."

Doubt slipped into the Anointed's eyes. "How could he have convinced the precinct to go with him, Holden? Your Captain was no idiot. I met him. A good man."

"A great one." Holden felt a desperate desire to destroy that sliver of doubt polluting her face. "Chapman could have manipulated Khlid or Sam. He was good at that— getting in people's heads, I mean. I've seen him crack hardened murderers like they were children."

The Anointed leaned back in her chair, considering Holden's words. She crossed her legs and flipped her braid over her left shoulder.

Holden couldn't help but notice how well her uniform conformed to her muscular body. Even her short-cut coat flowed well with her figure. He swallowed.

My friends are dead and I'm giving a demigod the eye. What is wrong with me?

"Inspector—"

"I am not an Inspector, ma'am." His throat caught at the audacity to interrupt her, but she just looked bemused.

"No?"

"In training to become one. Under Inspector Samuel. It's just 'Officer'."

She smiled prettily. "I appreciate your honesty, but I believe the label will apply nicely soon enough."

"Thank you, ma'am."

"Well, what I was going to say was that this is not your concern any more."

"No, listen, I knew—" Holden's voice seized as she raised her hand.

"No?" A tension filled the room. In a heartbeat, the Anointed's demeanor changed in some imperceptible way. Holden felt like a squirrel under the paw of a hound. He was not sitting across from a woman, but a predator; and he lived by her grace.

"I am sorry, ma'am." Holden was desperate to get her back on his side. If he came across as rational, maybe she would believe him. As she pursued those responsible, she would know the truth.

"Officer Sanders, you have been given great leeway today in light of the shock you are undoubtedly in." She lowered her hand "but do not overestimate my leniency."

"Of course, ma'am. Please just—"

"This is a matter of Imperial security. You shall obey my words as if they came from the Almighty itself. You are to refrain from any further inquiry into this matter. Am I clear?"

"Yes, but—"

"Good." The Anointed stood and paced the room once before slumping her shoulders and leaning against the far wall. "You've done nothing wrong, Holden. I'm sorry for your loss."

"Ma'am, please—"

"Avi."

"I'm sorry?"

"My name is Avi Cormick. You may use it if you please." It was a gesture of kindness, intended to smooth over her reprimand.

Holden tried, but saying an Anointed's name to

her face seemed wrong. Instead he just said, "Thank you, but please, I want to know more. If I do, I can offer insights. I know I can. I know the Seventh."

She gave a sigh and took her seat again. "As I said, a messenger from the seventh came and warned us. Your Captain sent hell and fury to meet the rebels. It was a trap. Who laid it, we don't know. I ran in the rain as fast as I could, but by the time I got there... Holden, I don't think you need the details."

Her voice shook with emotion. A memory danced across her face.

Holden looked away, feeling the loss all over again. His family had been butchered.

"It was a massacre. The mutilated dead were sprawled throughout the warehouse. There weren't even any Rebels left when I got there. A squad of the Red Hand arrived as backup, but all they could do was help carry the bodies. We sent a few soldiers to check on the precinct itself. That's when we received reports of fires. One at the Seventh, and one at a brothel nearby.

"B—Brothel?" Holden stumbled on the word.

"It's possible a rebel was seen, or..." She paused. "No. We don't know why. But it was burnt down by the rebellion with everyone trapped inside. Those monsters, they barricaded the doors."

Holden's stomach heaved at the thought. Dozens trapped inside, burning.

Anything to cover their tracks. The unholy bastards.

She continued: "We were just getting the fires under control when the first reports of off-duty officers being attacked in their homes came in. I had to return to the M.O.D., just to get addresses, but by then—"

Holden watched tears form in the Anointed's eye.

"I found families massacred. Children."

For the first time in his life, Holden realized how much pressure the Anointed must experience. Blessed beings chosen by the Almighty, yet still human. Something he had forgotten. "Ms. Cormick, I'm sorry."

Another tear rolled down Avi's face.

Holden did something he would have never thought possible. He leaned across the table and touched her hand.

A shocked look crossed her face.

Hardening against his own grief, Holden met her eyes. "You didn't fail. There is no one to blame but the rebels."

Avi wiped the wetness from her face. "It is my job to keep this city safe. In that, I have certainly failed."

Holden sat back in his chair and wondered for the first time what his future held. He guessed he would be transferred to another precinct while the Seventh was rebuilt.

"But thank you, Inspector Sanders." Avi cleared her throat and stood. "Of course, my presence in the city is to remain a secret. Your discretion will be appreciated. The Empire owes you for our failure. We will not forget."

"Wait." Something tickled Holden's mind. "Samuel and Khlid, why did you assume they were Rebels? They were killed too, but by who? Before you arrived? They must've been. Otherwise they would have been taken into custody, right? You would have wanted them alive."

The Anointed's eyes drifted, her mind going back to whatever had happened that night.

A chill ran down Holden's spine.

Her eyes snapped back to his. "Read the report, Officer Sanders. Feel free to send an inquiry to the M.O.T. if you wish to receive any clarifications on their findings."

As he was left alone to await whatever fate the Empire would give him, Holden thought over every word Avi Cormick, the Anointed, had said to him.

A MEETING IN NATURE

4 MONTHS BEFORE THE SEVENTH'S DEMISE

The forest made Chapman uneasy. Standing in the clearing provided some distance from looming foliage, but it introduced the feeling of being watched. He had been raised in cities. In the last decade, he had only really taken day trips from the massive Capital City, and always in a carriage. The idea of being so alone, surrounded by the wilds, felt dangerous, no matter how fervently the Empire claimed the forests had been hunted to the point that any threat was extinct.

These shadows used to hold six legged

beasts with eyes of fire. Serpents large enough to swallow a man whole. Flesh walkers who would take the form of those they encountered before—

Chapman halted his racing mind.

The night sky turned his discomfort into downright fear.

Both moons were new, an event that occurred only twice a year. The stars shone brightly, yet struggled to puncture the canopy above him.

Canopy is the word, right?

A snapping branch caused Chapman to whirl, drawing his pistol. He aimed at... nothing. Something small chattered, running deeper into the darkness.

Chapman holstered his pistol and let out a sigh. "Man was meant for cities."

His breath caught as cold metal touched the back of his neck.

"I would have to disagree. Knees, Inspector." The voice was cold and feminine.

Chapman's hand tensed, still resting on his sidearm. "Nature enthusiast?"

The sound of a pistol's hammer being pulled back was deafening.

"I won't ask again." The voice was firmer, but tinged with mirth.

Chapman dropped to his knees, placing his hands on his head.

A boot crashed into his spine. The force with which his face met dirt caused instant delirium. A sack was forced over his eyes. The unseen assailant's hands disarmed him of his pistol and began patting him down. Next, the sound of several sets of boots confirmed that surrender was the right move.

As a pair of hands lifted him back up to his feet, Chapman said, "Your invitation was a touch warmer than this."

That invitation had been delivered by a smooth woman who had approached him at his favorite tavern three nights prior. Chapman had thrown an uncertain greeting her way, but she had only smiled while tapping out a message on her mug in his people's silent language.

The invitation had consisted only of a date, time, coordinates, and the word "alone", but implied much more. Clearly, the Rebels had not only taken note of his off-duty proclivities, but had taken the time to delve into his past. How else could they know that Chapman was a descendant of the Islands of Yu'ib, and that he cared enough about that heritage to learn a dead form of communication? How else could they know that above all, he fervently desired to walk the dark shadows along with the rebellion?

"He's disarmed. No hidden nasties," a male voice snarled.

The bag was pulled from Chapman's head. A woman stood before him. She was stocky, her skin slightly lighter than his, and wore a parade mask covering all but her eyes and ears.

He could not tell how many remained behind him. It seemed like a bad idea to turn around and check.

The masked woman squatted in front of him and wiped a spot of dirt from his cheek. "Keep those hands on your head, Officer. The woods spook us as well. Almost as much as an Inspector nipping at our heels."

"I gather you don't spend too much time out here." Chapman would have laid odds that a frown blossomed underneath the mask at his accurate guess. He always had a knack for observing in others what they thought they kept hidden.

She stood and took a step back. Chapman took in her short green coat and plain trousers. Suitable attire for someone who did not want to be noticed, either in the city or out here.

"For nearly a year, as best we can tell, you've been dogging us. Why?" she asked.

Chapman met her eyes. "Hmm, Now why would someone try to contact the most wanted organization in the entire Empire? That's a stumper right there."

She met his eyes unblinkingly. "You go from cute to bothersome quickly."

"Fine," Chapman relented. "The Empire is built on corpses. Nations have burned." He risked turning his head now, and saw five more Rebels standing behind him with rifles aimed.

"Gods, you speak like a first year academic." The woman lay a finger on Chapman's chin, turning his gaze back to meet her own. "Tell us something any school child doesn't know."

Chapman hesitated for a single heartbeat before voicing what he had felt for years. "And it's all a lie. A doctrine of spiritual supremacy, based on—" he swallowed hard before continuing. He knew it to be true, but it felt no less sacrilegious to utter. "On a deity that does not exist. The Almighty isn't real, isn't a true god." He tried to peer through the woman's mask. He certainly couldn't read her reaction now. He felt compelled to continue in the silence that greeted him: "We've had our heritage stripped from us. Our futures dictated by a malicious myth."

The woman's reaction surprised Chapman. She let out a long breath, stood up straight, taking on a more casual demeanor. Pulling off her mask, she waved to those gathered behind Chapman.

With a sixth sense borne of years of Inspector training, Chapman felt the rifles being aimed away.

She was of the Ruzzai people of the North. The gold-tinted skin, dark curls, and wide brown eyes gave it away.

Her hood dropped next, allowing the moonlight to halo those dark curls. Gold twine had been braided and spun throughout it.

Yup, Ruzzai. And proud of it.

Chapman asked, "May I stand?"

"Yes, Chapman." She offered him a hand. "You've been fascinating to watch."

"I'm sure." He took the hand and rose to his feet. "I'm a blast to stalk. Everybody says so."

He had expected a well-trained, well-equipped, well-organized resistance laboriously working to undermine the Empire at every turn, but those before him fell far short. A disorganized mass of a dozen bodies stared back at him.

This is what strikes fear in the heart of the empire?

"Can't say you people live up to your reputation." Chapman turned back to judge the woman's response. "Years-old guns; commoners' clothing. You've extended a hand to me because—"

To his surprise, she was grinning broadly.

His brow furrowed. "What?"

Chapman's legs were suddenly not underneath him. He was being pulled to the tree line faster than he could have sprinted, slicing through cold mud. His left elbow painfully smashed into a rock. A taste of metal on his lips.

The dark forest loomed. Some massive creature stood tall, its eyes glowing as he sped inexorably toward it.

"No, n—"

Chapman rolled onto his belly and tried to grab onto grass, rocks, roots, anything. Anything to halt his scudding progress toward whatever that was awaiting him in the tree line. He was being pulled so fast, the skin tore from his hands where he tried to grab hold.

Suddenly, his legs were free, and he descended to the muck with a *whomp.* "Gah!" was all the cursing he could manage. He lay bruised and bleeding at the margin of the treeline. Looking into the darkness, closer now, Chapman could see the monster was a man in armor.

The man emerged from the shadows. His glowing green eyes dulled slightly within the square helmet as he released the Grohalind. He was well over seven feet tall. Even under the thick-plated silver and green Grip armor, Chapman could tell this was a wizard — one made of dense muscle, at that.

Chapman was a powerful man, but this armored behemoth could pull his arm off if he chose to.

"I'm sorry to disappoint, Inspector." The Grip's voice was gravel falling into a deep cave. "But we survive by not being very impressive."

Another gigantic Grip moved in from the tree line, bearing the same smooth, jointed head-to-toe armor and glowing green eyes. To Chapman, the extent to which he was now outnumbered and over-powered was almost comical.

Chapman looked back to the woman in the clearing. Her grin had only grown.

"Have you figured it out, Inspector?" she called.

The first Grip didn't bother with Chapman's hand, lifting him to his feet by the collar like an unruly puppy.

The Grip loomed over him. "We wouldn't have made contact if we weren't certain, Inspector. Call me Crom."

"Well Crom, what made you certain I could be trusted?" Chapman refused to let his voice tremble.

Crom gestured back to the Ruzzai woman. "Ask Pirka."

A rough hand pushed Chapman toward the clearing, nearly toppling him again.

"Okay", Chapman called loud enough for Pirka to hear. "What made you trust me?"

A look of regret replaced the smile on Pirka's face. "I wish I could say I saw you commit blatant treason. But I suppose it's good you're not that sloppy."

Chapman nodded in agreement. Flouting the M.O.D. was a good way to die fast.

"It was the small moments, Chapman. Drinking morosely after handing suspects over to the M.O.D. Turning your back on Imperials when you thought they weren't looking. Your cover is quite good, being a colossal asshole. But we know disillusionment when we see it." Pirka extended Chapman's pistol back to him. "Reading people is my specialty."

"So the Rebels are dependent on your judge of character?"

"I'm never wrong." There was a certainty to her voice that Chapman was tempted to believe.

"Well, then." Shaking off the last of his disorientation, Chapman noted there were now at least two dozen people around him. Most had removed their masks, though not the Grips. "What does the Rebellion need me to do?"

"Most likely?" Pirka gestured for him to follow her into the woods. "Die."

�֍ 3 ✣

BONDING

3 MONTHS BEFORE

Chapman had assumed that a night of walking in the forest, telling Pirka his life story, darkest secrets and all, would earn him a reciprocal level of access. But that had been stupid in hindsight. The Rebels made a show of revealing much, but gave him very little. He knew now they counted some Grips among their ranks, but how many? Their presence had only been to impress him —which it had— but was this the full contingent, or a fraction of it? Pirka could be their leader, or a foot soldier. They could number hundreds, or thousands. Or he might have just met the entire fighting force. He had no clue.

He had let his guard down amidst their parlor tricks all too eagerly.

Clever bastards.

The night air, bordering on frigid, did not make him more impatient. He would not allow it to. He was a man of discipline.

Now Chapman stood in a city alley in his civilian clothes, hoping he wasn't about to be subjected to another test. Like the last three times. He was far from trusted.

Last week, Chapman had paid a prostitute to dress as a noble and "escorted" her to a location of the Rebels' choosing. There, a dozen of them awaited him. An utterly pointless errand, designed to see whether he would follow orders. When he did, all the thanks he received was congratulations on not needing to be killed on the spot.

To add insult to injury, he came home one day to find his house had been searched. Had his Inspector's eye not clocked the slight displacement of his few possessions, he might not have noticed. He hadn't felt violated by it, only frustrated that the testing period was apparently not yet over.

He felt no anger toward their scrutiny. But he

was eager to begin working against the Empire in earnest.

No, not just eager. He needed to.

Pinpointing when exactly he had lost faith in the Empire was impossible. He had always figured traitors experienced some monumental, defining event. For him, it had simply been a series of quiet, contemplative moments. A processing of events on long walks or alone in a bar.

When he was younger, he believed in the cause. He may have never entirely believed in the Almighty, but the advantages of Imperial life seemed obvious. Cleaner cities, free church-run education, and holy medicine. Chapman was slightly too young to have served in the wars of two decades prior; without realizing it, he had noted that veterans of the battlefield always seemed to be the most zealous Imperials. He understood this, without ever having felt it himself.

Oh, how disappointed his mother and father would have been to see their son wear an imperial uniform.

But he saw clearly now.

I never took anything on faith. Now, the plain truth has appeared. The Almighty's direction was bringing humanity into a uniform direction, eliminating the possibility of failure.

"Are you ready?"

The voice from the sewer at his feet caused him to jump.

"Gods!" he demanded. "Why do you people do that? Is it funny to you?"

"Honestly?" It was Pirka. This was the first time he had seen her since the night in the forest. "Yeah. Now get in."

"The sewer?"

"Yup."

Chapman looked to the mouth of the alley. A drunk bystander, his back to him, helpfully blocked any prying eyes.

Letting out a sigh, Chapman slipped into the gutter.

Placing his feet to avoid stepping in the stream of street filth, Chapman looked to Pirka and said, "Do you also find it funny to make me do laundry?"

"Perhaps." The same toothy grin that had so galled him on the night they met spread across her face. "C'mon, we only have a couple of hours."

Giving up on dodging the sludge, Chapman followed Pirka deeper into the dark stench. "Until what?"

Pirka turned her head to look at him with mock concern. "Inspector, you have work in the morning. You need to get some decent sleep."

Chapman ruefully returned her smile. "Fine, be that way."

Arriving at a sewer intersection, Chapman marveled at the architecture. Over a dozen perfectly round tunnels large enough to stand in emptied slow trickles of vile fluid into a large black pool. A slow current pulled the city's liquid waste downstream to the river. While Chapman hated the Imperials, one couldn't fault their engineering.

"This way, Inspector." Pirka gestured to a small door at the far end of the pool. If she hadn't pointed it out, Chapman doubted he would have noticed it.

They both entered a small storage room, furnished with a table and a single candle. Two masked figures stood across the table from Pirka and Chapman.

Approaching, Chapman noted Pirka stayed on the same side as himself.

I'm not that easy.

Still, he appreciated the gesture in a way.

The silence lasted too long for his taste. "Interesting taste in decor."

One of the masked figures let out a bark of laughter. "You *did* earn your reputation." She said, "We have a job for you, Inspector."

"Shall I walk a prostitute to a bath house this time? Maybe a theater?" Chapman retorted.

The man on the left responded. "Inspector, this isn't some child's—"

"I know." He interrupted. "It's how I deal with tension. Relax."

The two figures exchanged looks with Pirka.

"Fine," the masked woman said. "You are to kill a man in three weeks time."

Chapman blinked. Silence seemed to be the safest response.

The man picked up, "He will be carrying a brief-case we need. You will take him off the street, as well as whomever he is with, and bring the case to us."

"What's in the case?" Chapman asked.

Silence.

"Of course," Chapman said drolly.

Pirka scoffed. "Chapman will end this man's life. He deserves to know."

Both figures glared at Pirka through their masks. Chapman wondered in passing whether this was all a performance for his benefit.

"Very well." The man looked back at Chapman. "Notes on a nightmare. The M.O.D. is..." The man took a deep breath. "The Empire is changing people. We've found corpses, twisted and disfigured. Something horrible altering..." He struggled for words. "Whatever these *changes* mean. We think they are preparing to use it. As a weapon, or to send a message. We've intercepted enough to be sure—"

"Listening to you struggle to tell me nothing is painful." Chapman made an effort to suppress his annoyance. "Why now?"

Looking to Pirka, the masked woman said, "To put the royal class in line. Their recent ventures into expanding their influence and power have not gone unnoticed by the Ministries. We've even had reports of them trying to pay off precinct captains to gain loyalty."

Chapman looked at Pirka now, too. The stout woman's face showed additional lines in the candle-light. She hadn't been sleeping well. Her coloring seemed off.

She met his eyes. "The Empire is still new, Inspector. The great wars ended less than two decades ago. Power struggles are the natural order."

"Oh, the sky's blue, you say?" he cut in.

She sighed, "Even when serving what they think is a god, people are greedy. Recklessly pursuing another crumb on the plate of power. Another atrocity is another opportunity. Maybe some of them up there care— maybe, but not enough to do anything. We want people to see what the Empire is doing. These people aren't being smote by the

Almighty in some great divine judgement. They've been poisoned, murdered."

Chapman had missed something in his initial assessment of Pirka. Even though she had struck him from behind at their first meeting, she had a pleasant, unassuming energy. Now he saw that was a part of her danger. If he looked deep enough into those eyes, he saw a mind like a dagger.

Over the next hour, Chapman was given all the information he could possibly want going into a mission like this. The researcher, his target, was described in detail, from his physical appearance right down to his smoking habits. If that weren't enough, Chapman would receive a clear signal when it was time to intercept him leaving an apothecary shop. The Rebellion was certainly meticulous. When the two masked figures began describing the various coats the researcher might be wearing, he failed to suppress a smirk.

They catalogued his wardrobe.

He tried not to think of how well they had probably catalogued his own life. Then again, it wouldn't have been hard to do.

"And one final thing," the masked woman said.

Chapman stopped massaging his drooping eyelids. "Promise?"

She no longer found his attitude amusing. "He has a family."

The masked man tensed at the words.

"I wouldn't feel right sending you to do this without telling you that."

Chapman wasn't sure he appreciated the honesty. Almighty's Hell, he wasn't even sure if this was all just the latest, most elaborate test. His frustration began to bubble over. He was done with their theatrics.

"Where are you going?" Pirka asked as he headed for the door.

"You said, 'One last thing.' We're done here. I know my way out."

Pirka opened her mouth to protest, but seemed to think better of it. Chapman thought even her small gesture of protest smacked of manipulation.

"Oh, and all of this?" Chapman gestured to the room around them. "Childish. Send me a letter next time; I'll burn it, for fuck's sake. Hell of a lot subtler than climbing into a sewer. We're in a city of eager witnesses, as if you needed to be told. You think people don't tattle about every oddity they see in their neighborhood? Eyes are everywhere. It gets back to the Officers of God."

He grabbed the door handle and yanked it open,

calling over his shoulder: "I could teach you how to *actually* be covert, but you seem to prefer—"

The words died on Chapman's tongue. Two Grips stood on either side of the door, looking down at him. The massive men wore no armor, but carried rifles, which looked puny in their immense hands.

Crom offered an apologetic smile. "Orders Chapman. Incase, ya know?"

They had been prepared to murder him if something went wrong. If he gave any indication of turning on them, their Grips, feared on battlefields across the continent, had been on standby to tear him to pieces.

At least I don't taste any metal.

"Sorry, Chapman," Pirka said walking up next to him. "There is a reason for everything. When fighting against a god, even a false one, every precaution must be taken. Let me take you for a drink."

Chapman left the sewer feeling hollow, yet his heart remained calm. His hands were dry. Chapman just wished he couldn't feel his father's disapproving gaze on his back.

What would he think of me, if he were still alive? His only son has agreed to murder a stranger — for these people?

🌸 4 🌸

ASSASSINATION

9 WEEKS BEFORE

The Ministry of Science researcher left the apothecary, and Chapman followed.

The agreed signal —a dropped kerchief from a watcher up high— had been unmistakable; yet, he still found himself verifying all the details. He wanted to be absolutely sure. This felt wrong. Killing while being fired upon was one thing — it had been self preservation. Assassination was quite another.

The address was correct; a tucked-away apothecary specializing in rare and hard-to-find ingredients. The man's stride was short and meek, matching the description Chapman had been given. About a minute into his walk, he lit a cigarette with a lighter from his breast pocket, just as Chapman had been told he had a habit of doing.

C'mon, man. Give me a sliver of an excuse here.

Each corroborating detail made him feel cold. A slight drizzle allowed Chapman to pull up his hood without arousing suspicion. Something so mundane on a regular day now felt somehow malicious. And indeed it was: a precaution en route to a murder in cold blood.

There was a bodyguard with the scientist, but he hardly seemed to be paying much attention. Even the best-trained soldiers could become complacent walking a mundane beat. It couldn't be much of an adrenaline rush escorting a scientist to and from a niche druggist.

It was shocking the lengths to which the M.O.D. had gone to hide their development of this twisted experiment. Sending a researcher into the field meant the quality of the ingredients mattered. It probably also meant they didn't trust their regular suppliers not to leak the details of... whatever it was they were amassing.

Trouble in cult paradise.

Tailing the two for a few blocks, it became clear they would head to the southernmost bridge of the

Merchant District. It was late evening, a quiet time in the area when most were already home from their commute. Even if witnesses saw Chapman murder the two, this wasn't the kind of neighborhood where policemen were eagerly summoned. So long as he hid the bodies well, the deaths would likely be discovered only after the M.O.D. summoned a search party.

It wasn't as rough as the Lower Districts, the area from which the Empire appeared to be harvesting victims; but the proximity to those neighborhoods comforted Chapman. In this locale, he was fairly likely to get away with murder.

Bleak thought there.

Taking a turn into a side street, Chapman decided to cut ahead of the two. Jogging through alleys, he reached the bridge as the last remnants of sunlight left the sky. Checking both directions, he verified he had beaten the men there. Then, he started humming loudly.

Swaying like a drunk, he stumbled out of the garbage-littered alley. Putting on a heck of a show, Chapman flopped onto the railing of the bridge and let out a loud groan.

I am either doing very well, or terribly.

He truly wasn't sure. Police officers weren't taught how to pull off assassinations, but it seemed like a decent front. His thought was that bystanders would steer clear of a belligerent, or unconscious, souse.

He lay there for several moments. His heart pounded in his ears as he stared into the black water a few meters below. It was so smooth, the first stars appearing in the sky sparkled back up at him. Only the slightest current, pulling along the leaves from the higher districts, caused any disturbance.

A pink flower caught his eye as it gently rolled off the stone support of the bridge and continued its journey downstream.

His left ribs began to protest his awkward position against the railing. This started to feel like an extremely dumb idea. At least his coat, hanging about his semi-prostrate form, would allow him to grasp his knife unseen. Otherwise, he felt completely vulnerable.

Footsteps caused a jolt of adrenaline in Chapman. He turned subtly to his side, affording himself the slightest view of whomever approached.

The researcher came onto the bridge, the bodyguard just behind. He seemed to be eyeing Chapman. The scientist was inspecting a yellow vial, likely part of his purchase from the apothecary.

Chapman's stomach sank. Pirka had told him the

researcher would be young, but his chubby face seemed downright adolescent.

You're going to kill a man —a boy— *who has seen all of twenty summers.*

The cold grip of his knife caused Chapman to shudder. This felt so wrong.

He steeled his nerves. No hesitation could be allowed. He slowed his mind. He was disturbed to discover how good he had gotten at suppressing his panic response.

Inhale... exhale.

Their footsteps grew louder as they neared.

Chapman exploded into action.

The bodyguard let out a cry of surprise as Chapman's body slammed into his. He tried to draw a pistol, but Chapman wrenched the man's wrist, the weapon spinning off into the water below.

Chapman's knife entered the guard's neck, and he ripped it free in one unforgiving pull. A guttural, gurgling sound overcame the guard's attempt to scream. Visible tendons and ligaments were flooded with spurting blood.

Chapman's five senses seemed to have tripled in potency. The splash of the distant pistol hitting water reached his ear.

With a swift kick, Chapman sent the man still clawing at his neck into the river below.

What, to Chapman, had felt like long minutes of combat had not been long enough for shock to measure on the boy's face. Finally processing the danger, the boy drew breath to scream.

A fist to the gut prevented that.

The boy began to collapse with a winded croak, but Chapman hooked an arm under his neck and brought him against his own chest.

Why hadn't he killed the boy with a quick stab as well?

Guilt. He didn't want to do it. He was prolonging the boy's suffering in cowardly hesitation.

"I'm sorry."

With that brief indulgence, Chapman stabbed deep into the researcher's chest. The feeling of his knife grinding against ribs made his skin crawl. He stabbed again, hearing the horrid, sapping sound of the boy's death.

When the weight against him went limp, Chapman let the body fall onto the railing.

Silence replaced chaos. Chapman's heart began to slow as he regained control over his breath. Less than ten seconds had passed, yet he felt as if he had run ten kilometers.

The boy was so still.

A voice in his mind screamed for him to run. It was beyond moronic to stand looking at the corpse of someone you had just murdered. But he couldn't bring himself to do it. This scientist had never done anything to hurt Chapman. He had simply fought for a cause he believed in. Imperial Will.

Imperial Will.

Those words snapped Chapman back to everything he had learned, everything he saw.

He picked up the boy's legs, and pushed him into the water below. The body would be discovered, but not immediately. The Empire would likely cover it up. The Ministries would never admit one of their own had been murdered in a slum.

Chapman's head hung low as he threw his blood-soaked gloves into a gutter and picked up the dropped case. After an overabundance of sensation, he was numb. He just felt the cold, wet wind on his face as he left the bridge behind.

I'm a murderer. Not a killer, a murderer.

The case dangled loosely from his fingers.

A case worth stabbing a man in the throat. Worth rending the heart of a frightened boy.

Arriving at the meet location, Chapman pulled his hood down. The dripping rain melted the blood away from his fingers. He felt so hot.

He pushed a rickety door open, entering an abandoned home. Four masked figures awaited him, long robes hiding their forms, seated at a rotting dining table.

Pirka removed her mask, walking over to give him a hug. Chapman rejected the gesture with a raised arm. Affectionate contact always made him uncomfortable; and right now, he was in no mood to placate her.

Chapman tossed the blood-smeared knife onto the ground at their feet. "Do you trust me now?"

The three other Rebels looked at each other, then revealed their own faces. They began to tell Chapman of their plan to sacrifice his precinct.

CANDLES BURNED LOW. A faint orange light danced across five faces. Only one of the Rebels, particularly pale, stood out clearly. The mood was tense. Those gathered may have chosen to trust him, but the plan laid out before him was another test in itself.

The Seventh would be tricked into catching the M.O.D. using a warehouse assigned for medical storage to house an experimental drug being used on their own citizens. Captain Williams, with Chapman's accidental endorsement, would be trusted to force this into the public eye. It would cost blood, and if one step of the plan went wrong, Chapman's fellow officers would be swept under the rug for nothing.

"They could *all* die." Not a question, but a statement Chapman let hang in the air. Pirka reached out to touch his arm, but he pulled away. "Stop that, please."

She hesitated, but nodded.

They've shown me their faces, but given me nothing. What do I do with faces?

"You are sending the Seventh Precinct to a slaughter." Every pair of eyes avoided his own. "All of them believe they are doing what is right every day. They may be brainwashed stooges, but they wake up and are driven to help. Each and every one. *You* sit on your asses, send out others to do your bidding, and judge when to toss lives away. Now, you will gamble with their lives, over this." He gestured to the briefcase he had killed to steal, now open. It contained no drug, no secret weapon, but a pile of scrawled-upon paper. "Vague notes on an experiment."

"And yet they are no more than the drudges of a false god," the pale man said. "And if we are successful, they will each of them do something *truly* good: push the scales of power away from the Empire's corruption."

Chapman tried to ignore his building frustration.

"After all of this work, your grand blow is to 'push the scales' incrementally? And risk the lives of dozens in the process?

"What more do you want from us, Chapman?" Pirka said. "You tell us your Captain Williams is a good man and we agree. When provided with irrefutable evidence, then, he will do what is right and make the crimes of the M.O.D. known."

"Unless they kill him first" Chapman retorted. "Bury him like so many others."

"Would they?" the pale man cut in. "The bodies are piling up, and we know the M.O.D. is already meeting resistance within the royal class. Religion and wealth struggle to coexist even here. Even with the military and the Anointed in their pocket, the Ministries have to play politics. They can't afford to alienate the former royal families *and* the police. Our spies tell us the M.O.D. believe the police are in their control. If we pull that pillar out from under them, the lies will start coming to light."

"This all comes down to a fucking power play!" Chapman didn't know why he was so angry. Maybe he had craved something more grand; more direct. But the long-term impact of this piddling plan... his mind began to put the pieces in place.

"What do you suggest then, Chapman? That we try to kill a mighty Anointed?" Pirka murmured. Her brown eyes gleamed in the dim light. "Dozens of us could die trying; and the Empire would suppress the news as easily as they would make a new Anointed. That leaves the Rebellion exhausted and with no progress made. But if we go the police route— we have enough for a fight. A fight. What you don't kno—"

The pale man raised a hand to silence her. "The Empire has found new land. More wars are coming, and we must act now to just *maybe* delay the inevitable. This entire society is built upon erasure, and driven by religious fervor. If we can quell the latter, we will forestall the former. And the Empire tumbles in due course."

With that, it all fell into place. Chapman's mind drew the final lines. "You plan on fleeing. New lands? You want to get there first. That's obvious. You're not rebels, you're refugees. You'll try to warn those you find there of what is coming in your wake.

"Okay, let's say it goes perfectly. You expose the Ministries' murder of civilians by sending the Seventh after the M.O.D. and their experiments. The police turn on the M.O.D. Nobles learn how radically they will be punished if they step out of line. They'll trust the police who made them aware, and support any attempt the police make to seize power from the Ministries. The Almighty will be forced to put off new wars while the political firestorm is dealt with. I can guess that buys you a few months, perhaps a year. Then what?"

No one responded.

"You're floundering. Your greatest weapon is your mystique; no one knows how many you number or how powerful you truly are. How many? How powerful?" He answered his own question: "Not many and not very, if your plan is to run. I'd say a thousand of you, total. Really only enough to secure supplies for a voyage and leave harbor safely. You've abandoned hope on this continent."

The pale man opened his mouth, but Chapman didn't let him speak. "I put puzzles together for a living."

"Exactly." Pirka's voice surprised Chapman. He looked to her.

"The Almighty isn't a god, Chapman, but it has its name for a reason. It creates devils capable of monstrous things. I watched an Anointed pull a man to pieces on the battlefield." Her voice shook with the memory. "She severed his limbs, one by one, for daring to shoot her in the back." She looked at Chapman with something close to disgust. "You're right. We number less than nine hundred and dwindling. How would you propose we fight?"

The question stung. He found he had no answer.

Pirka wasn't done. "You only missed one thing, Inspector. We've made contact with the kingdom across the sea."

The pale man hissed. Pirka ignored him.

"I want to bring forth an army, Inspector, but there are none left here. The people are either broken or afraid. So many have forsaken their gods for the comfort of the Almighty. My own child sings the praises of the Anointed. He calls them heroes; Warriors of God. He doesn't know where his mother goes at night. But in the mornings, I listen to him pray to the Almighty."

She finally met Chapman's eyes. "So how would you fight, Inspector? Our own children would turn us in. Do you think we have the footing here for war?"

Chapman had no response. Sometimes he hated his fast tongue. Of course they couldn't fight here. Every day the citizenry was indoctrinated more deeply. An ally existed across the sea. Getting to them was the only path.

Pirka wiped at her face and looked at everyone gathered. "Don't act like I'm the only one at their breaking point. Lui, relax."

The pale man looked torn between frustration and understanding. He clearly didn't want Chapman to know everything that had just been said, but what could he do? He stepped away and paced the room.

A heaviness settled over all of them.

"So we push." Chapman said. "But we do it right."

Lui looked to Chapman. "You have an idea, Inspector?"

"Yes." Chapman locked eyes with Pirka and indicated the briefcase. "Let me take a look at those notes. I have some —gods, don't laugh— I have some investigating to do."

After relocating to a makeshift study in the sewer, they were able to learn a great deal about the biological experiment known as the 'Drip'.

A weapon that even the boyish researcher didn't fully understand in his writing. The chemicals somehow changed their flesh and blood, something deep inside them. It rewrote their bodies to transform into something else. The chemical makeup of the Drip was scarcely mentioned within the notes — they could only surmise that the yellow vial the boy had purchased was likely an ingredient. Chapman wasn't sure what the end result of administering such a drug would be, and he was terrified to find out. It was impossible to imagine the pain of one's body tearing itself to pieces, only to recombine into something inhuman.

Most disturbing to Chapman was a single note, written offhandedly at the bottom of a typed page.

"Despite the adaptability among other species seen with variant A4-21, universal rejection still occurs among human subjects."

What the hell had it been used on before humans?

Using medicine meant for humans on animals could have sickening results. Chapman's own people, before the Empire banned the creation of unapproved medicines, had mastered painkillers and even a few tinctures that could accelerate the healing process. As a hobby, Chapman continued mixing some in his spare time. They had come in handy on more than one occasion; but when he was a boy, he had fed some to his sick dog. The poor cur didn't make it through the night. His mother had beaten him when she found out. Lesson learned.

The Drip seemed like a personal violation of his Yu'ib heritage. His people had used nature to heal and promote longevity. Whatever the Drip was, it walked a different path.

Reading along, Pirka felt the Drip was somehow related to the creation of the Anointed. Chapman disagreed. The Anointed were fully human, despite their strange abilities. The Drip appeared to confer certain inhuman abilities upon its victims; yet, the sketches of those tortured forms bore little resemblance to the intimidating grace of demigods —at least to his eye.

Mangled bodies with horrid tumors. Mutated limbs, reaching out, seeming to plead for a release.

A photograph fell from one page. Upon picking it up, Lui gagged.

The photo showed a dead man, stomach down, on a lab table. His body was bent and broken. Fluid was leaking from every orifice. His skin had split in several locations as jagged growths grew from his body. His spine was almost completely visible — where it was not coated by what looked to be masses of dead black slugs.

Chapman took the photo from Lui.

Certainly feel a bit less guilty about that murder. Who could stomach doing that to someone?

After hours of reading and debate, Chapman stood. "Tired. Home."

Lui raised a hand, "You need to— hey, wait!"

Chapman walked from the room into the greater sewer system.

Even the immense Grips standing sentinel had the sense to let him pass.

He heard Pirka laugh and say, "He's too bullheaded even for you, Lui."

3 WEEKS BEFORE

"He asked me to do it!" Tears streaked the gaunt, blonde-haired woman's face. "He wanted to die!"

Chapman read over the mortician's report in front of him. "I understand. Look, there are no armed men coming in to put you in ties. I believe you."

The woman's head collapsed into her arms. She shook with a relieved sob. "For weeks he begged me. The glass rotted his brain." Her breath came in a jolted gasp. "He was in so much pain."

Chapman repressed a scoff. Glass flowed in the streets. The black crystal filled thousands of lungs to help escape the brutal reality of poverty. "I know this will be hard, but I need you to walk me through what happened. You're not in trouble here Mrs. Vicks."

The woman took several more long, ragged breaths before saying, "Jin and I spent weeks together, smoking and—"

"Having sex?" Chapman kept his tone soft.

"Yes. He started to stare off, ya know? Not see

me anymore." Her tone took on an edge that pricked Chapman's ears.

"Did that bother you?"

"No! I wanted to know what was wrong, but he started talking about wanting to die." Her eyes locked with his. The hollow shine of glass gave her the gaze of the dead. "He didn't want to be here anymore."

Chapman pulled a cigarette from a pack on the table, put the smoke in his mouth and gave it a light. He passed the cigarette to a shaking, wretched hand across the table. "You gave him mercy."

Her hands covered her face, smudging the butt of the smoke across her cheek. "I had to. He begged."

"Tell me the rest."

"I waited for him to get as high as he could off the stash, then I wrapped my arms around his throat." The last words came out mixed in with a sob. "He didn't fight. He started to shake, oh god the shaking!"

"He had a seizure?"

"Yes." She pulled from the smoke, her eyes playing out the murder. "I asked Jin if he wanted me to stop, but he kept putting my hand back over his mouth."

"This was after the seizure started, while he was high on glass?"

The murderer's eyes met Chapman's before flinching away. "No, before."

"Before, when you got on top and put your hands over his mouth and nose?"

She began to cry into her arms again, shaking violently. A poor show.

"One of the interesting things right here," Chapman planted a finger in the mortician's report, "is that his eyes don't show that he smoked a large amount of glass before he died. There was a large amount of alcohol in his stomach though, Mrs. Vick."

She spoke from under her arms, head on the table. "He drank, I smoked."

"I understand it might be hard to remember. But you strangled him from behind with your arms?"

Through a harsh sob, "Yes!"

"See I thought you just told me you smothered him from above. The report here as well indicated his nose was broken. Seems like someone got on top of Jin here and put their full weight into smothering him after a few too many drinks."

The sobbing stopped all together. Glazed eyes refocused on Chapman.

"Mrs. Vick, did you kill Jin here in self defense? It's okay. You can tell me." Chapman leaned forward and kept his head low, eyes darting to the door.

Vick leaned forward, jumping at the opportunity. "Yes. I had to. I didn't want to be in that fucking room! He kept me there."

Gods, people are dumb.

Chapman leaned back in his chair and began. "Wrong. See there was no glass found in the room. Maybe an officer snatched it to resell, but I doubt it. There are no signs of assault burdening out dear Jin. No scattered bruises or even a scratch. He's clean for a junkie. Unless he's a dealer who wouldn't sell. Why wouldn't he sell? Simple, he was out. He didn't tell you that though, did he? Promise some glass in exchange for sex?"

Mrs. Vick's eyes widened.

"You see, the room was tossed before we arrived. Drawers emptied and even his pockets turned out. If you weren't still there, we might have chalked it up to a robbery. But you were still searching when the landlord knocked. Panicked, you made up a story of a lover begging for death. Good one, haven't heard it before. Long glass use can result in these dark thoughts."

The murderer began to stand, but stopped at Chapman's raised hand.

"Next time, not that there will be, be consistent with how the death happened. We can spot the difference between someone being choked out from behind and smothered from above. The smothering seems more violent though, I can see why you'd want to change it to something more intimate, a deadly caress from behind. A dark cuddle." Chapman smirked at his own remark. "Regardless, you killed him for taking advantage of you and promising glass when he had none. Am I wrong?"

"It wasn't— No. He lied!"

Chapman stood and headed for the door. As he pulled the door, two officers stepped in. "If it helps, he kinda deserved it. But murder is still murder Mrs. Vick."

Leaving the woman behind, he was already removing the case from his memory.

Chapman flopped down at his desk and let out a long, overly loud, sigh.

"Hard shell to crack?" Khlid walked to Chapman's desk and handed over a mug of tea.

"Easy to the point of mind numbing." He took the drink thankfully. It was hot enough to scorch his mouth. Still, he drank the caffeinated beverage eagerly. "Easy day?"

Khlid weighed him with those calculating eyes. "Could say that. Still not sleeping well?"

"Eh." He waved a hand. "Well enough."

Khlid put on a somewhat mockingly cheerful voice. "Remember, the Ministry says sleep is crucial. Fed, rested, and faithful and all that." She sipped her own mug and let out a satisfied sigh. Her eyes drifted to her husband, talking with some of the newer recruits.

Chapman followed her eye. Khlid's soppiness for her husband somewhat undercut her attempts at knowing irony. "Always the mentor. He's a keeper."

"Yeah, he is." Her lips quirked behind her mug. "Wanna come to ours for dinner?"

Chapman leaned back in his chair, picking the front legs off the ground. "Got plans."

"More mysterious skulking in the night?"

He nearly fell backwards. His arms flailed forward grabbing onto his desk. "Just—"

"Just following up on cases off the clock? Chap, you need a hobby."

Refraining from breathing a sigh of relief, Chapman said, "What I do with my time is—"

"Your business. But so is the weird shit I notice you doing on *my* time. I've watched you walk out of here with file after file tucked under your coat." Khlid sat on his desk. "You can't let this job become who you are."

Biting his tongue for possibly the first time in his life, he just shrugged.

It was the wrong move.

Khlid's eyes narrowed. "Not going to tell me off?"

"Why would I?" He kicked back in the chair. "You're probably right."

Khlid put her mug down and stared into his eyes.

He looked away.

Those damn eyes.

"I'm *what*?" She seemed genuinely startled.

"A goddess among mortals." Sam approached with a grin on his face. He kissed Khlid's cheek and looked at Chapman. "Any leads on the fires?"

Chapman picked a stack of papers from his desk. "Brick Folch. He's been connected to three out of five of the businesses hit."

"Strong connections?" Khlid's head tilted as it always did when thinking over a case.

"No. But that's what we have." He handed the dossier to Samuel as he stood. "Mind going over that with Williams? According to Khlid, you don't have plans."

"God, Chapman," Khlid exclaimed.

"Sure," Samuel said.

"Appreciate it." Chapman finished the tea in his mug.

Sam, a soppy spouse himself, remembered why he had come over to Khlid. "Oh, it looks like Williams made up his mind. I'll be heading out of the city. Day after tomorrow."

Khlid frowned. "How long?"

"However long it takes to figure out what those country bumpkins are getting up to." Sam had another thought. He lifted the file. "Wait, Chapman, why can't you go over this with Williams?"

"Meeting a friend."

Khlid's eyes bulged. "A *what?*"

Samuel lowered the file. "Really?"

Chapman stood. "Yup."

They exchanged looks as Chapman headed for the exit. He heard Khlid mutter something to Sam, but couldn't make out what. He did hear Sam's reply: "Khlid, no. He's got a right to pri—"

Great. Took me about five minutes to get Khlid on my back..

He passed Holden on the way out and gave him a pat on the shoulder. "Have a good one."

"You too, Inspector."

Coming out into a warm night, Chapman took in the moons. They shone brightly in the sky. The city was clearly visible on nights like these. The street lights were off on such nights — some form of conservation. Of what, he couldn't say he understood.

Got to talk to someone at the Ministries about how that works. Could be helpful for a case... or over-throwing the Empire. Either way.

He walked home at a slow pace. The night was

lovely, and walking always calmed his mind. Not much else did these days.

"Inspector!" A merchant closing his shop waved him over.

Chapman obliged. "Evening."

"Seventh, right?" the tall portly man said, pointing to the number seven on his badge.

"Nope."

An awkward silence. *People never— whatever.*

Chapman forced a grin, "Bad joke. Yes sir. How may I help?"

The merchant smiled and forced a "ha!" before continuing, "wanted to say thank you for—"

Chapman stopped listening. He waited for the man to stop talking before saying, "Of course. Just doing our jobs."

"Well, take this as thanks." The merchant handed him a trinket: a remarkably well-carved bit of wood, depicting an Inspector. "Not much, but a hobby my son's gotten into. You can even see the seven there."

Chapman examined the thing, and felt wrong. "Talented boy."

"Indeed he is." The father's pride was clear. "Wants to be an Inspector himself."

Cold. Chapman felt cold to his very core. "Oh. That's very nice."

The merchant talked some more, but Chapman walked away, still staring at the wooden figure. The tiny officer looked proud, noble even. The length of his palm, the carving had little weight, but it lay heavy in his hand.

As he turned the corner onto the next street, Chapman considered tossing the figure into the gutter.

Why does this bother me so much? The boy wants to be an Inspector. Nothing wrong with that.

Except there was.

Children throughout the city positively pined for Chapman's job. Hell, plenty of grown men and women did, too. He was seen as a religious figure by many. Something akin to the priests of old.

And it was all a lie.

His job, his uniform, were an open threat to the civilian population: *Keep in line. Your betters have important work to do.* Yet the people embraced the threat as security. The Imperials, and the nobles and monarchs they had conquered, no longer looked after their people. They were blinded by wealth; opportunity; and, of course, that very same threat from an even higher source.

All power lay in the Ministries' hands, and Chapman and his fellow officers played a key role in that. They kept the streets quiet while nations' histories were erased and cultures rewritten. That merchant's child would grow up thinking of himself as an Imperial citizen first. He would be told every day of the glorious victories of the Empire, and how they freed the people from horrid kings and queens. Some aspects of pre-Imperial cultures were "approved"; yet they were nothing more than watered-down decoration, a thin pretext of some sort of new identity. Last month, Chapman had spent over an hour watching imperial men try on clothing brought in from the southern island nations. They had no idea the colors had been dulled to fit the uniform Imperial pallet and necklines raised to reinforce 'Imperial Decency'. All a grotesque *purified* version of the culture crafted by a once free people now undergoing imperial reduction.

Chapman thought when his mother tried to teach him how to cook a traditional Yu'ib meal; of his father's insistence that he pay attention. Gods, Chapman wished he had. His brain retained what he had deemed "useful" and dismissed the rest.

He was second-generation, and the value of what had already been lost broke his heart. The Imperials were winning. All they needed was time.

Arriving at his home, Chapman took a moment to look over his neighborhood. Mr. Drik across the street was reading to his boy on their porch. The sound of a couple laughing came from a second story flat across the road. It was peaceful. It was a lie.

The front door squeaked as he entered.

Pirka stood from his dining table. "Maybe a couple paintings. Carpet over there. Hell, even a few plants."

"Did you really just resume lecturing me from yesterday?" Chapman pulled files from under his coat, and placed them on the table. "What you asked for. Weapons shipments."

She poured him a drink from a bottle. "You walked out."

He took the glass and surveyed his place. It seemed she hadn't searched it this time. Or had done a better job hiding the fact. "I didn't— I *don't* want to hear it."

"Yeah, but you need to. Almighty, Chapman, you own one chair. What do you do with visitors?"

"Hasn't come up." He walked into his bedroom, starting to change out of his uniform.

"That's even worse!" She called after him.

"That's even worse." He whispered under his breath.

As he entered his kitchen in more comfortable clothing, he saw Pirka inspecting the service pistol he had left on the counter.

"Will I be using that tonight?"

"Nope." She placed it back in its holster. "Just you and me chatting tonight."

"Feels weird."

"Why?"

He began to put back on his shoes. "Shouldn't we avoid being seen together?"

"Do you not own another pair? Bit more casual footwear."

"Nope."

"Gods." She rubbed her hands over her face and ran fingers through her curly hair. He always wondered how she did that without catching knots. "Okay, let's say your Captain Williams sees us. What's the problem?"

"I— I don't know. It's dangerous." He finished lacing his boots.

"As far as anyone knows, we're on a date."

"No one will believe that."

Pirka raised her brows. "Rude."

Chapman rolled his eyes. "I would just feel more comfortable if you wore one of those ridiculous parade masks"

A sharp elbow caused Chapman to nearly double over.

Pirka sported that cutting grin causing her eyes to narrow. "Still not able to avoid chewing on that foot I see."

"I didn't mean—" Chapman wheezed.

"Save it." They both walked out the door and down his front steps. "Think of it as co-workers getting a drink."

"I don't drink with co-workers."

"If you weren't so cute, this night wouldn't be worth it." She shot him a wink and slipped an arm through his, running her fingers over his tattoos. "Relax, I know you don't see people like that. If it makes you uncomfortable, I'll stop. I just enjoy a good tease."

He'd never seen her like this. Pirka had become one of the most consistent figures in his life over the last few weeks, but this was far beyond her normal pleasantries. "It's fine."

They walked for some time. Pirka hummed a tune he did not know as the thoughts rolled around his head.

Halfway over a bridge, Pirka stopped humming. "Alright, what's bothering you?"

"Just thoughts."

"Care to share?"

He shot her a look. She had that same smile as always. In a sewer, the forest, or on a pretend date, Pirka always seemed to manage to enjoy the day. "The cost."

"The cost." She unwrapped her arm from his. "Of fighting, do you mean? Of what—"

"No," Chapman cut her off. "Not the cost of what we're doing. The cost already paid."

"Oh." Pirka's eyes dug into him.

Chapman took a moment to think his words over carefully. Instead of the long outpouring of thoughts, he simplified it all to, "Those masks you wear to hide yourselves. They are from a time before the Empire ruled this land right here. Before the Almighty descended. The masks were a part of a summer holiday, a wild bacchanal. Most only wore the masks."

Pirka's eyes glimmered with this new knowledge. "Sounds like we're all missing out on a good festival."

Chapman only replied, "Can what they have taken truly be recovered? Is there anything left *to* recover, besides the signifiers of the societies we've burned?"

"I don't know. But I do know that the longer we wait—"

"The worse it will get." Chapman was surprised to find comfort in Pirka's simple response.

They arrived at a tavern and took seats at a booth near the back. Getting drinks took longer due to the crowd, but the noise provided privacy. Still they leaned close not to be heard.

"Do you know any stories of your people?" Chapman asked. "I don't know much of the Ruzzai."

Pirka's eyes lit up. "Many. Countless. What do you want to know?"

He thought for a moment. "Can you tell me a love story?"

He could see her rolling through a catalogue in her mind. "Drakkil and Raech. They were lovers torn apart by tragedy."

"Kinda spoiled the ending there," Chapman said over a sip.

"Oh, hush." Pirka setted in to tell the story, putting a leg in the booth. "The Ruzzai were very proud of their arts. Cities went to war over the most beautiful pieces. People died for them."

"Seems extreme."

Pirka shrugged. "The master artists told the Ruzzai's story. Art was politics for the nobles, and as with all politics, it escalated and people died." She pointed a finger into the table. "Drakkil was an apprentice to the greatest artist the Ruzzai ever produced. His style was beautiful, yet savage. Imaginative, yet precise. But the master painter would never agree to work for a noble family. The nobles hoped his apprentice wouldn't be so rigid. The young man became the subject of a bidding war. He was offered palaces, land, fortunes, anything he could want. But he turned it all down. Instead, he promised to follow in his master's footsteps."

Chapman had leaned forward. "Which was? What was his master's name?"

"Crizon, but that doesn't matter. His self-imposed duty was to depict an unbiased history of the nation. Not the version that suited a royal family." Her whole fist came down on the table. A few nearby people looked their way. "Beautiful vision. But if you tell those in power 'no' long enough, you become the enemy.

"So he continued to paint the people's history. It showed the corruption and pain brought about by the nobles' petty warring. The people came to support Drakkil, protecting him and his work."

"Protecting?"

"Oh, there were attempts to destroy it. Think how furious it made the lords and ladies to see the greatest artist in the nation showcasing their atrocities? Eventually, an assassin's blade killed Drakkil's master Crizon. Drakkil was left, at sixteen, with this vast responsibility. That's when Raech came to his side. A young woman who had run from her own noble family."

"Why?"

"Fuck, Chapman, let me tell it!"

"Why though?"

Pirka rubbed her eyes. "Because she was abused, Chapman. She was being forced into a worthless life amidst terrible people. She took the valuables she could carry with her and sought out the artists who had opened her eyes to the atrocities of her own people.

"What she found was a scared boy, mourning the loss of the man who raised him. Murdered for a legacy he was now tasked to continue. So, she took up the cause with the now-master artist."

"Master at sixteen? That's amazing." Chapman felt a sudden, irrational urge: he would have given all of his possessions to see this boy's work.

"Yes, he was. Raech told him of the true impact of his work, how the nobles were forced to see the suffering their actions had caused. How the people really saw them. Drakkil and his master had broken unity not only between, but within the houses.

"So Drakkil got back to work." Pirka poured some of her drink on the table and smeared it with her palm. "With Raech at his side, telling him the detailed personal relations between the noble houses, Drakkil was able to expose affairs, backstabbing, incest, murders, and more. All put to canvas and shown to the people. Surrounded by guards, Raech would tell the stories at each unveiling. The people learned exactly why so many of their own had died in countless petty wars. The cause solidified and a rebellion was born."

Chapman felt a pit form in his stomach. "The two fell in love?"

"As the young and passionate tend to. They became a figurehead for the people. A beautiful couple pulling the curtain back on the corrupt? That's the kind of story that moves nations." Pirka swirled her drink. "Finally, the noble class agreed to allow the people to have a say in the government. A people's house was formed and allowed to vote on laws. All due to an artist and a storyteller.

"After their wedding, Drakkil began painting only Raech."

"Only her?" Chapman found it hard to believe.

"Only her. Again and again for months. Drakkil would tell his friends he could never get it perfect; he could never truly capture her beauty." Pirka took the last swallow of her drink. "Until she died."

Chapman sat back in his chair. "How?"

"When you defeat those in power, they will find their revenge. Raech's father saw her as an embarrassment, the daughter who betrayed the family and ruined their standing in high society. He sent men with knives. She was butchered in the street.

"When Drakkil heard, he collapsed to the ground and had to be carried home. For days, he mourned, unable to accept her death. The people found and killed the father, but it was no consolation to the artist. His heart had died."

"What happened to him?" Chapman almost didn't want to know.

"He refused to eat or drink. The artist wasted away until his body gave out."

Chapman rubbed his head. "Well, that—"

"That's not the end, Chapman." Pirka's eyes lit up. "Drakkil's art became cherished by all. Even the ruling class began collecting it. Over time, nearly all of it was split up and placed into collections across Ruzzai."

"So I could still see it in—" the realization hit Chapman. "Oh."

"Yes, Chapman. When the Empire invaded, the art of the people became rather problematic to have lying around. Symbols of rebellion, of the people's voice and power? Burned. It was all burned."

"Are there recreations?" Chapman's voice was not hopeful.

Pirka put her head in her hands. "That's the most *Chapman* question you could have possibly asked."

Later in the night, after several more drinks, the two of them stumbled back to Chapman's home.

"I still don't even know what you do," Chapman slurred.

"In the day?" Pirka lay down on his slim bed. "I'm an administrator at the docks. I help the empire keep track of its shipments from our shores, to the Mythril islands, even out into the Endless Ocean."

"Do the others know you're here?" Chapman lay on the ground next to the bed.

"Fuck, no." Pirka said. "Lui would lose his mind."

Silence filled the air for several beats before Chapman said, "Then why these visits?"

"'Cause we both need them." Pirka patted his bald head from above. "We have a new lead, by the way."

"Oh?"

"Yeah. Our next target. Blackmailed the right guy to steal the right document from blah, blah, blah. Name of Crunner." Pirka rolled to her stomach and let out a deep sigh. "Chapman, why did you turn coat?"

Chapman paused before saying, "Why did I join you?"

"Yeah."

"Boredom."

Pirka grunted. "I'm serious."

"So am I." Chapman stared up at the ceiling. "I

don't know what the future holds, but any world with the Empire is bleak. We used to be so much more, didn't we? Free, our own people. Like yours, the Ruzzai." A yawn escaped him. "I saw these children in the market district singing a nursery rhyme. They were skipping to the lyrics, clapping and smiling, and it was about how we burned crops, starved *thousands* of people to force a surrender of the Tuthæ." The pain came out in a laugh. "The children had the white hair of the Tuthæ. They played to the lyrics of their ancestors' deaths. Before their time, but they think their ancestors were ignorant fools for defending their homes. How is that what we teach?"

He received only a soft snore in response.

"Well, anyway, yeah. Because I am bored."

Chapman pulled a pillow to the floor and tried to join her in sleep.

5

AN UNEXPECTED FACTOR

THE NIGHT BEFORE

"And there he goes." Pirka removed the looking glass from her eye and carefully returned it to a case at her side. She wore a brown coat with trousers meant for running. Her curly hair had been done up in a tight bun.

Chapman, on the other hand, was in his full Inspector's attire. Badge gleaming in the moonlight and all. He had to look like an Empire man through and through for this to work.

Lowering his own looking glass, Chapman slid back from the edge of the rooftop and let out a long breath.

To execute justice, one must wield darkness as a weapon of one's own.

The quote from one of Chapman's favorite pre-Imperial academics had become an internal slogan. Most non-Imperial writing had been heavily censored or erased altogether during the wars. But Chapman now had connections to black-market books. It was a risk, but the reading had become precious to him.

Pirka already stood over him, smiling with that slash of a grin. "Let's go, Chap. Won't capture himself."

Chapman and Pirka made their way down the fire escape attached to the roof. On five separate nights now, they had trailed this man to the industrial section of the city. They suspected him of working with the M.O.D. on moving the 'Drip'.

They climbed down the last few rungs and walked into the main thoroughfare. Few people moved about in the evening glow. Workers walked home with shoulders hunched against the cold and ignored anything not directly in their path.

One child was begging for scraps. Chapman slipped the boy a coin from his pocket as Pirka shot him an appreciative look.

Reaching a corner they knew their man would pass, Chapman and Pirka took positions: she, across the street, he, scanning the faces of the men and women returning home from work.

Crunner Huicks, the worker Pirka had set them on, turned the corner and walked in Chapman's direction. He was occupied, fiddling with some smith's puzzle — a popular trend among the working class. They believed solving the complex workings of the pieces proved some form of intelligence. A childish belief to Chapman. His own inability to solve the damn things had nothing to do with his dislike. Nothing.

"Crunner." Chapman called when the man was within three meters.

He looked up in surprise, nearly dropping his puzzle. The man looked tired. The lines on his aged face ran deep. A faded scar marred his chin, probably a gift he had received on the job.

Crunner recognized Chapman's coat and badge and his eyes bulged. An Inspector knowing your name was rarely a good thing.

"Yes, Inspector?" He shoved the puzzle into his coat pocket. "May I be of assistance?"

Chapman closed the distance between the two of them and took on a mildly aggressive demeanor. "We have a witness who says he saw you with the Jackson boy before he went missing. I'm afraid I must ask you to come with me to answer some questions."

"Jackson boy?" A mixture of concern and fear played across Crunner's face. "I haven't heard of no missing boy named Jackson."

"A likely story." Chapman reached into his pocket and pulled out his Inspector's ties, making sure to show his gun. "Are these necessary, or will you come willingly?"

Chapman stood well over a foot taller than the man and, aside from the underlying muscle of someone who put in a hard day's work, Crunner did not come across as ready for a scuffle. The conclusion of the exchange was guaranteed. The only question was if Crunner would resist. Some did, out of fear or anger, even when they were innocent.

The man did hesitate, but after letting out a sigh he said, "Guess I can spare a minute for some questions, but I ain't done nothing wrong."

Putting his ties away, Chapman shifted his tone. "If I may be blunt, our witness is... shoddy. I don't think this will take long." He grabbed the man's arm —not too roughly— and began to walk him down the street.

Pirka moved across the street following the doomed man.

After several blocks, Crunner spoke up. "Uhh... Inspector?"

Chapman assumed he might be catching on that they weren't heading toward any precinct. While most did not know every station location, the darker streets Chapman led the man down didn't scream 'police this way'.

"Yes?" Chapman replied in as disarming a way as he could. He still held the man tightly by the arm. It was possible the man was wising up to the fact that there was unlikely to be a precinct down these dark alleys.

"I think we're being followed." Crunner's eyes kept darting to the street behind them.

Pirka, keep your damn distance.

"What?" The less Chapman gave Crunner, the more the man would have to explain. A simple but effective delay tactic.

"I saw— that is, there has been this woman. I think." Crunner strained to look behind them again, but Chapman increased his pace. "Which precinct do you work with, Inspector?"

Chapman wracked his brain for the closest station. "The sixteenth. What did this woman look like? Would anyone want to hurt you?" Keep him split between two subjects.

"Shorter, I believe. Darker skin than my own.

Lighter than yours. It was just the way I saw her walking. Skulking is all." Crunner looked behind them once again. Genuine fear started to radiate off of him. "No one I know wants to harm me. I keep to myself. Honest and true."

Exploiting the man's fear, Chapman looked behind them as well, picking up his pace to a near jog. "Who is she, Crunner? Don't lie to me."

Crunner's voice cracked. "Honest, I don't know!"

The man's shorter legs pumped to keep up with Chapman's longer strides. It was cruel, but playing up the man's fear was his best bet. The fact Pirka had forced Chapman into this ploy annoyed him.

"Stay close and move silently." Chapman hissed. "She has a knife."

Ducking his head in an exaggerated show, Chapman broke into a jog, causing Crunner to run. They entered a darker alley, emerging deeper into a dead industrial part of town. They were as isolated as they could be within the capital city. A couple of dirty children darted by. A drunk passed out in a gutter was the last soul they saw before Chapman stopped at an abandoned brick shed attached to an empty factory.

"Get inside." He barked.

Crunner obeyed with gusto.

Chapman followed him in and closed the door behind them.

Crunner's eyes were fixed on the door. His breath came in ragged drags. "Do you think we lost her? She had murder in her eyes, Inspector. Murder. I saw it!"

The human mind is bizarre.

Fear had brought out the man's imagination, it seemed. Chapman doubted Pirka had been close enough for Crunner to see murder, or anything else, in her eyes.

He latched the door and leaned against it, waiting.

"Smart, Inspector." Crunner backed into a lone table in the room and sat against it. "She coulda seen. Honest, I don't know who she is. You believe me, don't ya? I'm just glad—"

Crunner noticed the restraints attached to the table. His brow furrowed. Concerned eyes darted to a lamp, already lit when they entered the shed. "Inspector..."

A knock came at the door. Chapman let Pirka in.

THE TOE POPPED off with a squirt of blood. The clamp Pirka had kept in her pocket was designed for carpenters, but it served this purpose well. Crunner's screams were muffled by the scarf Chapman held to his mouth. The restraints attached to the table rattled as the worker thrashed. Pirka lazily plucked another toe. The lack of effort required to break the man was pathetic.

They hadn't even asked him a question yet. For all the man knew, they were doing this for some sick pleasure. A murderous couple killing strangers at night.

A sickening snap renewed the screams. He howled as Pirka tore the last tendons away and tossed the digit to the side.

The man convulsed. His limbs rammed against the restraints as he pounded his body into the table. Snot flew from his nose as his tears mixed with thick sweat.

Pirka nodded to Chapman.

Keeping one hand over the man's mouth, Chapman drew his pistol and placed it at his drenched temple. Crunner quieted his uncontrolled whimpers.

Chapman spoke for the first time since they began. "Do not scream or I'll kill you. Understood?"

To Chapman's revulsion, hope sprang into Crunner's face. If they were going to ask questions, maybe he could get out of this alive.

It was important to let him keep thinking so.

Crunner slowly nodded.

Chapman pulled the scarf from his mouth. blood stained the fabric.

"Please," he breathed. "Please. I have a family. I want to see 'em. You don't have—"

The sound of the gun's hammer being cocked silenced the whimpers.

Pirka pulled the man's head to face her. "How many soldiers guard the warehouse?"

"Only a few." The man replied quickly, meeting Pirka's eyes. His eyes did not waver. They screamed for her to believe him. Chapman wasn't sure if he did.

To Chapman's surprise, Crunner required no more prompting. Without being asked, he spilled every detail he could think of: barrels filled with frothing, pungent black fluid, which he claimed would lurch toward anyone within reach. According to him, it was possible to hear the liquid sloshing towards you if you drew too close. A couple of careless men had even been touched. Those unlucky few had never been seen again after members of the Red Hand had silently escorted them away.

Pirka looked at Chapman and curled an eyebrow. If nothing else, the man's blubberings corroborated much of the information the notes had provided.

Pirka looked back at the sweating Crunner. "How much of it is there?"

"Heaps!" Crunner tried to kick the pain from his foot. "Some was just sent out."

"Why?" Chapman and Pirka asked together.

"Why in the fuck would they tell me?"

Chapman roughly shoved his pistol's barrel into the Crunner's mouth. "Could they be sending their message to the royal class so soon?"

Pirka only exhaled in response to Chapman's question. Her eyes moved, weighing scales no one else saw.

Turning back to her subject, Pirka asked, "Is it kept anywhere else?"

Chapman removed the barrel from his mouth.

"No. *No.*" Crunner tensed as Pirka moved towards his feet. "Please, I'm telling you. I heard that science lady say it. She's in charge. They wanted to ship out from one central location for some... I don't know, *something* they have planned. Please, no more!"

Pirka looked back to him, a false apology in her eyes. "I am sorry. We need to make sure we get everything from you we can."

"No! N*wumpf*"

Chapman put the scarf back in place. "He's scared, but not broken. Keep at it."

The words were more for Crunner than Pirka. Attacking the mind was Chapman's job.

THE SMOKE BURNED Chapman's lungs. He normally avoided the habit, but today was different. The feeling of Crunner's neck breaking under his hands...

A poster along the side of the shed caught Chapman's eye. One of the countless pieces of propagandic art displayed throughout the city, it depicted the capital as a glowing golden beacon in the distance. The foreground was flooded by a faceless mass of people in darkness, basking in the slivers of warm light provided by the glowing city. Those in the front had begun crawling toward salvation. The people had no distinguishing features aside from recognizable bits of clothing from conquered kingdoms. The words along the bottom read, "THE ALMIGHTY FUTURE".

He had been forced to look at pieces like this for as long as he could remember. A constant backdrop to growing up in the Empire. Before they had filled him with a vague pride, but now they twisted a knife into his spine—shame, pain, anger, a fire being stoked again and again.

Does this justify what I've done here today?

Chapman pulled at the cigarette again. It did, and it didn't. Today, the cost had been too high. Tomorrow it wouldn't be. He hoped in the end, the balance would pan out to allow him to sleep at night.

Chapman ripped the poster from the wall.

He leaned against the brick, repeating the slogan in his mind.

To execute justice, one must wield darkness as a weapon of their own.

To execute justice, one must wield darkness as a weapon of their own.

To execute justice, one must wield darkness—

"You okay?" Pirka stepped into the abandoned courtyard.

"No." Chapman flicked the cigarette into the gravel. "But I will be."

"Good. We'll need to dispose of the body."

"Yup. River works."

Pirka closed the door firmly. "Well, we know how well guarded it is now."

"Are you sure?" Chapman met her eyes. "Torture doesn't always produce the most accura—"

"*Hold!*" The cry came from an alley across the courtyard.

Chapman turned to see who had called out.

Pirka ran without even looking.

Seeing the uniform of two Imperial soldiers

coming from the shadows, Chapman cursed under his breath.

How under the two fucking moons?

This would undo everything. If Crunner's corpse was found, the Empire would know that the Rebellion had discovered the Drip. A worker going missing could be written off, but a body? A trail had been laid for the Empire to follow.

Gravel crunched under Chapman's boots as he sprinted to catch up to Pirka.

"Hold, or we will shoot!"

The two reached an already-broken door to the nearby factory, and plunged into the darkness within.

Chapman caught up to Pirka and grabbed her by the forearm, hissing, "Wait. They saw our faces."

She looked at him with confusion.

Out of view of the door, Chapman went back to the entrance and pressed his body to the wall. Pirka followed his lead, pulling a knife from her pocket.

An alarm whistle sounded from just outside.

Fuck.

Chapman had hoped the soldiers would be incompetent enough to forget to sound an alarm. A slim chance, but you never knew.

The whistle continued to blow as the first soldier sprinted into the darkness of the industrial building, and, immediately thereafter, Chapman's tattooed fist.

Blood sprayed into the air as the soldier's nose collapsed with a crunch. It was followed by guttural choking as the young man tried to cough up the long whistle, and a few of his own teeth, that had been forced down his throat

A blast of pain exploded into Chapman's side. He looked down to see Pirka, holding back a bayoneted rifle, as the second soldier struggled to plunge it deeper through his coat.

Chapman spun away and grabbed the wound. At least an inch deep.

Simultaneously, Pirka knocked the rifle away and stabbed at the man's chest.

No longer underestimating her, the soldier dodged and tried to get a shot off.

Pirka easily swatted the weapon away and sliced the man's hand. The rifle hit the floor with a wooden clack.

Chapman wanted to help, but the soldier whose face he'd mangled was getting to his knees, groping for a pistol at his hip.

Launching himself at the man, Chapman pulled the pistol himself and tossed it away. Any gunshots here would only help his colleagues locate him and Pirka.

The soldier rolled away from Chapman, avoiding his tackle.

Both got to their feet. Chapman closed the distance first. The soldier swung with heavy desperation. Chapman blocked it with his upper arm. Off balance now, the soldier couldn't retract his blow fast enough. Chapman slammed his free fist into the soldier's elbow.

A crunch.

The soldier screamed.

Chapman was strong enough to send the man to the floor hard. He heard the air evacuate his lungs. He got on top of the desperate man.

The soldier wildly tried to buck him off, but Chapman's weight was overwhelming. His hands closed around the man's neck.

Finding a grip was difficult as the struggling man tore at Chapman's coat. He found the gash in Chapman's side and pressed his fingers into it.

Now Chapman screamed, knocking away the intruding hand. He pinned the wrist to the ground and strangled the man with the other. Blood from the man's nose and mouth made Chapman's hands slip.

With the last of his strength, the soldier raised his broken arm high and slammed it down on Chapman's arm, causing Chapman to buckle at the elbows.

Chapman used the momentum to slam his forehead into the man's already broken nose. A far more significant crack was heard. Chapman was unsure what exactly had broken this time, but the soldier was consumed by a dazed look.

Placing both hands back onto the bloody neck, Chapman said, "I'm sorry!" through clenched teeth.

The soldier had little fight left in him. His good hand beat at Chapman's chest and arms, but it was over. He stared fearfully into Chapman's eyes with a dark acceptance.

A weight crashed into Chapman's back, sending him forward over the man beneath him. Something metal skittered across the floor. Chapman's face exploded in pain as it met concrete.

The soldier Pirka fought had thrown himself into Chapman in an attempt to free his comrade.

Chapman rolled to his feet. He saw Pirka manage to knife her assailant in the gut. He bellowed in pain and collapsed backward, the knife still in him.

Pirka reached down and pulled the knife free. She rammed it home again and again. Neck, chest, side, face. The man fell to the floor, dead many blows since, silent.

The younger soldier was struggling to his feet. Chapman kicked him to the floor and stomped on his head. Again. Only when he heard a definitive crunch, did Chapman stop.

He looked to Pirka.

She was searching the dead man. "Someone must have watched you accost Crunner. They called for backup and tailed us. It's the only way." Pirka seemed to have regained much of her composure. She tore off the dead man's sleeve, using it to wipe the blood from her face. "So they're watching the workers. How did we not think—"

An alarm whistle sounded. Far too close for comfort. They were searching for the soldier who had sounded the alarm.

"No time." Chapman stood, offering a hand. "Come on."

"You're covered in blood." Pirka tore another chunk of fabric from the soldier's shirt. "Here."

Chapman cleaned off the best he could with a few swipes.

"Where's your gun?"

Chapman looked at his holster. "Shit." Not only was his Inspector's coat torn, his sidearm was missing. He looked around desperately. It wasn't under either of the men.

The alarm whistle sounded again.

"Let's go." Pirka said, getting to her feet. "We'll find it later. Go!"

Boots on gravel could be heard outside. Chapman and Pirka disappeared into the maze of disused industrial buildings before finding refuge in the sewer. They moved through the black stink of the city's mess for hours. The occasional grate provided enough light from the moons for Chapman to check his wound. Blood trickled onto his leg, but not enough to cause an immediate worry.

Pirka had escaped the scuffle mostly unharmed, though she vomited once the adrenaline wore off. He rubbed her back and whispered comforting words and she shook. Chapman took strange comfort in seeing her hands tremble. She felt the guilt, too. No matter the situation, good people were disturbed by killing.

Pirka wiped bile from her lips. "I can't take much more of this. Crunner seemed like—?"

"This way," Chapman cut her off, pulling her past a split she normally took home. Pirka raised her eyebrows, eyeing him. "We should stick together. I have medicine at my house. I'll need your help getting ready for my shift in the morning. And if the Drip is being sent out now, you'll need me out there. Unless you have another secret Imperial District Inspector in your pocket?"

They exited the sewer at an alleyway roughly two blocks from Chapman's home. Surprisingly, his elderly neighbor sat on her front porch. He worried under the light of the moons she might be able to make out his condition, until he heard her soft snores. "We're fine. Let's go."

Chapman walked straight to the bathroom, undoing his shirt.

Pirka followed Chapman in and helped him strip down. "Gods, Chapman. That isn't pretty."

Chapman looked at the wound. No, it was not. At least an inch deep, he had pushed the blade out at an angle, worsening the damage to his stomach.

He pointed to the cabinet. "One of the purple vials."

She handed it to him after taking in the several dozen concoctions. "What will it do?"

"Prevent infection, stop bleeding, make me pull myself together."

She watched him work with fascination. Small bubbles emerged from the fluid as Chapman pulled off the cork. Pirka suddenly smirked, giving his naked body a clear once-over. "Ya know, Chapman, most would consider you—"

"Good for most." Chapman gritted his teeth — an intense burn settled in his throat after swigging the vial down.

Pirka went back to the cabinet. "Anything here to give a man a libido?"

"No, but hand me the pouch with white powder."

She obliged him.

Chapman took several snorts of the drug. His pupils dilated and his mind lit a fire.

"The hell was that?"

"Another painkiller." Chapman winced his way down into the tub as Pirka pumped in several splashes of lukewarm water. "Help me wash. I can't miss any blood."

Pirka helped him cleanse the blood from his body. She marveled at the scrapes on his face, already disappearing. "That stuff's amazing. Why isn't it on every street corner?"

"Extremely difficult to make." Chapman said. "And tied to the Yu'ib. The Empire doesn't like relying on old medicines. They consider it weakness. Not that they could manufacture them anyway."

Pirka nodded in agreement. "How'd you learn?"

"My mother. One of the few lessons I actually paid attention to."

After a few moments of silence Pirka said, "What else can I do?"

"Do you know how to sew? The rip in my coat."

"Not well, sorry."

Chapman hesitated. He didn't need anything, but he honestly felt no desire to be alone. Casting about for an excuse to keep her there, he picked up the white vial. "Here."

She took a snort from his palm and immediately stood up. "Whoa, *wow*. Chapman, how— how in the — what is th— GODS! You could punch me in the face and— everything is numb!"

He lay back and rested his head. "I have to get my gun back." He closed his eyes, trying to relax his tense back. "Please, find it."

Pirka sat back down, twitching slightly. "Alright. but they will be watching that area. Give me time."

"No one has our description now. At least not yours. I'm not sure who all saw me arrest Crun— Crunner..." Chapman took another snort. "They might assume it was a stolen uniform, but in a few days, Inspectors will probably have to answer questions."

The colossal strain Chapman had put himself under finally began to settle in. He was so unbelievably tired. Sleepless nights, constant doubt, running around the city nonstop and relying too heavily on his tinctures were all catching up to him at once. He had been on work binges before, but these last weeks had been emotionally draining on an entirely new level. Tonight had nearly been the final straw.

Chapman opened his eyes and met Pirka's

dilated gaze. "But I'll have served my purpose by then, won't I?"

She looked away.

He lay his head back down.

They sat in silence, knowing what was to come.

"I'll get your gun back, Chap." He heard Pirka stand, but he didn't open his eyes. "Rest while you can. You have a few hours."

Chapman lay in the shallow water, his mind floating.

Sleep came.

6

HEARTFELT

THE MORNING OF THE DEMISE

"Enough!" Captain Williams' voice boomed off the walls of the Seventh Precinct. "All of you have cases. Either get to them or get in my office for a discussion about time management."

The gathered dozen Inspectors of the Seventh murmured to each other as they dispersed. Only Khlid and Chapman remained. She tossed him a smile as she and the Captain went to her desk. Williams was already relaying details of a reported murder at a mansion belonging to a minor royal family just outside the city.

It had to be what Crunner had spoken of. A family had been hit. The Ministries were moving to put fear into the hearts of the noble class. Their purses and manufacturing would slowly be moved into the coffers of the Empire.

Chapman snatched a ball meant for children that he kept in his desk, and loudly began scooting his chair over to Khlid's desk. Several officers shot him annoyed looks.

The Captain didn't look up, but took a deep breath at the sound of rubber skittering across wood.

Khlid looked more bemused.

"What?" Chapman lifted his hands up. "You're not going to send me on this? Oh, you're right. I guess the M.O.D. wouldn't want me on this. Not like royals are important or anything. I certainly don't have the best record of anyone in—"

The Captain let out a sigh and hung his head. "You okay with this, Khlid?"

She shrugged. "A pain in the ass can be a decent motivator."

"And I'm known for my ability to cause procto-logical pain, Cap. None better in the business." Chapman bounced the ball off the side of Khlid's desk to emphasize his point.

"Shut up and get over here." The Captain still

looked stern, but Khlid was losing the battle to hide a smile.

Inside, Chapman wanted to scream. His mind raced over what was to come.

"The woman who reported what happened, she's still not entirely coherent." The Captain's deep, experienced voice cut through Chapman's reverie. Chapman respected few minds above his own; Captain Williams' was one of them. "There is apparently a hanged boy out front."

"Almighty." Khlid exhaled. "How many officers can I take?"

"As many as you need." The Captain's eyes focused on Chapman. "Do whatever must be done to get to the bottom of this, Khlid, but be careful. Something tells me this is the start of something."

"The cornerstone of solid police work, *feelings*." Both of them looked at Chapman. He raised his hands again. "I'm being serious."

Khlid turned back to Williams. "Any suspicions you wanna let me in on?"

The Captain didn't look away from Chapman. His eyes narrowed.

Chapman forced himself not to look down at the gash still visible in his coat. At least he knew his empty holster was concealed.

"Captain?" Khlid repeated. She glanced at

Chapman, then back to the Captain. "Do you two have a new game or something? I know children enjoy staring contests, but—"

"No, Khlid." The Captain glanced over Chapman's coat once more before looking back to her. "I want you to go into this one clean. And honestly, we haven't seen a family this high up attacked before. Not since the wars."

The Captain turned his back and headed to his office.

"That was... odd." Khlid turned to Chapman. "What— actually, No. I don't care. Follow my lead and don't go anywhere without my say-so. Deal?"

Chapman bounced the ball off Khlid's desk again, avoiding her eyes. The woman was one of the few people Chapman had trouble lying to. "Deal."

Knowing what they were about to see, Chapman forced away any thoughts of the last few months. He muted the screams of Crunner. The look of desperation in the dying soldier's eyes. Pirka's story of Drakkil and Raech. All of that was locked away. He had to walk into this investigation as though blind. With Khlid watching him, any step out of place could be disastrous.

No treasonous thoughts would enter his mind. On this outing, he was Chapman, the loyal Inspector to the Empire.

. . .

PIRKA PULLED his pistol from her pocket and handed it to Chapman. It was dinged-up and scuffed, but aside from that it looked unharmed.

"Thanks."

Pirka straightened her coat. "One of the street kids picked it up. Luckily they don't know how to keep their mouths shut. An Inspector's pistol was news."

"Where'd he find it?" Chapman asked, looking down from a second-story window to the market square below. He had told Khlid to meet him there; sure enough, Khlid and Sam paced around, clearly searching for him. From the shuttered inn room he had hired for the hour, he took morbid amusement in the game.

"Said it was under a vat. The kids often rummage through once search parties are done. Even just looking for a half-smoked cig..." Pirka trailed off, following his eyes. She seemed unsettled to see the two Inspectors circling. "Is there a problem?"

"Lots." Chapman thought of Khlid's eyes scanning him that morning, testing the walls he tried so hard to keep in her way. "But nothing I can't handle."

"Do you enjoy being with them?" Pirka's voice was cold.

"Yes. I'm convinced Khlid has a bunch of unpaired shoes at home from how often she leaves a boot in someone's ass." Chapman smiled at a memory of Khlid chewing out the Captain himself for showing up late. "But they've devoted their lives to this system of destruction. A system that has taken this continent into an abyss. Whether they know it or not."

"I hate them for not knowing what they do." Pirka rubbed her arms.

Chapman felt an urge to do the same. "We all pay the price for their blindness."

"There are more guards than ever around the warehouse, Chap. It's too late. The Seventh has—"

"Don't," Chapman cut her off. "They signed up to protect the people no matter what. We are showing them their true enemy. Take that vial of Drip and start your whispers."

Chapman hoped he wasn't lying to himself. If Khlid and Samuel knew the full truth, they would want this too, right?

I know Khlid would. I'm certain of it.

Pirka took a step toward him, registering the strange look on his face. "What are you planning?"

"I think... I think I'm going to get Samuel out of

the way." Chapman focused on Sam, looking over a stand of apples. "He'll make things messier. Khlid I can get on the right path."

"You think she won't go to the Captain?" Pirka was focusing on the female Inspector, a glint of distrust in her eyes.

"She will. I'll invite her to come to the warehouses by the docks with me. She'll say no. I'll go myself. She'll bring an army in pursuit." Chapman turned his eyes to Khlid. "The woman doesn't let others walk away until she's done with them."

"What if she tries to arrest you?"

Chapman walked away from the window and sat on the bed. "She will. Khlid never flinches from the truth."

Pirka sat next to him and started rubbing his neck. The tension there felt like rocks. "You can do this."

"I know." He took a long breath. "I just thought we had more time. Sounds dumb."

"Not dumb." Her fingers dug into his muscles. "We all did. If everything goes well—"

"It won't."

She ignored him. "If it goes well, the scandal will give the police power over the Ministries. The Seventh will bring the Drip to light so that it can't be swept under the rug. William's the type of Captain to make sure of that. The public support will sway away from the Ministries. The people will begin to see the imperial power grabs for what they are."

"Is it enough? The Ministries already seized the Pruit's production capabilities. They will have enough steel."

"And the agents we leave behind will make sure the noble know just how that happened —not that the Pruits were smote by the Almighty for some holy reason— that they were killed for strategy. Once this vial you nabbed is shown as proof, the royals will organize. Why are you pushing back now? You helped craft this plan."

Below, Khlid looked to be growing frustrated with her failed hunt for him. "Because it's real now," Chapman replied as he headed to the door.

"Chapman, the Seventh can come out of this on top. You're acting as if their defeat is a foregone conclusion."

He turned back to Pirka before leaving. "Whatever happens, the fallout will be uncontrollable."

"That's the point. Our people will do their job."

"'Our?'"

Pirka met his eyes. "This plan is messy and rushed. I can admit that. But we have a chance."

Chapman nodded. "I know there are still angles to this you haven't told me."

Pirka just nodded. "I'm sorry. What comes next, you won't be a part of. If you're captured..."

"Wield me as the shadow."

Pirka looked confused by the words. "What?"

But Chapman was already out in the hall.

CHAPMAN CLOSED HIS FRONT DOOR, leaving Khlid to heal in his home's bathroom. He had dosed her with enough Yu'ib' medicine to heal a gunshot wound to the chest. The rather harsh hit to the head he had inflicted on her at the tavern would have put her down for the night otherwise. After getting rid of Samuel, he had hoped Khlid would have trusted him enough not to force him to resort to violence. Now he had to leave his best friend bleeding alone in a cold tub. Chapman hoped his mother's medicine would be enough to revive her in time for whatever she went up against tonight as a result of what he had to do.

Well, time to burn it all down.

His job was now simple. Pirka had told him this morning the workers at the warehouse were already destroying any evidence of the Drip's existence. Where it was being moved was impossible to tell. Ships were being prepared nearby. It could vanish off the face of the continent, re-emerging after the

Ministries had succeeded in making their accusers look foolish. Then there would be no stopping them.

The Drip had to be brought to light now. Chapman had to slow down the cover-up long enough for Captain Williams to send the Seventh. If they arrived in time, all could be exposed. By this time tomorrow, the people would see the experiments done to the defenseless. They would care. Right? The royal houses could push openly to remove the Ministries from power. And maybe, *maybe*, the police could live up to their intent and serve the people by securing that removal of power. They would find the ability to unify against tyranny.

If; could; maybe. For these uncertain words, I may send the Seventh to their deaths.

Every bloody action Chapman had taken these last few months now rested on all of these elements falling into place.

And I might not be alive to know if it was worth it.

He made his way towards the warehouse district as quickly as he could without drawing attention. His side still mildly burned, and the effects of the huff he had sniffed were long gone. There was adrenaline, but it was undercut by a deep weariness.

Rain began to fall on Chapman as he arrived at

the warehouse. His bald head was frigid, but he welcomed the sensation. He felt hot.

Chapman watched from a corner as two cargo doors were closed behind several carts being brought out of the rain. They would quickly be loaded with however much of the Drip was stored here and be taken away, never to be seen again.

I've got to slow them down without giving away that the Seventh is coming.

Chapman realized he had not thought this step through. Perhaps he had hoped deep down to ride in with the Seventh, guns blazing. If so, that hope had always been faint. Now he stood alone, wet, feverish, and needing to slow an entire M.O.D operation. And the longer he waited, the less time he had to execute an impromptu plan.

Mind racing, Chapman methodically circled the building, moving from alley to alley. The warehouse itself was secluded in the middle of dozens of out-of-use facilities, retired when the wars ended. The cover provided was brilliant. No prying eyes except for the occasional wandering—

Oh, how did I not see that.

The abductions of the homeless suddenly made much more sense. Just wait for one to wander too close to your trap. The Empire didn't even need to hunt for them.

Well, gods' damn, sometimes simple is smart.

Chapman entered a closed-down facility behind the warehouse the M.O.D. occupied. The industrial equipment was wrapped in muslin. Huge boxes filled with gods-knew-what lined the walls. He saw nothing he could use to stop a labor force from covering up—

Simple is smart.

Chapman walked into the facility's abandoned management office and pulled open drawers: bits of paper, a forgotten, half-empty bottle of booze, and a massive ledger provided everything he needed.

He pulled a lighter from his pocket and lit the corner of a dusty paper. It went up beautifully. The book caught fire next. Within moments, the wooden desk became an inferno. He threw all the furniture on top of the blaze for good measure. No one in Warehouse Two could possibly miss the roar of flames licking through the greasy window.

Shouts sounded below as the fire was spotted. Ignoring the heat and danger, Chapman looked down at the gathering guards and workers.

"What are you all standing around for?" he shrieked mockingly. The tone in his voice annoyed even himself, and he loved it. "Somebody call a fire team!"

For a moment, the assembly beneath him just

stared at the mad Inspector and his inferno. "What's that? You can't? Why ever not? Come on, you worthless drudges, are you going to let me burn it all?!"

A few of the guards below shook off their amazement and headed his way. His performance complete, Chapman tipped over a barrel once used as a table and rolled it to the top of the staircase. He pulled his scuffed pistol from his holster and crouched behind it. Above the crackling behind him, he made out perhaps a dozen sets of stomping boots. He would guess over half were soldiers made up to look like civilians, but it didn't matter. The result would be the same. He would die fighting them.

As the sound of commotion reached the bottom of the stairs, Chapman gently shoved the barrel. Even empty, it was heavier than some men. The loud *CONG, CONG, CONG* as the barrel heavily descended each stair sounded dangerous enough.

The sound of steps halted, followed by a domino cascade of screams as oak and wrought-iron slammed into fragile flesh and bone.

He looked down at the aftermath, and any amusement he felt left him. At least two men were dead or dying. The rest had halted, looking horrified from their mangled comrades to the mad Chapman, silhouetted by flames.

The glint of a pistol being raised made Chapman dive for cover down the hall.

The men swore at him as they pursued. By the time they reached the top of the stairs, Chapman had dipped into a side office at the opposite end of the hall from the fire. Ramming a latch in place, he searched for anything to barricade the door with. A flimsy desk and poorly-built chair were all that greeted him.

Okay, didn't think this through.

His eyes lit on the open window. It was open. A fire escape just beyond shone to his eyes like the light of the Almi— like the light of the old gods.

As the door to the office splintered with the force of several burly men, Chapman hoisted himself out into what was now a considerable downpour. The men charged Chapman with weapons raised. Two shot haphazardly, missing Chapman by inches.

Definitely just workers.

On the street below, more laborers pointed up at him, cries of alarm echoing off the brick.

Up we go, then.

Chapman climbed the fire escape, which sent a stinging vibration through his hands as it was struck by bullets. The M.O.D. had actually armed their workers. Luckily they hadn't trained them all that well. That was a decided edge. Stealing a glance behind him, Chapman saw the workers were hesitant to follow him. Any civilian, even under direct orders, would be nervous to kill a man in Inspector's regalia.

The fire escape terminated at another office window. The braver laborers were only one flight below him now. Chapman pulled at the window, but it resisted. A lock visible on the inside made him curse.

Break it?

His pursuers' hands reached the top rung just below him.

Nope.

Chapman jumped and grabbed onto the gutter. The metal groaned loudly in protest and Chapman lifted himself. As hands reached for his feet, he pulled himself over the roof ledge and to momentary safety.

He rolled over and stared up at the sky. Rain pelted his skin. It felt so nice.

The clang of a bullet ripping through metal made him jump.

"For the love of the gods, stop shooting!" Chapman shouted down. He was genuinely angry on behalf of his unskilled, expendable pursuers. They were bound to take friendly fire.

"Good advice, Inspector." The voice from behind was calm and soft.

A chill shot through Chapman's spine. Still crouching, he turned to see a woman dressed in black sharing the rooftop with him. She stood within leaping distance, looking down at him.

A hand appeared on the ledge, followed by a face. A bearded soldier glared at Chapman with bared teeth before following his eyes to the woman. His own eyes went wide, and he let himself fall onto his comrades below.

"I'd like to think so." Chapman said as he stood. He knew deep down what he faced, but he had to ask. "Anointed?"

The woman nodded. She held a white mask in her right hand; a pair of clawed gauntlets in her left. He was no threat to her. She didn't feel the need to pretend otherwise.

Well. I'll prove her wrong.

"Why? I thought you all were—"

"Every city has one, actually." She laced the mask into her belt, the rictus grin it bore stared directly at him. "When one of our men was found tortured, well, it felt like a good excuse to get out of the office. You've stepped in the Ministries' way, dear."

Chapman's mind raced. If this Anointed was still

here when the Seventh arrived, they would all die. He had to draw her away. Far enough for... for what? For the Seventh to raid the building, secure evidence, call for backup, and for that backup to arrive? His heart sank.

No... it can't go like this. They'll all be butchered.

He stood up straight and met the woman's gray-eyed gaze. "I guess I have to kill you, then."

A grin split her lips. "Is that so?"

"Well I really—"

The Anointed became a blur. She tossed her clawed gauntlets into the air. Chapman felt his back slam to the metal roof. The air was purged from his lungs.

The Anointed slapped him with an open hand.

That mere slap was hard enough to turn Chapman's vision to dancing colors. For what must have been seconds, he tried to refocus his vision.

"Would you like another?" The voice cut through his daze like a knife.

"Yeah, I'd love one," he gasped, trying to regain his breath.

The woman laughed. It sounded like the bells of hell to his ears.

Well, I stalled them, and I've brought the Seventh to the slaughter.

· · ·

THE ANOINTED lazily shoved Chapman into a chair. A man tried to fasten Chapman's arm into a restraint, but Chapman struck. His fist sent the man careening to the floor. Chapman tried to stand, but the demigod's open-palmed strike to his chest sent him right back down, gasping again.

"Certainly do find the fiercest for the force, don't they?" The Anointed slipped on one of her gauntlets. "Harm anyone else who works for me and I will bisect you. Do you understand?"

Chapman could only cough in response.

"Good boy."

A woman in a black coat entered the room carrying a medical case. She bowed her head to the Anointed. "You asked for samples?"

Her accent was strange, one Chapman couldn't place.

She nodded towards Chapman. "Flood him with the Drip. Break him completely. I want everything he knows. Understood?"

The white-coated woman grinned in response. "Of course." He felt revulsion at the pleasure on her face.

As she stepped toward him, two large men entered the room with her.

"Mistress Cormick." A voice in the hall called.

The Anointed turned. "Yes?"

"Officers have been spotted out back. This Inspector wasn't alone."

The Anointed, Cormick, turned to Chapman and donned her mask.

She leaned in close and said, **"I hope you don't love these people."** The mask altered her voice, disguising it into something booming, yet smooth. Her whispered words vibrated in his mind like a foghorn. She was within an inch of his ear now, caressing his face with her one naked hand. **"I'm going to have fun with your friends. I haven't had a good hunt in so long. Thank you, Inspector."**

Chapman lunged at her once again, desperate to inflict any harm. His fist smashed into her mask. The Anointed's head snapped to the side as Chapman landed one of the hardest blows he had ever thrown. He tried to follow it up with a second.

The Anointed caught his hand. Her head slowly turned back to look at him. **"That was stupid. I'll stop being gentle now."**

OVER THE YEARS, Chapman had been beaten, stabbed, even shot—scars littered his body. He thought he knew pain; he thought no torture could surprise him. None of that compared to what the

Anointed could do. The pains of hell were reserved for the dead, but she had brought them to him.

Delirious, spluttering, half himself and half a broken mess, he clung to what little sanity remained through the pain.

As the white-coated woman plunged the needle full of Drip into his arm, the sensation that burned through him was beyond the imaginable. A symphony of agony consumed reality.

The gunfire from outside ceased to exist. The vile, grinning woman in the lab coat left his vision. All that remained was the exquisite, hellish feeling of his person being ripped to shreds. Like a million insects burrowing through his bones.

He screamed. He screamed until the sensation reached his head.

The last thing his mind processed were the words, "**Give him more.**"

Three hundred eighty seven, three hundred eighty eight, three hundred eighty nine, three hundred ninety, three hundred...

The sound of a key turning in the door to Khlid's cell broke her concentration. She lost track of her count — the stones in the wall.

Damn.

The jail door was opened. Four men entered, all with the shining green eyes of Grips. Wearing their full heavy armor, they eyed her as if she were a wild predator.

As Khlid climbed to her feet, the growth that had spurted from her mangled leg scraped across the floor. Twisted like a gnarled root, Khlid could now feel the cold stone below her— "claw" was still the only word that seemed remotely accurate.

The men tested the bars of her cell. She had tried to break them. The harder she pulled, the more the creatures within her had pulsed; replacing muscles, digging into her bones. Slowly but surely, Khlid's body was being replaced.

The transformation wasn't merely corporeal; it was also altering her senses. She saw differently now. The edges of objects seemed shaper; certain colors were growing more vibrant. Fine details in fabric jumped out. Sensations on her skin felt catalogued in a new way. Her ears could pick up individual voices from the street far below. Even her thoughts seemed to process differently, reaching conclusions through connections the still human part of her struggled to understand.

Am I even me *anymore?*

Her life had been taken long ago. Khlid was a dead woman walking, awaiting the end of an experiment she had not volunteered to be a part of. They had forced her onto countless cold medical tables to be violated. Her ever-darker blood drawn from her. Concoctions injected into her flesh. They beat her, then measured how quickly she healed.

The answer was, *quickly*. As a man had cut into her stomach, Khlid had snapped a leather arm restraint and clawed off half his face. She was becoming the weapon they wanted.

His inspection of the cell bars' strength complete, one of the Grips called an all-clear. A man and woman in black coats entered the room, followed by the Anointed Avi Cormick. Khlid's blood boiled at the sight of the raven-haired woman.

"Well," Avi said, looking Khlid over. "You're looking better by the day."

"Come in and take a better look." The fear the Anointed had once brought her was completely gone. She had accepted her death as something past. "You might miss some of the details."

Avi turned to one of the researchers. "Note the new markings on her face. The pattern is emanating from the jawline and eyes."

Khlid flinched at the words. In the month of her captivity, her own image had never been revealed to her. She could only infer from the comments of those observing her.

"You're the greatest specimen we've ever had." Avi turned back to Khlid, a smile on her lips. "You and Chapman. You didn't just survive; you thrived. But I'd say you've edged him now. His reaction was... less sophisticated. Shame I had to tear him in two."

Khlid leaned against the bars. If the Anointed got closer, she wanted to be ready.

Avi took on a parochial tone. "You both reacted so well to a brew meant to create monsters." Avi stepped in, still just outside of Khlid's reach. "It turned you both into something so beautiful. Yet you are my masterpiece, Khlid. It took only minutes for the Drip to consume Chapman"

Avi licked her lips.

"No surprise there. We positively flooded him with the stuff. Yet you have now received even more Drip than he, and continue to evolve. It's clearly related to the Drip we found already in your system. That was certainly a shock. But let us focus on one mystery at a time. Inspector Whitter, please. You will spare future subjects much pain with your cooperation: What is it that you and Chapman had in common? What are we missing here?"

She leaned forward, pressing Khlid to answer.

Now.

Khlid lashed forward, hurling as much of her arm between the bars as she could manage. Her clawed hand gnashed into the Anointed's shirt, but she was too slow. Khlid was faster than she had ever been — but not faster than a demigod.

Avi turned out of reach without even blinking, the question still hanging in the air. Only a small tear in her shirt evidenced of Khlid's futile assault.

Two of the hulking Grips stepped forward. The Anointed waved them off.

"Inspector—"

"Don't call me that!" Khlid barked, retracting her arm. "I'm no servant of the Empire."

Avi blinked before saying, "You don't share blood with Chapman, no heritage, not even a diet from what we can tell. Did you fuck him? It would explain why so many speak of your husband hating him."

Khlid shot the woman a disgusted look.

"We know you spent time alone with Inspector Chapman before his attack on the warehouse. We know it got violent. I had hoped that meant there was still a shred of loyalty in you." Avi stepped well within reach, daring Khlid to try and attack her again. The Grips moved in behind her. "Maybe Holden might provide some new insights."

Khlid exhaled. "He's alive?" She knew her mistake immediately.

Avi smiled at the leverage she had so easily uncovered. "Indeed he is. Spending his days drunk and weeping, last I heard. Certainly seems to miss his dear mentor."

No. Fuck you, no.

Holden was the closest thing Khlid and Samuel had ever had to a child. For a decade the couple had guided the lad away from his parents' deplorable ways and into... an active servant of the Empire. He would be a willing servant to this creature.

Her stomach twisted.

"I'm keeping a close eye on him. Give me a good reason, and I will have him assigned to a better precinct out of the Lower Districts." Avi stepped so close Khlid could smell her breath. "Keep what happened to yourself, and perhaps our scientific inquiries will require more subjects from the Seventh Precinct. I could certainly use more like" — she gestured to Khlid's claw— "you."

Khlid made a fist with the gnarled talon. "I have no idea why I survived!"

"I don't believe you."

"It's true. And that means you failed."

Avi blinked at the retort, then smiled. "Spot on, Inspector."

Khlid lashed out again. Her claw met flesh. She reveled in the feeling. Avi hadn't pulled away. Khlid dug in deeper, glaring into the Anointed's eyes.

They hadn't changed.

"Spot on." After a beat, Avi pulled away, the claws unsheathing from the flesh of her stomach.

Khlid watched the demigod's skin heal in moments. She had barely had time to draw blood.

"Arvin." Avi turned to one of the Grips.

He stepped forward in response.

"Bring me the apprentice—"

"No!" Khlid interrupted. "It was just a painkiller. That's all he gave me!"

Avi turned. "Chapman gave you a painkiller. What was it?"

Khlid continued, anything to cause the subject of Holden to fade from their minds. "Something purple. I'm not sure. I know his mother had taught him many of his people's traditional medicines. It had to be one of those."

"And how did the Drip get into you?"

"I was investigating the Pruit murders. I was first to discover Lord Pruit. His blood, it—" the taste had never truly left her mouth. "It got into a cut."

"A cut?" Avi said, her young eyes looking deep into Khlid's. "Where?"

"On my leg. When he fell onto me." The lie was pathetic. She had already given them what was important. But it might, *might,* slow whatever they had planned. "It healed up. I never mentioned it to anyone but Sam."

Avi said to the Grips, "Keep an eye on Holden. If we see better results with the Drip, he may live longer."

"Please." Khlid tried to look as defeated as she could. "He serves well. Holden would never do anything against the Almighty."

"That is good to know." Avi said, starting for the door. "One can always use another reliable pawn."

She stopped and looked back at Khlid. "The Almighty would reward you greatly if you accepted His power."

Long after Avi left, Khlid stood still holding onto the cold bars, planning how she could fulfill her promise to murder the woman.

❧ II ❧
WOUNDS

7

CRACKS

77 DAYS LATER

"I don't enjoy starting my day by beating officers." The gravelly voice barely registered as another fist slammed into Holden's gut, causing vomit to spill on his assailant's arm.

"Nasty cunt."

The sting of a ringed backhand cut a gash into his face. A hand twisted painfully in his hair and forced Holden to look his captor, Sergeant Rict, in the eyes. Well, eye. The brutish man had lost the right one to a thief's dagger years ago.

"You're going to be our new plaything." Spittle splashed into Holden's face. "Understand?"

Holden nodded. He had struggled, sworn, and swung wild fists at the officers. A gratifying dribble of blood leaked where Holden had managed to pistol-whip the fat face of the man now holding him down.

But now, that fight was extinguished. Each of the six uniformed officers had taken their turns showing Holden what they thought of his noble attempt of reporting their abuses of duty.

"Let 'em go." Rict barked.

The two officers holding his arms dropped him roughly into the alley grime. Holden couldn't have picked himself up if he tried. His stomach convulsed with pain. Both of his eyes were rapidly swelling shut. Blood poured from his nose and mouth. He tried to draw in breath, but blood caught in his throat, causing him to cough in pain.

Through shallow gasps, he managed, "Hospital, please."

The Sergeant placed his boot on the back of Holden's head and ground his mangled face into the dirt. "We know where you live, boy. You violated the uniform. Don't think one beating is payment enough."

Holden felt the boot lift from his head and heard the Sergeant snap his fingers. The sound of steps exited the alley.

Consciousness slipped away. For how long, Holden was not sure. He awoke to a light rain cooling his burning skin. He had never hurt so completely. Every command to move a muscle was met with sharp protest. As he vomited blood, the stabbing of cracked ribs caused Holden to scream. Bile leaked from his nose. He couldn't even curl into a protective ball.

Two days prior, Holden had come across six officers of the Fifteenth Precinct abusing several brothel workers. He had gone directly to the only Sergeant of the Fifteenth he knew, Rict. This morning, when Rict had offered to take Holden to the M.O.D. for a full report, he had been stupid enough to trust him. It wasn't until they were in the alley that Holden spotted the same six officers tailing them. Far too late.

Holden planted a fist in the filth below him and pushed himself to a kneeling position. The world swam before his eyes. He plunged into the grime again.

Almighty, please.

He thought back to the Seventh. The precinct ran so cleanly. The worst corruption he had ever witnessed in the Imperial District was sloppy paperwork. It had never occurred to him how unique the Seventh was; how rare. In his sheltered world,

Captain Williams, Samuel and Khlid had built something precious and delicate: a police force built on order and service. Through blinded eyes, he saw it clearly enough now. The service had been to protect the higher districts and nothing more. After the massacre, Holden had been assigned to the Low District with the Eleventh Precinct. Everyone on the force knew the Eleventh was where the Empire assigned officers it no longer wanted to deal with. It would bring shame to dismiss an officer— better to assign him to the area of the city filled with untouchables. No one in the Ministries cared who lived and died out here. Laying in the sludge, bleeding into the gutter, his own body had become evidence of that truth

"Mister?" a young voice called. A child.

Holden raised his bleary eyes. He lost his stomach again. He made out a shape approaching.

A slight pressure on his arm; someone kneeling over him. A small hand rummaged through his coat pockets. It dipped into several before noticing the sidearm tossed to the corner of the alley by Holden's attackers.

The boy began to walk towards it.

"No!" Holden managed to cry out. The child hesitated between him and the pistol. "Don't."

The boy brought him the gun and placed it in Holden's limp hand. "You'll die here."

"Get Krolf. Please." Holden sputtered.

Everyone knew the aged Krolf. One of the herbal healers of the district. He didn't charge for his work, but the community supported him in whatever way they could.

Holden did not even realize he had lost consciousness again until he awoke to the softness of a pillow under his head. Dirty sheets were pulled over him. The chills of a fever already roiled through his body. His only relief came from gentle pressure over his wounds: bandages. The old man had found him. By way of the child or not, Holden didn't know.

PAIN WAS the worst way to be awoken. Whether from a hangover or injuries, the result was the same. Holden let out a holler as the sensations registered with his conscious mind.

Something clattered to the floor.

"Shit, Holden!"

It was the clipped voice of Recki, a fellow officer of the Eleventh and the only one Holden would call a friend. She herself had been assigned there after reporting a senior officer for an assault.

Holden felt her cool hands press onto his head. "You scared me half to death." Her voice had the sharp, cutting accent of the lower districts. Her reassignment back home hadn't been a welcome career move.

He wanted to speak. The urge to tease Recki for showing concern for him was strong, but the pain rolling over him was stronger. All he managed was a defeated groan.

"Don't move, you twit." Her hand was replaced by something wet and cool. "I let the Captain know you got jumped. You have the rest of the week off. Just rest."

Holden's mind went back to the alley. The sting of the Sergeants ring.

"No." He wasn't even sure why he said it.

"Yes." Recki seemed exasperated. "You're late half the time anyway. You can take the time off."

He felt frustrated she had misunderstood his intent, but he knew it wasn't her fault. He didn't give a shit about the precinct. The protest was against the pain.

Holden focused on his breathing. It was difficult to get enough air when a deep breath would send pain shooting through his ribs.

"You could have died, Holden." The concern in Recki's voice was raw. "Keep that fat head down.

You aren't on the Inspector track here. I want to get 'em, too, but there's nothing to win."

Her words stung. Holden had once wanted to become a Captain. He wanted to use his position within the Empire to protect the vulnerable. At the Seventh, he had felt that he could. When he tied a thief's wrists and threw him in a cell, it felt like justice.

Down here, the reality was different. The thief he left rotting in a cell might have a family, and that family would go hungry for lack of stolen rations.

Tears seeped through his swollen eyes. The pride he had once felt so misplaced.

Through tears, he croaked, "I'm sorry."

"Hush." Recki stroked his face and hair. "It's okay."

She understood. Holden knew she understood like few others.

Holden shook his head, letting a sob painfully shake him.

Recki carefully got into the bed next to him. She cradled Holden as he wept. He wept for those he had hurt. At the loss he still felt. Above all, he wept at the black despair into which he now plummeted.

. . .

IT TOOK two days for Holden to be able to walk more than a few cringing steps. Krolf had fed him painkillers like candies, as well as a series of tinctures he claimed would stave off infection from "the filth you decided to nap in."

Now Krolf watched him try and navigate the stairs down into the main room of his home. A look of concern deeply etched itself onto his elderly face.

"More painkillers." Krolf spoke the words around a knuckle he gnawed on while thinking. "Still amazed you didn't get an infection."

Holden carefully lowered himself from the final step, feeling pride in the progress. "I drank my weight in your potions. I'm amazed I don't piss blue."

The elderly man barked a single laugh and went to one of his cabinets, pulling down several vials.

Lowering himself onto a stool at a table nearly overflowing with medicinal equipment, Holden asked, "When can I get back to work?"

"Don't." Krolf didn't turn from his table. "They did this to you, no? Stay away. You need a new start, boy."

Holden looked down at his hands, paler than he ever remembered seeing them. His nails were ragged and torn. Half-healed cuts mixed with fresh scrapes. Life in the Lower District was harder than Holden had ever thought possible. Before being assigned here, he had walked the streets of these districts. But there was a stark difference between passing through, and the reality of living. Ignoring the hungry faces had been so much easier when he did not recognize them. Now, Holden knew what life was like here. Yesterday, he saw grown men steal bread from a child. Cold-hearted desperation for survival turning regular people into animals in a pen. The worst part was learning it wasn't the people's fault. The empire had failed them. The food rations for the poor were disgraceful. Barely enough to survive on, while priests read from gold-laced scripture.

"I can't quit my job," Holden said, shaking his head.

Khlid and Sam put me on this path. I can't leave just because they're gone.

A hopeful memory flashed in his mind, of a woman clutching her bleeding boy, running into an alley. She had gotten away from the police raid. Many others in the illegal shelter had not, but he had saved them from the beatings.

I can correct this ship.

As if in mockery, pain from his ribs jolted him.

Krolf slammed a cup on the table in front of Holden. Tea sloshed violently within. "Then don't expect more help from me. I don't help the dead."

Eyes widening, Holden tried to protest but Krolf cut him off.

"I know those officers, Holden. They play with their food before they kill it. Those tinctures ain't cheap. I've used more than I can afford getting you back on your feet. If you go get yourself killed, it was wasted medicine." The lines in the healer's face deepened. His beard quivered slightly as he pointed his finger at Holden. "Don't stay in the city lad. Go."

Holden felt the plea in Krolf's blue eyes.

Maybe he could move to a smaller city and start over.

The faces of the seventh forced themselves to the front of his mind. Grief pulsed in Holden's heart.

Holden crumbled, feeling the hopelessness return. "I can't." It was a pathetic retort, but it was all he could muster.

FIVE DAYS LATER, Holden sat in a pub. His legs and back were healed, mostly, yet he was still unable to bring himself to stand up and walk into the Eleventh for the first time since the attack. He was usually late to his shift since starting there, but always due to his own negligence. This was different. This was fear.

Rubbing his face felt good. Pulling his skin and pressing on his eyes brought some relief from the headache pounding away. He had hoped drinking might kill the anxiety roiling his gut.

"Another!" An officer he knew, Jirrem's, voice cut through the air with his nasally rasp. "Come on! Hurry! We have streets to protect! You want us to be properly quenched, don't ya?"

Two other officers sitting at the table with Holden hollered in agreement.

A distressed young woman came to the table and refilled each of their mugs. Holden did not envy the task of taking care of four officers, but the pounding behind his eyes prevented him from sparing her an apologetic look.

His mind was instead focused on examining his life since his reassignment. He had left the M.O.D. after meeting with the Anointed determined to find the Rebels responsible for killing his fellow officers. For days, he read every report from the Ministry of Truth with a fervor unlike any he had ever felt. He wondered if that was what it felt like to think as quickly as Chapman.

The details didn't add up. No answers had been given as to why specific events of the night played out as they did. How Rebels had run amok in the streets, setting fires and murdering at random, and yet how almost no one witnessed them. Holden had tried and failed to track down the two witnesses on record. Ghosts.

The Empire was hiding something. Holden had become desperate enough to wait outside the M.O.D. and follow random officers about the city, trying to find any suspicious activity. Nothing came of it.

He had been lied to, and he had no tracks to pick apart. How much of the report was lies? All of it?

One question burned above all in his mind. Why in all the Almighty's wisdom had an Anointed been on standby ready to respond to such an attack, yet still been too slow to catch even one witness?

Bullshit, bullshit, bullshit.

When he had finally been reassigned to the Eleventh, Holden had been too busy to continue hunting ghosts. His life had been consumed with raiding thief dens, getting into brawls with gangs, and becoming embroiled in futile attempts to report the open corruption and abuse of his fellow officers.

He saw the physical toll every morning in the mirror. Khlid's strict exercise regimen was hard to stick to when he usually awoke in an empty bar, the hovering staff too afraid to try and kick out an officer of God. Instead of morning calisthenics, he was stumbling and vomiting bile in alleyways. In the last month alone, the last of his muscular youth had been replaced by a gaunt and sallow affect. Eating less than a meal a day and puking it up in the morning would do that.

Disgusted with himself, Holden pushed his mug away and forced his sore body to stand.

"Oi! Where you going?" Jirrem snatched Holden's stained coat sleeve with his reedy hand. "You don't have to report in for hours yet."

"I'm already late."

Jirrem's eyes widened and he addressed the table. "Well I guess that means I missed a whole shift!"

The other two officers Holden didn't know laughed through untrimmed beards with rancid breath.

The fatter of the two said, "Captain's back on the glass. He won't notice for another week."

Renewed laughter pushed Holden towards the door.

Sam would be rolling in his grave if he saw these men in those coats.

Holden stumbled on a boot, falling heavily on all fours. The stickiness of the wooden floors made his stomach want to heave.

Getting to his feet as fast as he could in his drunk and injured state, he was ready to drag the owner of the boot. Several curses died on his lips as sunken emerald eyes looked down at his own.

It was not a natural green. No one was born with eyes that faintly glowed. Those eyes reminded Holden of a recent hurt he had afflicted on someone undeserving.

He put a hand to his chest and said, "Apologies."

The behemoth of a man looked drunkenly at Holden. He seemed not to fully register what had occurred. Holden suspected he was under the influence of more than alcohol. Memories of war drove men to seek out dark reliefs. Grips above all.

The large man nodded vaguely in response, causing fat layered over old muscle to wobble.

Holden took his leave as fast as he could. Those eyes weren't noticeable only for their color. They seemed to glow with the pain of the past.

Sunlight brought Holden's head from a dull throb to a sharp sting. The morning air should have been refreshing, but in the Lower City, the stench of the street was suffocating. Holden often thought back to the cleanliness of the streets of Imperial Districts he'd patrolled. It had been impossible to tell then just how spoiled he had been. Holden had never seen the realities of the city he lived in. Now, he couldn't escape them.

Walking to the Eleventh took Holden far longer

than it should have. He moved at a shuffle, barely lifting his legs. His right hand kept unconsciously touching the holster at his hip.

Why am I here?

The thought had haunted his dreams ever since the Seventh was massacred. Why had he been allowed to live? Why had the Almighty seen fit to spare him, yet killed everyone who helped make him who he was? Was there something he could have done? Was there something he could do now to make it right? The thought was insane, but his mind seemed certain it was all somehow his fault.

He had not even been in the city at the time; yet he often woke up hearing the screams of the Seventh dying, his family butchered by traitors.

Chapman. It had to be Chapman.

Just the thought of the man brought rage into Holden's heart. Khlid and Sam were not guilty of treason. It was impossible. He would prove it one day. He would find out exactly how Chapman had tricked everyone into this and clear their names.

Apparently, his treasonous body had never even been found.

He could still be alive, and if he is, I will rip the truth from him.

Holden imagined ramming Chapman's head into a wall until his fingers felt the bricks.

Remembering just how large Chapman was, Holden decided shooting him in the knees at a distance might make a better start. The arms, too, just to be safe.

Stupid worthless tattooed bastard.

Then there was his gut. His gut told him it wasn't Chapman. His gut wanted him to continue down the ghostly path, the one he had started down when those two witnesses—

No! It's Chapman. It has to be.

Arriving at the Eleventh, the sound of the precinct washed over him. Several officers sat in a small circle laughing. Most ignored the few civilians waiting at the front to be seen.

As he walked by, those officers not totally oblivious to him openly stared at his still-visible injuries.

Holden found his desk in the pool and nearly fell into the lightly wooden chair with a creak. His sergeant gave him a disapproving look. Holden returned the look with a universal rude gesture. Having survived his beating and shown up to work, he could get away with a good deal. Holden had a golden ticket to be as disrespectful as he desired.

He pulled several dark green leaves from a pouch he kept beside his desk and began to chew them. The relief to his nausea came slowly but it was noticeable. Then a portion of it returned: it was

Chapman who had taught him this lesson in herbology..

Tea.

The thought pushed him to his feet and he walked toward a table with a kettle on a small burner.

"You're looking extra worthless today." Recki popped up on his right as she always did. Holden would have sworn she was half a fairy from the children's tales. The short brown hair and angled face completed the portrait of a fae. Although he didn't imagine fairies were so lethal, or had police uniforms.

"Appreciate the kind words."

"The Inspectors' exam is being given again next month. I figured with your experience as an apprentice—" She shrugged innocently. "You'd like to help me study?"

"Nope." Holden lifted the weak tea to his lips.

"Ah." She grabbed the cup of tea from his hand just before he could take a sip. "None of that for you until we talk about your plans."

"Plans?"

"You stopped seeing Flip."

Holden shot her a dangerous look.

Recki blew a raspberry in response."Oh, Pththth." She pulled the cup away from his reaching hand. "You've missed too many meals to be intimidating. At least Flip fed you."

Frustrated, Holden started to pour himself another cup, but Recki pulled the pot away. Holding the two containers of liquid as far from him as she could, the visual brought Holden a glint of amusement. "Would you just—"

Recki turned her back and began to walk back into the pool. She turned her head and said, "Tea is at my desk if you want to chat."

And that is the best officer in the entire Eleventh.

Officer Tripps approached with an empty cup and looked after Recki. "Sooo... the no tea is your fault I assume?"

Holden shrugged and walked back to his desk.

Recki was a beacon of light to Holden in an otherwise continual nightmare. She helped him adjust to his new life as well as anyone could, teaching him how to survive a precinct like the Eleventh. Plus, having someone who made it a priority to rib him as often as possible was refreshing when everyone else seemed to treat him like a refugee. But he knew Recki wouldn't have cut it in the Seventh. None here would.

And neither did you. *You let them all die.*

Holden collapsed back at his desk and began to look over a paper containing his assignments for the day. Regular neighborhood check-ins, a follow-up on a missing woman, children seen playing with a gun, reports of glass— a vicious, mind-altering concoction sold by the city's shadier apothecaries— being dealt to children, and a meeting with an officer from the Second Precinct to possibly connect two cases. Standard officer of God work. He just had to stand up and get moving.

His eyes felt so heavy.

Holden glanced at the board. He was partnered with Officer Tyth, which was an assignment he didn't hate. Tyth was weird, but he didn't talk too much and could be trusted with a gun. He was probably already out working, having given up waiting for Holden to report in.

Folding the day's assignments into his pockets, Holden stood and walked for the door. Recki threw him a grunt of disapproval, which he returned with a wink.

HE CAUGHT UP TO TYTH, who was with the family of the missing woman. No one had anything new to report to one another, and the two left, making vague promises about a continued effort.

"Just remember, we are always available to help. Day or night." Holden released the husband's hand

and turned his back, putting the family from his mind before the door was shut.

Tyth was already off the stoop lighting a cigarette from his pocket. "Did you hear we might get one of those pumps for water? No more hand-cranked showers."

The steam-powered pumps Tyth was referring to had previously only been available to the wealthiest of the Empire. But as things continued to progress, it seemed the law would soon enjoy such new privileges.

"Yeah." Holden pulled his coat tighter against the wind. The hints of winter were coming. "We'll have to find some other grunt work for the recruits to do."

Tyth let out a large cloud of smoke and tapped ash onto the cracked cobblestone. "Late again."

The way Tyth spoke, every word was slurred and blended together, mixing his consonants more often than not. Holden thought his voice was rather pleasant to listen to. Years of smoking combined with a Kallick accent made him sound like a friendly bear, dangerous only to others. It matched his hooded eyes and stress-lined face.

"Sorry." Holden pulled the papers from his pocket to check the location of the kids seen with a gun.

"Are you?"

Holden blinked at the words and looked over to the man.

Tyth didn't meet his gaze. "If you were sorry you'd stop doing it. You feel bad, maybe. But you're not sorry."

"Feeling bad and being sorry—"

"Are not the same thing. And you don't even feel bad about being late." Tyth pulled his own copy of the assignments from his pocket and checked the address. He began walking.

Holden had no choice but to follow. "Are you getting in the business of analyzing fellow officers then?"

"Just the ones worth a thought." Tyth rubbed his hands together, summoning warmth. "Everyone knows what you've been through. Must be tough."

Irrationally, Holden wanted to lash out at the extended concern. "Been a breeze."

They walked in silence for a few blocks before Tyth said, "The Whitters, Samuel and Khlid, did they—"

"Stop." Holden picked up his pace and hunched his shoulders. Tyth was just snooping. More than a few had done that. The married Inspectors had become known as the notorious traitor couple. The type of story people told over drinks. Manipulated by the insidious Chapman, they had been drawn into rebel plots.

They didn't—Chapman couldn't...

His mind flinched away from the thoughts.

Tyth caught up to him. Holden felt a hand on his shoulder. "Look, I'm sorry mate. It's just kin—"

"Stop." Holden jerked his shoulder out of reach. Anger rapidly consumed by repressed grief bled into his voice. "Please, just drop it."

"Holden, I'm not— okay, sorry."

They continued walking in the morning air.

Flicking his cigarette away, Tyth asked, "Are you sleeping well?"

"Tyth, one of the things I like about you is how little you talk." Holden didn't look at his partner, but he was sure there was hurt on his face.

"You just seem like you could use an ear." Tyth pulled another cigarette from his pocket. "That's all."

"Noted. No, I don't."

Arriving at a poorly-kept home for orphans, Holden took in the conditions the dozens of foundlings lived in. The house was comically over-crowded with kids, ranging from those just learning to walk to those bordering on adulthood. They darted about, lay in the sun, or giggled in huddles. While dirty, at least they showed signs of being well fed.

As soon as they saw two Inspectors approach, many of the older children vanished, stepping into the alleyway or running flat-out down the street.

Some of the younger ones ran about them, laughing. Holden kept an eye on their hands. One boy, no older than three, caught his attention. He was watching silently from a second story window, his thumb jammed firmly into his mouth.

"The Empire needs to do more," Tyth said, taking it all in. "This is inexcusable."

Holden nodded in agreement. "The wars took a toll."

"Right, so now we shouldn't be looked after? Those left without parents are an assumed cost of conquest. We should get another petition to the M.O.D. They have the money. Stop pouring it into defense when there are no enemies left."

They stepped onto the porch as the front door opened.

A tired-looking man with gray hair, the father of the house, greeted them. "I figured when the older ones went running."

Tyth showed his badge and said, "We've received reports of a child with a gun. You wouldn't happen to have seen anything, would you?"

The man grunted. "Just stories. A few weeks back a boy here bragged that he had had a gun. Just tales, Officer. Said some woman bought it off him. An excuse to explain some money the older kids found him hiding, which I bet he'd stolen."

Holden and Tyth nodded.

"He *did* have money, though?" Holden asked.

"Aye. Like I said. Probably stole it." The man leaned against the frame of the door and eyed the officers. "If there was a gun here, you'd be the first to know. I ain't letting kids get their hands on a firearm. Rivalries in this house run deep, ya see."

"I can imagine." Tyth said, taking the detail down in his notebook. "Can we speak to the boy? We have to follow up."

"Aye, though I don't rightly see the point." The gray-haired man moved out of the doorway and gestured inside. "He'll be upstairs in the first room on the right. Kindly is his name. Wait!" He put a gnarled hand on Holden's arm. "I don't like ya smelling of booze around my kids."

Holden pang of shame. "Had to rustle some drunks last night." He pushed past the man, lowering his head.

"Uh huh."

The home was a wreck. Holes littered the walls. Stains seemed to take up more space on the furniture than the original colors. The sounds of children screaming, some in play, others shouting in anger.

Squeaking stairs brought the two of them to a room filled with as many beds as would fit. Barely enough space between mattresses for a grown man to walk.

Two officers of God suddenly looming in the doorway silenced every child in the room. Eight pairs of wide eyes stared at them.

"Kindly." Holden said. Seven boys and girls all pointed to a towheaded child on a dirty mattress. "Thank you. Everyone else out."

"Ididn'tusethegunhonestitwasjustthereandthewomantookitrightoffoofme! Promise!" The torrent of words made no sense to Holden, but Tyth actually nodded in understanding.

"It's okay, Kindly." Holden said. "You're in no trouble with us. Take a deep breath for me."

Kindly took quite possibly the fastest breath Holden had ever seen.

"Would you mind trying that again?" he asked. "Slower this time."

Kindly took an even faster breath. Holden was worried the child would hyperventilate.

Tyth caught the boy's attention. "All we need is the truth, and we'll leave ya be. You can even tell your friends you told us to beat it. Deal?"

The opportunity to look good in front of his friends did seem to reassure the boy. His eyes still darted between the two officers with amazing frequency.

"Did you really find a gun?" Holden asked it as calmly as he could.

Kindly's eyes darted again. "Can you officers really tell when peoples is lying?"

"Yes." Tyth and Holden said in unison.

Kindly nodded before saying. "It were silver. Shiny and the like. It's why I asked for a full silver from the woman."

The officers exchanged looks.

Holden continued the interrogation. "What else can you tell me about it? Any markings?"

"Had a number on it. Seven."

Tyth's eyes shot to Holden as his own widened.

A beat passed before Holden put a hand on his own weapon and drew it.

Kindly nearly leapt out of his seat.

"Relax, it's okay." Holden said. "Just want you to verify something for me."

The boy's breath became shallow.

Holden turned the gun in his hands, feeling his own heart race. He showed the seven on the butt of his own gun. "Like this?"

"No." Kindly said.

Relief hit Holden like a carriage.

Kindly continued, "The seven were surrounded by leaves."

Tyth actually stood as Holden's eyes shot through the boy, trying to detect some hint of a lie. His heart pulsed and full sobriety took over.

"An Inspector's mark." It wasn't a question from Tyth. More like an involuntary spasm.

Holden kept his wits enough to ask, "Kindly, what did the woman look like? Tell me everything you can possibly remember and I will buy you a new set of clothes today."

HANDING the father of the house several coins from his wallet, Holden instructed him to buy Kindly the best outfit available. He promised to come back and check to make sure the boy was given the gift.

He wouldn't.

Without looking at Tyth, Holden began marching down the street.

A woman, not matching Khlid's description, went looking for and retrieved an Inspector of the Seventh's sidearm.

"Holden." Tyth caught up. "This has to be reported to the captain."

"Why?" Holden didn't look back at him.

"Rebels, the butchering of a precinct, bunch of officers dead, an Anointed—"

"And you want the same to happen to the Eleventh?" Holden said the words as coldly as he possibly could.

"Well... I don't—"

Holden interrupted again. "The Rebels butchered a precinct. If they find out we're onto them, what's stopping them from doing it again? Are you sure someone in the Eleventh isn't with them? I say we forget this and go about our job."

Tyth went quiet. Holden could feel his mind racing.

In reality, Holden itched to chase this down. He just didn't want a single soul from the Eleventh involved. He had to find this woman, alone. No one bought a dirty gun off a kid who would obviously blab. She'd been looking for it. She would know something. No one would prevent him from questioning her personally.

I'll finish today's shift, and then I'm done. I'll walk away from this fucking job and get to the bottom of this on my own.

He considered asking Recki to come with him.

"Holden." Tyth's voice sounded cautious. "This could lead to the people responsible for what happened. You want to walk away?"

Lining his voice with false fear, Holden responded, "Yes, Tyth. I can't... the M.O.D. handled it. One pistol won't lead anywhere. What do we have? A vague description of a woman from a child. You want to track her down? Go right ahead."

Holden realized that, even keeping his intentions secret, he had nothing better to go on. He didn't care. He would still run it down the best he could.

As the sun crept below the city's buildings, Tyth and Holden entered the Eleventh. Fresh officers preparing to work the night shift bustled about. Two slept on their desks. Holden kicked the leg of one, causing him to snort loudly as he sat up straight looking about.

Recki leaned against Holden's desk, waiting for him. Her black officer's coat was unbuttoned, revealing a plain white shirt.

"Been waiting long?" he asked, tossing his own coat over his chair.

"Don't mind." Recki said, openly looking at his injuries. "Pain?"

"Not bad. Kolf's drugs are—" Holden pinched his thumbs and middle fingers, a gesture meaning perfection.

Recki smiled slightly, her one dimple flashing. "Good! I miss tossing you around the mats." She threw a few light jabs his way teasingly.

"That so?" Holden whipped his hands up and slapped her final hand away.

"Ooooooooooo." they said in unison, exchanging grins.

"Holden!" The Captain nearly screamed his slurred words, just feet behind Recki.

They both turned to look at him in surprise. Captain Trimmer was clearly high, his eyes nearly entirely white. One of the strange effects of glass.

"Get to my office!"

Recki just shrugged saying, "A woman went in there earlier. Maybe someone from the M.O.D.?"

A sudden ache in Holden's stomach warned him of danger.

8

CONFESSION

Walking up the creaking stairs, Holden noticed Recki openly watching him with a guarded posture, nervously picking at her nails. He had to suppress a grin. Her concern was oddly reassuring.

The Captain flopped down into Holden's chair, staring at nothing. The motion pulled the last tails of the Captain's shirt free of his stained trousers. A wondrously disheveled man.

A smile died on his lips when he entered the Captain's office. Avi Cormick sat in the Captain's chair, a smile on her face.

Holden could have vomited.

"Hello, Officer Sanders." She leaned forward, seeming to stare into his soul. "Please take a seat."

Holden stood unmoving. His mind screamed for

him to run. He didn't know why, but he wanted to flee. Not just from the room, but from the city itself, and never return. As soon as he thought it, he felt she must somehow know and disapprove of his plan. Was it insane to think the Anointed could read thoughts?

"Holden." The Anointed voice was soft, yet firm. "Please, sit."

Forcing himself into motion one leg at a time, Holden sat across from Avi Cormick, the woman who had told him a cascade of lies about the slaughter of the Seventh just two months prior. The cracks in her story had been visible immediately — indeed, she hadn't seemed to care that they were— and it had nagged at Holden every day since. Why would Captain Williams not call in nearby precincts for aid, who would have been able to respond far faster than the M.O.D., unless he had a reason to believe they wouldn't help the Seventh?

If they were truly going to get rebels, no answer could be found. Lie. How had Khlid, Sam, and Chapman all been killed, but none of them had been taken into custody while other rebels escaped? Convenient. How did the rebels have the ability to hunt down and kill dozens of patrons and workers of the brothel that was burned? Impossible. How would they even know where they live? Only imperial records would be that comprehensive. At first, he had been willing to chalk it up to the secretive nature of the M.O.D. There were plenty of 'official' reasons Inspectors, let alone one still in training, couldn't be given the full picture. But the more time passed, the more his mind fought against the smile the Anointed had left him with. He now refused to fall into line without a question. Holden owed Khlid and Samuel more than that.

Avi leaned back and steepled her fingers. "Don't worry. The Captain just thinks I'm some M.O.D. higher-up following up on... the incident. And I suppose that is true. You haven't told anyone about me, right?"

"Course not." Holden managed.

She looked at him, as if expecting more.

All he could think to say was, "You look good in civilian clothes."

The Anointed grinned at the compliment. "Still charming, I see."

Holden could bring himself to offer no more. Instead, he pulled a cigarette from his pocket and lit it. Maybe doing something with his hands would hide his frayed nerves.

As he exhaled smoke, Avi asked, "How have you been, survivor?"

"Not well." Holden gestured to the building around them. "You stuck me in a shithole."

The Anointed blinked in surprise.

That's right, I am done with Imperial posturing.

Voice shaking, Holden continued. "You lied to me. Khlid and Sam weren't a part of the Rebellion, and you knew it. Chapman was, but you just lumped them in with him because— I don't know why. You didn't even bother to lie to me properly. Almighty, not even the official report aligned with your story. I guess you thought an apprentice Inspector, not even thirty, would never dare to doubt you?"

Holden leaned forward and ashed his cigarette. He knew he might be signing his death warrant, but Avi was in civilian clothes, and the Anointed only drew blood in uniform. He would at least live long enough to walk out of the building. So he dug on.

"But I did. I do. I don't think the M.O.D. hunted down any Rebels. Why would you want to take down the one group who justify your ever growing power?" Sweat began to pour down Holden's back as the Anointed tensed. "I think you stuck me here to blind me. Take a traumatized man and stick him in the shittiest precinct in the city. Put him in a sewer, so he won't smell the bullshit you're feeding him."

Holden sat back. All of this had been festering inside of him, waiting to come out. He drew breath and spoke what could be his final words: "For this conversation to continue, you need to admit one thing."

Avi blinked once before saying, "And that is?"

"You're here to make sure I won't cause any trouble." Tears formed in Holden's eyes. "You don't give a shit what really happened in that warehouse."

The Anointed stood up, her boots sounding heavy as she slowly walked to the door and shut it.

Holden closed his eyes, pondering if she might actually be willing to kill an officer in a precinct after all. He said a prayer to the Almighty under his breath.

Instead of pain, or the oblivion of death, Holden felt a soft hand on his chin.

Opening his own eyes, he saw Avi's own gray gaze. She smelled of sweat, but not horribly so. Her breath was that of tea and mint. He felt her nails ever so slightly touching his skin.

God, she is stunning.

"I'm so sorry for your pain, Holden, but I am not your enemy. I also do not work for the M.O.D. None of the Anointed do. We do not control what they put into the reports. Any discrepancies that caused you pain, I am sorry for."

If he didn't know any better, Holden would have thought she wanted him to kiss her.

"I... " Feeling fat tongued, Holden tried to will away the tear slipping down his cheek. "I know you're not my enemy."

Avi leaned back against the desk and let his face go. "Then why are you starting a fight with me, Holden?"

"I'm not."

She quirked her brows. "I don't enjoy petulance, Holden. Do you think I personally assigned you here? Do you think I know anything beyond what was handed to me in reports? I am no spy. I am a soldier. I spent that night doing exactly what I told you, running in the rain, trying my best to save lives. To you, that makes me part of some conspiracy? Now there are lies being told, but to the public, not to you."

Guilt rocked through Holden. How had he been stupid enough to think she had anything to do with his placement here?

"As for not hunting down the Rebels..." Avi walked to a window looking over the street. "Holden, do you know exactly what the Anointed's purpose is now that the wars are over? Of course you don't; no one does."

Holden watched her take a deep breath before continuing.

"We are each assigned a city to protect. Every

man, woman or child is considered our personal responsibility. The Rebels have killed one thousand and forty seven people I value as my own. Your comrades included."

She's kept count?

"The real reason I came to see you here today is to warn you. Rebels have infiltrated the Ministries. That may explain some of the... discrepancies that so bother you. They are certainly within the police precincts as well, so be careful who you trust, Holden."

Is that why the Captain didn't call for help from the precincts, or another lie? Is Avi an ally?

"As for the guilt of your mentors," Avi slumped back into the Captain's chair, "I don't know. I won't lie to you and say I believe their innocence, but I need you to admit you are not unbiased in this matter."

Holden sat up straighter. "I know them better than anyone else still walking—"

"Exactly, Holden."

Silence between them. Holden's mind balked at her insistence, but a part of him knew she was right. Officers were to recuse themselves from working on cases involving anyone related to them.

"Have you found anything I should know

about?" The Anointed asked the question with just enough intensity to prick Holden's ears.

"You told me not to pursue the case." Holden wished he had kept the cigarette lit.

"Weak dodge." Avi's expression made him feel like a child caught with his hand in the sweets jar. "Holden, I need a friend out here. Someone not filtered by the M.O.D."

Keeping anything from the Anointed seemed pointless. Maybe she *was* his ally. He did believe that if she found anything, she'd tell him. Avi didn't... *feel* like the rest of the M.O.D., and she certainly didn't display the false swagger of other highly placed figures he had met. She struck him as someone trying to do a job.

"Can I ask you something?" Holden pulled out his lighter and lit a new cigarette.

"Of course."

"Have you found anything you haven't told me?"

She leaned forward and cocked her head to the side. "Of course, Holden. But nothing that would help you yet. When I do, I'll be at your door. Day or night."

Holden believed her. He hated himself for it, but something in those eyes made him believe she was just as eager as he was to get to the bottom of all of this. He relented. "Do you know anything about a missing gun?"

Her expression lit up at the question. "No, that hasn't come up."

"A boy in an orphanage named Kindly found a pistol. It was from the Seventh. Best I can tell, it had to be related. Too weird not to be. Best part: it was an Inspector's pistol."

The Anointed gave a faint smile unlike any he had seen from her before. It possessed a coldness he found unsettling. "Is that all?"

"A woman came searching for it. Specifically that gun. She knew it had been lost. She bought it from the boy."

Avi licked her lips. "Holden, I need you to tell me everything."

9

A BRAVE COWARD

Jotch Holdir, a portly balding man, was not known for his courage. He was painfully aware of just how meek he tended to be. Speaking to others outside his immediate family made him nervous and his list of friends was, well, empty. But that was exactly why he pushed down the fear welling in his gut as he felt the lock click on his editor's door.

For you, Michael.

The office was clean, almost barren. The desk, a single chair on each side, was simple. A tall filing cabinet stood on the opposite end of the room, Jotch's target.

Months of preparation had led to this moment — this mission— as he thought of it. He had spent weeks carefully watching the movements of the security guards here within the Ministry of Truth, too afraid to jot down any notes that might be discovered. During that time he had also frequented the roughest pubs he knew, trying to find someone to teach him how to pick locks. It turned out you couldn't entirely learn it from a book. It wasn't until he sought out new, "adventurous" speakeasies that he succeeded.

Jotch had been introduced to a kind woman with lovely red curls and golden skin. For a month's salary, she had taught him how to pick several different types of locks with simple tools, which had cost extra.

Standing inside an office he once hoped would eventually be his, Jotch found himself slightly *enjoying* the adrenaline of being on the cusp of a criminal act.

Closing the door behind himself, knowing the next patrol wouldn't be by for at least two minutes, Jotch hustled over to the cabinet.

It should be row three, column seven.

After checking to make sure the drawer was actually locked, Jotch made quick work with his tools, earning a satisfying *click* in under a minute. The drawer slid open smoothly, revealing dozens of cases yet to be taken to the archives. They would be kept here for a year in case clarification or revision was necessary.

Jotch glided his hand over the dates until he arrived at one in particular: the day after his brother's murder. The date of the massacre of the Seventh Precinct.

It was missing.

Did they move it to storage early?

After double-checking the drawer, Jotch began to pick the lock beneath. Perhaps they had misfiled it.

Yes, the most catastrophic event in the last decade of the Imperial City just happens to be misplaced. Fool.

Pocketing his tools, new plans began to form in his mind. If his own editor wasn't allowed a copy, one person in the building had to have it.

Jotch pulled the door to David's office open and walked directly into Rowyn, the security guard for the floor.

Rowyn looked down at Jotch with a mixture of confusion and concern. "Everything okay, Minister Holdir?"

"Yes, how about yourself?" The awkwardness of the question was painful to Jotch's ears.

"Everything's fine." The guard cast a glance at the empty office behind Jotch. "May I help you with something, Minister?"

"Ah, yes." Jotch stuffed a sweaty hand into his pocket and removed a draft he had been working on earlier in the day. "I need David's approval for a date change. His door was open, but no luck. Any idea where he might be?"

Rowyn relaxed slightly. "Aye. Up at the top floor in some briefings. Should be back in about an hour."

"Well, shit." Jotch adjusted his glasses and looked down the hall, mind racing. "This really needs a stamp."

Rowyn let out a soft cough before saying, "I could take you up. Just gotta stick by my side, of course."

Forcing a look of relief through his abject terror, Jotch said, "You wouldn't mind?"

"Course not." Rowyn clapped Jotched on the back as they both headed toward the lift.

Jotch had to force himself to pay attention to the small talk Rowyn put forth about his baby sister while they rode up in the ridiculously slow lift. Jotch felt himself dehydrating as his nerves pulsed with energy. They would emerge onto the top floor, where the highest Minister worked, and Jotch would ask clarification for a date he knew was right, all while hoping by some miracle he would have a chance to dip into the Head Minister's office. Undetected.

I'm going to die. I'm going to die. Oh, God, I am going to die.

The lift door finally opened and the two stepped onto the gray and blue marble of the M.O.T. Jotch felt faint as two security officers questioned Rowyn about the purpose of their visit before ushering them through.

The new electric bulbs blazed into Jotch's eyes, amplifying a nascent headache. Noisy typewriters clacked away inside his skull. A woman's cackle from a boardroom caused him to jump.

"Uhh... you okay, Mr. Holdir?" Rowyn's face was twisted with concern.

"Ah, yes." Jotch gulped. "Just need some water."

"Let's sit you down." Rowyn placed a hand on Jotch's shoulder and lowered him onto a bench in the hall, also made of fine marble. Waving over another guard, Rowyn asked for water. While the man jogged off, Rowyn asked, "You look like a curse landed on you."

Jotch tried his best to look amused. "Thanks, Rowyn. Not like I'm about to see the boss."

The guard grimaced an apology.

"Do you know where David will be? I don't know which room holds the editors' meetings." Jotch accepted a glass from a returning guard with thanks.

"I believe room seven 'round the hall there." Rowyn pointed.

"That—uh, great. Thank you. Can you take me there?" Jotch's throat felt tight.

"I really don't think that's such a great idea, Minister." Rowyn's voice was low and sincere. "You're looking like you might drop your breakfast."

"I'm fine!" His voice was too loud. "I just need to get that signature."

The receptionist at the front was glancing at him now, too, with open concern on her face.

Oh, shit.

Rowyn put his hands on Jotch's shoulders, forcing him back into his seat. "You're sweating something awful."

Oh Almighty, I can't breathe.

Jotch tried to loosen his necktie as Rowyn began to fan him.

"Get a doctor!" Rowyn was shouting.

Jotch realized he was laying down on the bench.

Rowyn was lifting his legs up, sending blood to Jotch's head.

Why is he doing tha—

Blackness consumed him.

. . .

JOTCH CAME BACK to the world as three men stood over him. He recognized Rowyn and his bespectacled editor, David, but there was a third man his mind could not place.

"Never seen a grown man have a fainting spell before." Rowyn's hands still fanned Jotch's face.

"Mmmokay." Jotch's words sounded as if it they came not from himself, but the lips of a drunk in another room. His thoughts seemed to be over there, too. "Just had a fall."

Almighty, but I sound loopy.

"Take the man into my office."

Four hands grabbed Jotch and helped him into a room he didn't recognize. As his vision cleared, he saw large tapestries and a magnificent black desk.

Jotch was plopped into a comfy chair and a wet towel pressed against his head.

The world returned to focus.

Minister Quil —The Minister of Truth himself— looked down on Jotch with worry in his brows. "Is more water on the way? Who is clearing the broken glass? Give him space! He needs air."

The hands pulled away from Jotch.

He noticed David in the corner, eyeing him with suspicion. Likely wondering what had brought Jotch up here in the first place. This was only the second time in his career Jotch had even set foot on this floor.

"I'll get water, sir." It was Rowyn's voice.

"I can't—" Jotch had no idea what to say. One of the most important men in the entire Empire was fanning him with a book. Jotch tried to take the book for himself. "I can do that, sir— Minister. Your Truthness, uhh—"

"Writer, do not worry!" Quil said, the badge of his utmost rank shining in the light. He pulled the book from Jotch's reach and continued fanning. "We're all a bit overworked these days. David!"

Jotch's editor stepped forward.

"Rowyn said this man was here for a date confirmation. Take that paper from his pocket and get it done."

David did so, snatching the paper from Jotch's pocket and all but jogging from the room.

To his amazement, Jotch realized he was nearly alone with the Minister of Truth in his office. Two guards stood just outside the open door, but that was all.

"Well! Some color is returning to those cheeks." The Minister finally slowed his fanning. He extended a hand. "My name is Quil. Jotch, I believe, correct?"

"Y— yes." Jotch's name must have been mentioned the moments he had passed out.

The Minister of Truth knew his name.

His handshake was firm and quick.

Quil stood and went to his desk. He pulled a bottle from a drawer and poured two glasses.

He handed one to Jotch. "Do you need a minute? We can sit here and drink. We all need breaks these days."

"Thank you, Minister."

"Don't think twice." The Minister sipped and gestured for Jotch to do the same. He did. "May I ask you something while I have you here?"

Jotch nodded.

"David... is he ready for a promotion?" The Minister tented his fingers. "Think it over carefully and be honest. I'm your boss's boss's boss. I can smell lies."

The wink he tossed at Jotch almost made him spit out his drink.

Not having much choice, Jotch thought about David: How he had chewed out several Writers for mistakes that were the Editors' fault. He thought of David looming over him, even though — because? —David knew it caused Jotch to make more mistakes with his mechanized writer. And finally, he thought of how this was probably his last day in the M.O.T., whether he succeeded or not.

"No, sir. Frankly, he is terrible at the position he has now."

The Minister blinked.

"He puts blame on others, as no leader should, especially when the mistakes are entirely his own. He takes credit for things he didn't do. His drain on morale is palpable. Every single Writer under him simply hates their job because of *him*." Jotch slammed the rest of the drink, feeling a rush in his blood. "If anything, I'd demote him."

The Minister didn't blink for several seconds. He stared at Jotch before taking a deep breath.

"Jotch, if it wasn't for your stellar reputation I might punish you for those words. But they felt true. They actually match some whispers I've heard before." The Minister stood and walked toward the guards. "If you'll excuse me."

And just like that, Jotch was alone in the Minister of Truth's office.

He stood, wobbly legs threatening to betray him, and lurched toward the desk. His eyes desperately scanned the files splayed before him. Well over a dozen case files; were any of them... no.

Jotch's eyes bulged.

All of them were related to the Incident. Tabs

atop each file claimed they were reports on other, more innocuous matters. Yet within each folder were details on the same subject. That horrendous night. A fast reader, Jotch swiftly synthesized the purpose of these files.

They're working on a cover story. In fact, a narrative to smooth over inconsistencies with the first *cover story.*

Jotch had written the original false report. He knew how flimsy and rushed the explanation was.

What sounded like the end of a conversation reached his ear.

Panicking once again, Jotch's mind screamed for him to do something.

Selecting a form within a file that bore several red tabs, Jotch stuffed it inside his pants. He tried to mask the sound of paper crumpling with several coughs before re-tucking his shirt. He swiftly restored the files to the way he had found them, then fell back into his chair, all but hyperventilating.

Seconds later, the Minister walked back into the room carrying a glass of water.

"Here you go."

The glass was cold, and beaded with condensation.

"Are you okay, Jotch?"

"Feeling somewhat better. Ready for work." He forced a grin.

The Minister of Truth patted his shoulder. "I almost believed you for a second. Jotch, you forget, I had your job once. I know what the stress is like. I'll be back in a few minutes to check on you. I told the guards outside you're officially taking a mandated break in here. Take all the time you need. In fact, if you're still here when I get back, we'll play a game of chess. Deal?"

Jotch nodded.

The Minister left, closing the door behind him.

"Th—thank you." Jotch's voice echoed in the large room. Under normal circumstances, he would have been delighted to take the Minister of Truth up on a game of chess. It had been ages since he had a decent game.

CLOSING the door to the Minister's office behind him, Jotch nodded to the two guards. He hoped the folder's worth of paper stuffed into his pants wasn't very noticeable.

The smaller of the two guards walked Jotch to the elevator and bade him a nonchalant goodbye.

Jotch returned the gesture as the doors closed.

The moment they did, he fell against the wall

and nearly shrieked from the thrill. He rang the bell for the ground floor and the cart began moving.

Of course the guards here wouldn't suspect him. For Almighty's sake, he had brought them his mother's pastries. And the Minister was known for being sweet to his underlings. The further down the ladder, the nicer he was.

By his math, Jotch would have roughly fifteen minutes to get out of the Ministry before the papers were noticed missing. Then he would begin the second phase of the plan: contacting an apprentice Inspector who had lost his mentors to this lie. According to everything Jotch had read on the man's history kept at the M.O.T., the officer was his best bet in finding an ally willing to help. Jotch had carefully examined many candidates connected to those who perished that night. Holden, still actively on the force, would be both open to the truth, and connected enough to get Jotch out of the city.

His glee was cut off as a wave of nausea hit him. His breakfast indeed hit the floor.

10

THE HUNT FOR A BRAVE
COWARD

voiding eyes within the precinct was easy for Recki. Most paid her little mind as she went about her business. Being invisible was a talent she had carefully developed over the years. When she wanted to be seen, she would be. It was about posture and positioning. Small exploitations of the human mind.

This current situation required all of her talents. The Captain was of no concern. The aged man was in the middle of the officer desk pool, sitting in Holden's chair. Her commander stared at his own trembling hands, a common side effect of glass, oblivious to the activity of the bustling precinct. No, her obstacle came in the form of officers going about this damn business.

As she casually maneuvered toward the office

door, close enough to hear, Tyth accosted her.

"You know, Recki, I'm free this evening."

The man stood directly between her and the captain's door. "That's nice," she replied, trying to peer past him.

"There is a show going on at Poe's Pub just a few blocks over. Right on the water. It starts in about an hour." Tyth pulled something from his pocket and handed it to Recki. "Would you like to go?"

Almighty! Move, you horny mule!

"Sure." She snatched the paper from his hand. "See ya there."

The officer's face forced itself into the focus of her vision, a broad grin on it. "It should be a great—"

"Is that what you're going to wear?" Recki put on a stern face.

"Uhh." Tyth looked down at his stained uniform. "Well, it's—"

"You'll need to change. Meet you at your place in thirty." She flashed him an impatient grin. She wasn't sure how he would take the dismissal, until he damn near leapt down the stairs, presumably to freshen up for his date with himself.

Bah, she thought, tossing the ticket into a bin.

Nonchalantly, Recki leaned against the wall next to the door — out of view of most.

Pressing the side of her head to the wall, she

strained to hear.

The sound of the doorknob turning caused her to leap back, then stumble. She bounced to her feet and scrambled as far as she could.

Ahhhhhh! The internal scream was an art she had mastered.

Acting remarkably casual, Recki put one arm high into the air and pretended to be stretching against the railing. A totally, completely, normal activity to be doing outside the Captain's office.

Holden and the woman —remarkably beautiful, with gray eyes and an angular face— exited the room. She looked right at Recki. "A friend of yours?"

Holden smirked. "Indeed."

"Does she often exercise outside the Captain's office?" The woman turned to Holden and looked him far too deeply in the eyes.

"Couldn't think of a better spot myself." Holden returned her look rather flatly. But Recki recognized the small signs. Holden was aroused.

Bloody idiot.

The woman softly touched Holden's shoulder and pulled him down to kiss his cheek. "Be well. If you need to talk, come to the M.O.D. You're on the guest clearance list."

Holden actually stammered. "Yu— absolutely, Avi."

He's embarrassing.

Holden watched the woman go all the way down the stairs.

"Cough cough, Holden."

The man actually jumped before turning to her.

"Almighty, your flirting is like sandpaper on a baby's ass."

Holden put on an indignant look. "I got a kiss!"

"Then why aren't you leaving with her now? Coulda had a tumble for sure." Recki looped her arm through that of her friend.

"'Cause I want to keep breathing." Holden walked her down the stairs. The woman was already gone.

Huh. Fast.

"Oh? Is she dangerous?"

"As dangerous as any Anointed." Holden whispered.

Recki froze. A look of shock lifted her brows.

Holden stopped in time with her, having anticipated the reaction.

"Are you joking?"

"Nope."

"You just met with an—"

"Yup."

"She is—"

"Mm-hm."

"And she just—" Recki touched where the woman kissed.

"I was surprised, too." Holden stepped forward with a shit-eating grin.

"I'm bringing you home again tonight."

Now it was Holden's turn to freeze in his tracks.

Two officers close enough to overhear looked up from their desks.

Recki lowered her voice and said, "Well, if magic snake kisses give royal girls kingdoms like in the fairy tales, then maybe a kiss from an Anointed will make a tumble with you worth it this time."

Holden cracked a laugh.

After several drinks, a few laughs, and a bit of flirting at their favorite spot, they did end up walking onto her porch, properly drunk. Holden's hand traced its way down the small of her back onto her ass, pulling her closer.

Recki flashed him that wicked grin, leaning in and inviting more.

He pulled her into a kiss. She bit his lip; he liked it.

The door wasn't even shut before Holden tugged open her shirt, exposing a tattoo of thorny vines climbing her ribs.

Feeling his lips on her neck made her frustrated that he wasn't already naked.

Hair pulling, cursing, and hot breath all blended together. Holden always fucked her with a mixture of passion and aggression she loved. His fingers entered her, causing her to bite him with a moan.

"Easy Reck. I'm still heal—"

She grabbed his cock and licked his neck to shut him up. Holden growled as he pushed her back onto the kitchen table. His head sank between her legs, kissing her thighs before delving deeper.

His efforts were rewarded with a small cry of pleasure, the first such sound of the night. Her fingers knotted in his hair. Holden had gotten to know her body well; now that they each had some practice with the other, she found herself bothering her neighbors soon enough.

Recki sat up and pulled Holden up to her. She bit his lip once more before whispering into his ear, "fuck me."

Holden hungrily obliged.

Enjoying the bliss rolling through her body, Recki watched as Holden walked to her sink and pumped them both water. His broad shoulders and lean body still excited her. Though admittedly, he had been far more attractive when she first met him.

He returned to where she still lay on the floor

and handed her a cup, which she drank greedily.

Holden was not the best she had ever had, but he was a damn good ride.

"Go get a blanket," Recki ordered him.

"Shouldn't we go to bed?"

"Not ready to stand."

Laughing, Holden picked Recki up and carried her to her room. They lay like that, wrapped together for some time.

She played with his unwashed dark hair and stubble. "How's your mind been treating you?"

"Same, but I have something I'm set on."

"What's that? Also, you were late again today. I smelled the booze."

He let out a long sigh. "Yeah. Listen. I might not turn up at all one day soon."

"Holden, you can't quit." She tugged on a hair he had clearly missed shaving more than once.

He winced. "I found something. A lead."

She sat up. "What did you find?"

Holden told her of the child with the gun, and the mystery woman who had purchased it.

"I... okay."

He blinked in surprise. "I'm not a mule, fool, dolt, or idiot?"

"No." She lay her head back on his chest. "This is important. More important than the Eleventh. But keep coming into work, at least until you get some traction on this, okay?"

"Deal."

When he began to snore she rolled out of bed and walked back to the kitchen. She had chocolate in her icebox and zero intention of sharing it.

Enjoying the treat, the feeling of being naked and satisfied, Recki thought about Holden. He was a good time, but she planned on settling down with a woman. Since the day she met him, she had known Holden would be in her life forever. He was too decent a man not to keep close. She had a slight fear he might fall in love with her, which would snap an axle on an otherwise wonderful journey.

Shoving off that possible drama, Recki considered her job. She liked being an officer well enough, but she was no loyalist. The Empire was just the system she survived in. It provided protections and dangers, just like everything else. The city was what she was loyal to. She knew every street and corner. Thousands of them burned into her mind. The world outside was a complete mystery to her, one she had zero desire to see.

So what do I want?

The question haunted her most of the night. She had escaped the harshest conditions, risen high, and... her mind flinched away from her assault.

And now I'm still not back where I started. I own this home. I control my day and life.

She wasn't even thirty and the home was completely paid off. Something no one in the history of her family had ever managed, to her knowledge.

I am Recki fucking Tamlin.

Recki returned to Holden, nuzzling into his warmth. She hoped the oaf would stick by her side at the precinct a bit longer.

Maybe we would both do better in private security?

THE NEXT MORNING, the two of them resumed their constant poking. Recki shamed Holden for being out of shape, though he was still far healthier than most officers at the Eleventh. In response, he pinned her to the kitchen table and repeated his performance from the night before.

"Come on, shift starts in two hours. We got to get a run in. We can swing by your place." Recki stretched her calf with a grimace.

Stretching is unholy.

"I wanna hit the—"

"So help me God, if you say bar..."

"Tavern."

"Holden!"

"I need a drink." Holden avoided her glare and tried to put on a jovial tone. "Just a couple to start the day."

"You need to get your shit together." Recki didn't hide her scorn.

Holden turned his back to her, lacing his boots. "I'm recovering."

She scoffed. "A couple drinks to tolerate the day. Yep, solid steps to recovery."

He put his hands on his knees, boots still unlaced. "I just need—"

"You'll never get to Inspector—"

"The Eleventh doesn't *have* Inspectors!" Holden shouted. His fists clenched as he stood. "They took me off the—"

His chair clattered to the floor, cutting him off.

Recki did not flinch. She looked at him with open contempt. "In control, I see."

The anger in his eyes vanished as quickly as it had appeared. He picked up the chair.

Recki didn't comfort him. He didn't deserve it. "All you do is drink, fuck, and half-ass your job, Holden. You've been through it. I've been through it. This is where they put us. They want us out of the way. It's on *us* to look out for ourselves. You won't get better until you work on you."

"I know, Recki." Holden sat back in the chair. "I

know. I don't think I can be an officer anymore."

"Well, that is for you to decide." She left him sitting there. Holden knew where the spare key was. He could lock up.

Stepping out into the sun, she took a moment to feel it on her skin. The day was warm and bright. Even the lousy start to the day couldn't ruin her run. Seeing the city rush by as she cleared her mind was the perfect form of meditation.

Blood pumping, Recki shattered her previous record for the route she had taken. To her surprise, Holden still sat on her porch, gasping for breath in his exercise attire. Sweat dripped from his face in thick lines. "I didn't get very far."

She opened her mouth.

"Don't." His finger went up. Holden drew in another large breath before saying, "Oh my god, my chest is going to explode."

"Please tell me you didn't just run in those filthy clothes you left here weeks ago?"

Holden nodded.

"Almighty, Holden." Recki couldn't keep the amusement from her face. "I could run to yours and be back before you catch your breath."

Holden raised a different finger.

Laughing, she took her friend inside to wash.

. . .

"I'M JUST SAYING, if we pooled our money, we could get one of those fancy new pumps. No more working up a sweat in the shower, Recki! Think about it!"

She pushed open the door to the precinct, rolling her eyes. "And whose place would we have it installed at?"

"Well, we spend more time at yours." Holden seemed to be seriously thinking it over.

"'Cause yours is a hole."

"Hole?"

"Hole."

"A nice hole?"

"Sure."

He flopped down in his desk chair, smiling the most genuine smile she had ever seen on his face. "This news will take time to digest. Who knew I was living in a hole?"

"Everyone who has been there. No need for the M.O.T." Recki sat at her own desk and began reading over the morning reports.

HOLDEN'S HEART RACED. The top of the morning's report detailed the hunt for a traitor named Minister Jotch Holdir. As there were no leads, the report only detailed why he was wanted. Holdir had stolen files related to the slaughter of the Seventh Precinct.

Recki read along with him. "Holden, don't—"

It was too late. He was already on his feet, running to the Captain's office, taking the stairs three at a time.

Throwing the door open, it bounced off the wall and crashed into Holden as he saw a member of the Red Hand sitting at the desk, badge reflecting the name prominent on his chest. The man had white hair and dark eyes. A feature common to very few regions of the Empire. Thick muscles were visible through the man's shirt. Under normal circumstances, Holden might have tried to flirt with the man.

"So, knocking isn't a thing here," the man said, lowering his pen.

Holden walked to the desk, not taking a seat, "You know who I am. Has he been found?"

The muscular man's eyebrows arched. "Oh, do I know you?"

Holden was taken aback. He thought everyone near the M.O.D. in the city knew of his assignment here. "I'm the surv— I lived— the Seventh. Officer Holden Sanders."

Recognition lit in the man's eyes. "Ah, I knew you were here, but not your name." He gestured out the still open door. "I'm glad you weren't a part of the crew working here last night. Almighty, they're useless."

Holden didn't argue, but he smelled deceit. "Where is the Captain? Who are you?"

"The M.O.D. doesn't like what they have seen from a few of the precincts. Certain captains are being reprimanded and replaced. I'm Sergeant Marx. You'll report to me."

"The fuck I will."

"Excuse me?" The Sergeant stood from his chair.

"The M.O.D. has no jurisdiction over officers. You—" Holden realized he had no reason to fight this battle. He was being lied to in some capacity, but he could not tell why. He was frustrated and done with this game. "Fuck it, I don't care. Has he been found?"

"The missing Minister?"

"Almighty, Yes!" Holden's heart was racing. He had no idea why this Minister would have taken those files, but he would steal them from him if it was the last thing he did.

Marx leaned back in his chair. "That is none of your concern. Given your connection to the case, I'm taking you off the manhunt. There is plenty of work to be done with the city going into lockdown. Gates and docks to watch. You'll be— where are you going?"

Holden tossed his badge over his shoulder. "I quit."

Recki caught up to him as he dropped his coat on the staircase, heading to the front door. "What're you doing, Holden?"

"Leaving."

"They won't let you." Recki said, keeping stride with him.

A cry of "Officer Sanders!" echoed down from above.

"Too bad." Holden pushed open the door and walked into the sunlight. The sounds of the busy street cut off whatever Recki said next.

He started running.

Got to get home and think of a plan. I know where the M.O.D. will look first. I just have to stay ahead. Inns and pubs are already being swept. I'll start with... stables?

Thinking through the monumental odds in front of him, Holden realized how stupid he had just been. Even if he was forced off the case, he might have been able to get close once the man was in custody. Now?

Pushing open the door to his home, Holden began to reconsider. If he did manage to find this

Jotch, he could finally get the truth. Those files had to contain the unfiltered truth; otherwise the M.O.D. wouldn't have cared *this* much about his stealing them. They *were* hiding something. This was all the confirmation he needed.

Holden walked to the kitchen table he used only as a bar. He uncorked his favorite whiskey, racking his brain for a way to get ahead of the search parties. He had even spotted one emerging from an alley on the way home. The soldiers with rifles and dogs had caused the crowds to split like water over stone.

Maybe he's hiding in one of the abandoned warehouses. That's where I'd go.

"Uhh... excuse me."

The voice caused Holden to drop his glass and cough on the whiskey traveling down his throat. He wheezed, trying to draw his pistol as tears welled in his eyes. His back slammed against the wall and he continued to sputter, seeing a figure standing in the doorway to his bedroom.

"Who—"

A man matching the exact description of the missing Minister walked into the light.

"My name is Jotch." The short man gestured to his own chest. "You're Holden, correct? The apprentice of Khlid and Samuel Whitter?"

11

ABUSING FRIENDS

"Could you please lower your weapon?" Jotch said, trying to step out from where the pistol was pointed. "I've never had one pointed at me before."

Holden did not oblige. Instead, after he got over his coughing fit, he pulled ties from his belt and tossed them at Jotch. "Put those on, now."

Jotch glanced down at the ties and felt a pit in his stomach.

"Mr. Sanders, if you—"

The sound of the pistol's hammer cocking shut him up. "I won't ask again."

Jotch leaned down and picked up the restraints. He laced his hands through and pulled the clasp.

I can still talk with ties on.

"There," he said. "Can we talk now, Officer?"

Holden holstered his pistol. "No." He closed the distance between them and turned Jotch around. A foot to the back of his knee sent Jotch painfully to the floor. It was even dirtier up close.

"Ouch! Oh, Almighty, Officer, please."

"Why are you here?" The officer pat him down. "Where's the report?"

"Oh, so you heard? Good." Jotch tried to get to his knees, but Holden roughly held him down. "Now, listen here."

A hand knotted in Jotch's hair, and his head was slammed into the wooden floor boards.

"Where are they?" Holden growled.

Jotch tried to clutch his head. The pain was explosive.

Holden slammed his head once more. "Tell me, you shit."

"On your bed!" Jotch cried, desperate to make him stop.

Holden picked up the smaller man by the collar and dragged him into the bedroom. As soon as the officer's eyes landed on the papers, he dropped Jotch and ran to them.

Jotch curled into a ball, clutching his head and suppressing tears. The pain was extraordinary. He couldn't understand why the officer had attacked him. Did he not realize he was here to provide the truth?

The sound of the front door opening froze both of them. Their eyes met, wide with panic.

"Holden?" A woman's voice said, boiling with frustration. "Holden, where are you? That asshat that replaced the captain is trying to put together a posse to come arrest you. He sent for backup from the M.O.D. You just made yourself a wanted—"

The short, rather pretty owner of the voice appeared in the doorway. She glared at Holden before noticing Jotch on the floor.

"What the Hell? Is that—"

"I have the papers!" Holden said with a fervor that scared Jotch, and the woman, judging by her flinch.

She recovered and stepped toward Holden with both hands up. "That's good, Holden. But why's he here?"

"I don't know," Holden said, looking at Jotch. "But he brought the truth with him. Is the door locked?"

Holden walked past the woman as she knelt to Jotch. "Are you okay?"

"He attacked me," Jotch whispered. His voice trembled. He had never even been hit before.

The woman's eyes softened a moment. "My

name is Officer Recki Tamlin. But just call me Recki, okay? You're safe."

She placed a comforting hand on his head before standing and whirling on Holden as he reentered the room. "You attacked him!"

The accusation stopped Holden in his tracks. "He's a fugitive."

"Was he resisting?"

Holden didn't answer.

"God damn it, Holden. You're better than that."

He pushed past her and stepped over Jotch before returning to the papers.

Recki knelt to Jotch once again. "Where are you hurt?"

"He—"

"I knocked his head," Holden said, cutting him off. "He'll be fine. Wasn't that hard."

Recki bared her teeth. "Holden, a man wanted by the entire city comes to your place, and you don't take two seconds to realize he's seeking refuge? You didn't stop to think maybe he was *bringing* you the evidence you've been looking for?"

Holden stopped his reading and looked at Jotch. "I... I'm sorry. This—" he gestured to the papers with his eyes afire. "This is it!"

Jotch managed to sit up with Recki's help. "Yes, I know. Which is why I expected a warmer welcome."

Recki stood and went to Holden's side, looking over the papers as well. "What do they say, Jotch?"

"Well," he said, still clutching his head, "the truth is far different than what my editor passed on to me. It was about steel. Steel and... something else. Something even classified reports wouldn't come right out and name."

The fervor still in his eyes, Holden dropped the paper he was reading and turned on Jotch. "What? What was it?"

"I don't know, you mule." Jotch got to his feet with some trouble. The ties were quite obnoxious. "It looks like your mentors found out the Ministry of Defense murdered the Pruit family so they could confiscate the family's steel production." Jotch looked over the papers. "The Pruit family tried to sell outside the M.O.D. to enrich themselves. They were made an example of. Something terrible was done to them. Something beyond an execution. Soon the M.O.D will let rumors of the truth trickle to the royal families. The most influential families within the empire will believe they will be struck by the Almighty itself if they work against imperial will.

"You don't know what exactly was done to them?" Recki asked.

"The original reports of the murder investigation are all gone." Jotch eyed Holden, failing to keep the disdain from his look. "Your mentors were trying to expose the truth. Some kind of power play unfolded there and I still don't know all the pieces to it. But the military was willing to butcher an entire precinct to cover it up."

"I knew it." Holden's voice shook with passion. Papers crumpled in his hands.

"Oi!" Jotch said, reaching to save the documents.

Recki moved, wrapping her arms around Holden. The man openly wept in her arms. She silently cried with him.

"It's okay, Holden. You were right. You knew, and you never betrayed them." Recki ran her hands over Holden's face and kissed him. "We can expose this."

A sob shook the officer. "Oh, fuck, I told her, Recki. I told that woman about the boy. She had to be a part of the cover-up too."

Jotch felt extremely uncomfortable. He was clearly witnessing an intimate moment between lovers. He stepped out into the kitchen, allowing them their privacy.

Almighty, this is a hole, Jotch thought, cleaning a glass in the sink as best he could without soap before gingerly drinking from it.

Splashing cool water on his head, Jotch felt some relief from the assault. He spent several moments taking deep breaths, calming himself not just from the attack, but from, well, everything. He had spent the night hiding under this stranger's bed, hoping for a protector. Instead, he had received a drubbing.

"Mr. Holdir?" Holden's voice was calmer.

He opened his eyes, turning to the voice. "You can call me Jotch."

The officer gave a slight smile. "You can call me Holden. Thank you. I'm so sorry for hurting you. I have no excuse."

Jotch thought of agreeing there, then shrugged. "A stranger— a fugitive— was in your home. Also, safe to say you're probably not over what happened."

Holden didn't respond.

"And why would you be?" Jotch refilled his glass, pumping more water. "We're all on edge."

"Yeah, we both have enemies."

"That explains the—" Jotch gestured to Holden's partly healed face.

"Yup. Thank you, for all of this."

"Of course." Jotch dried his face with a stained towel. "I'll call us completely good if you do me one favor."

"And that is?"

"Get me the hell out of this city."

IN HOLDEN'S LIVING ROOM, Recki kept one ear on the conversation in the kitchen while she sorted through the documents in Jotch's file. Something there shocked her. She grabbed the file and stepped into the kitchen. "Where's Khlid's death certificate?"

"What?" Holden asked.

Recki held the thick stack of papers out. "I was looking at the files. The death certificates for everyone involved that night are here. "Chapman, Captain Williams, a bunch of brothel workers, officers, families of officers, but no Khlid Whitter. They're even alphabetized. Khlid isn't there."

Holden took the file, flipped through the pages and said, "They must have forgotten it."

"No." Jotch said from the other side of the room. "She's alive, Holden. Promise to get me out of the city, and I'll tell you where she is."

Jotch took them back into the bedroom and showed them a transfer of custody. "I spent last night hiding under your bed reading these reports. There is a prisoner transfer. It gives some unspecified agent full legal *ownership* of 'former Inspector Khlid Whitter'".

"Impossible," Recki said.

Holden remained silent a moment before saying, "Okay, I promise to get us *all* out of the city, after we get Khlid. Fair?"

"Not at all," Jotch interjected. "You can't get her out. Khlid's been brought into the highest cells of the M.O.S.. Called 'The Playground'. It's where the most radical experiments are carried out. You won't be able to get her out. It's nearly as secure as the M.O.D. itself."

"I'm going to get her," Holden said. His heart felt like steel. "I'm going to kill that lying witch and free Khlid."

"Holden." Recki's voice attempted calm. "Think this through. That's an Anointed you're threatening."

"An Anointed? What?" Jotch took the form from the officer, fearing he might crumple another priceless part of the puzzle. "If an Anointed is involved, an attempt at rescue would be beyond moronic. I gave you the truth. I hope it helps. Now I need my favor in return. Just—"

Holden headed back to the kitchen.

"Holden!" Recki yelled after him. She scooped up the papers in a messy pile.

They both left Jotch with his mouth hanging open.

"What are you going to do, Holden?" Recki said. "Run into the Ministry of Science guns blazing?"

"Don't be stupid." Holden said, opening his rifle cabinet. "I'll sneak in."

Jotch scoffed. "Are you a child?"

They both looked at the Minister. Recki looked as though she shared his assessment. Holden's eyes flared with anger.

"I get that Mrs. Whitter was important to you, but suicide, which this would be, helps no one." Jotch gestured to his ties. "Could you?"

Recki stepped over and removed the restraints.

Holden took a deep breath. "I know it's desperate, but I cannot leave her."

Recki nodded in agreement. "Exactly. Which is why we need to be careful. You think it was a coincidence that a member of the Red Hand happened to take over our precinct the day these papers went missing?"

"So we're all traitors then?" Jotch didn't know why he asked the question, but it produced complete silence for several seconds.

Holden was the first to speak. "Are we, Recki?"

She met his eyes. "Never thought of myself as a loyalist, just a fighter."

Holden felt oddly aroused at the glint in her eyes.

"Don't worry, Holden." Recki poked him. "I knew you'd figure out the Empire was shit soon enough. I'm used to being ahead."

"I don't suppose either of you know how to

contact the Rebels?" Jotch looked between the both of them. "No? Damn. They must have ways out of the city."

Recki's face flashed with realization. "We gotta get you both out of here."

"Why?" Jotch and Holden said in unison.

"Holden, you just tossed your badge at a member of the Red Hand."

"What?!" Jotch backed into the bedroom. Fear was ablaze in the man's face.

"Ah," Holden said. "Yeah, there will be a follow-up."

Recki looked to Jotch. "And he told that Red Hand he was looking for you, Writer. So you're coming with me."

"He can't stay with you," Holden interjected. "Everyone knows we're close. You'll probably be interviewed."

Jotch began to take quick, shallow breaths. "I thought I would be safe here." The man's voice cracked slightly.

"Deep breaths." Recki looked somewhat amused. "We have a wonderfully powerful friend who no one knows Holden was extremely close with."

The Writer's breath slowed.

Holden felt a knot form in his stomach. "No. Not Flip."

"Yes. Flip." Recki walked towards the Writer and took his arm. "You'll need a cap. Holden, you have one?"

"Not Flip," Holden repeated, knowing it was pointless.

Recki stuck out her tongue as she snatched a hat from his coat rack and plopped it on Jotch's head. "Now, Mr. Minister, we're going to see Holden's ex. The one he stopped seeing without telling him, or me, why."

"Well." Jotch looked as if some semblance of calm was returning. "At least I might get a show."

12

CLOSED DOORS

As they stepped out of Holden's front door, Recki said she needed to grab some things from her place. Tucking the bulging folder under her arm, she darted off. Neither man had time to interject. An awkward silence fell between the two of them.

Holden began walking.

Jotch had to take several rapid steps to catch up. The painful lump on his forehead, covered by the ugly cap he now wore, didn't exactly make him feel chatty. Still, he hated being uncomfortable around strangers. At several points during their long walk, Jotch tried to initiate conversation with the officer, but all he received in return were curt "yes" answers.

Arriving at a small house near the middle wall of

the Capital City, Jotch was surprised by how tired he felt.

Holden strode through a waist-high gate and onto the front path before pausing halfway. Following behind, Jotch looked him up and down. "Is there a problem?"

"Many." The officer continued toward the home.

Looking back onto the street, Jotch watched a carriage roll by. A neighbor hanging laundry stopped to wave at Jotch. He returned the gesture noncommittally. It all seemed excessively ordinary. Still, Jotch felt watched.

Knocking started him back into the moment. Holden was pounding his fist on a thick wooden door. "Flip. It's Holden. Open up."

Jotch caught up to Holden at the door, his tension radiating from him.

Holden pulled a kerchief from his pocket and tried to hand it to Jotch. The thing looked thoroughly used.

"Umm... why?" Jotch did not want to offend the Inspector, but he wasn't about to take a snot rag.

Holden didn't even look at him. "Your nose is bleeding."

"Ah." Jotch pressed the rag to his nose and began wiping.

Several more moments passed.

"Flip, I know you're home. Open the door!"

Jotch looked around. The nice neighbor lady was staring. "I don't know if yelling—"

Holden's glare made Jotch jump. "Right, never mind me, then."

Holden seemed to be trying to glare the door open. "Who exactly is Flip?"

"He's a Grip."

Jotch was amazed. "He can access the Grohalind? And... he's just living here like an ordinary person?"

"He's reached his limit. He can't access it anymore without risking torching himself." Holden flat-out punched the door this time.

Jotch jumped in response, then tried to mask it by running his hand through his hair. The cap fell from his head. "Flip the Grip. That's fun." He picked the cap back up and plopped it in place.

Caps are so... blah.

As Holden turned to Jotch in annoyance, the door was finally jerked open.

The largest man Jotch had ever seen consumed the space. He loomed like a mountain made flesh. The man bore a similar energy to the bears held in traveling circuses. A tired strength, worn down in an irreversible way. If Jotch had worked out every day of his thirty-two years and never skipped a meal, he doubted he would be half as muscular as the man before him.

"Good God," Jotch said aloud, before planting a hand over his mouth. "I mean, hello."

Flip looked over Jotch once before dismissing him outright. "Get off my stoop, Holden."

Holden didn't balk an inch. He pushed Jotch in front of him and said, "He needs protecting. I have nowhere else I can—"

Flip began to close the door.

Holden barked, "It's about the Seventh."

The behemoth paused.

Jotch noticed his glowing green eyes for the first time. They were truly spectacular.

Flip opened the door fully. "All right, you have five minutes."

THE HOME WAS SIMPLE, but nice. The sparse decorations, mostly industrial in look, went well with the space. Jotch particularly liked the curtains pulled back over iron hooks. "Your home is lovely."

Flip grunted in thanks, before looking to Holden. "What is this?" The man's dark skin made the green of his gaze stand out even more on his brick-like face.

Holden sat in a cushioned chair, gesturing for the

other two to do the same. "You know the suspicions I had? The theories we went over and over?"

Flip settled in on the couch, next to Jotch. "It was all you would talk about after sex."

Jotch choked. Both men looked at him.

"Sorry," Jotch said. "Guess I'm used to a bit more subtle—"

Holden cut him off. "Well, they're not just theories anymore."

Flip leaned back on the couch. "Explain."

Holden and Jotch began speaking at the same time. Holden's face flashed with frustration, but he gestured for Jotch to continue.

"I work— well, worked, I guess— for the Ministry of Truth. I stole evidence that proves they lied about what happened to Holden's friends." Jotch rubbed his chin. "Now, I gave that information to Holden here in the hopes he would get me out of the city. Payment, so to speak."

Flip's eyes narrowed. "Why, why, and why?"

"What?" Jotch was thoroughly confused.

"Why did you steal the information? Why choose Holden? And why do you think he'll help you?"

"Ah," Jotch said, looking at the young Inspector. Holden looked curious too, actually. The man had been too excited to ask these questions on his own.

"My brother was killed. Half-brother. He worked at the brothel that was burned. Before he went home that night, he came and saw me. He told me of a female Inspector seeking refuge, terrified of something that was coming after her. The Mother at the brothel helped her. She was a good woman from what Michael said of her. He left, eager to see me look into his story. The next day I was handed a report claiming he died hours before he even visited me. In the files I stole today, it reports how everyone who may have seen something that night was murdered to cover the M.O.D.'s ass. For what, I still don't know. Records within the M.O.T. were used to locate where they *all* lived. Massacred just for helping. Simple as that."

"I'm sorry," Holden said.

Flip put a hand on Jotch's shoulder. "You're doing this for your brother?"

"You're damn right," Jotch said. "When the report was put on my desk to write, his name was there. It said he died in the fire. Obviously, that was before he came to see me. I thought as soon as they noticed he was related to me, they would get rid of me as well. But I just received an apology and a bonus for having to report on my own brother's death. My editor personally commended me for 'doing my job even in the worst of it'. Asshole."

Jotch took a breath. "To your second and third questions: from that point on, I used my M.O.T. position to research the surviving members of the Seventh. What I needed was someone within the police who already suspected that my colleagues and I had been feeding them horseshit about the Seventh's massacre. Under the circumstances, Holden seemed like my best shot. I just didn't know you would have quit your job. Now, my companion here is a rogue Officer of God. The rogue survivor. Not exactly someone they'll let through the gates unmolested."

Holden shifted uncomfortably at the moniker.

Flip stood and walked into the small kitchen. He put a kettle on.

"Well, I started planning," Jotch continued. "I wanted to get the truth. I was able to get trickles of information through clarification requests. Holden is one of the few; and he's been written up for disruptive behavior several times since his reassignment to the Eleventh.

"I figured if I could bring him some proof that the massacre of his friends was part of a cover-up, he'd be willing to pay me back." Jotch coughed, knowing it sounded like a stretch. It had been. But it was all he had. "So I did. Now we all know that Khlid's alive, we —"

"Khlid is alive?" Flip's voice boomed. It more than matched his size, like a boulder falling into a cave.

Holden sat forward. "Yes. And we have to get her out of the M.O.S."

Within half an hour, they had caught Flip up. In retelling the details, Jotch realized it couldn't have been a coincidence that the Red Hand had seized control of the Eleventh. Passively watching Holden had probably been their plan to catch Jotch. There was one small comfort, Jotch thought to himself: *no one* had expected Holden to suddenly walk away from his career. That had fouled up the Hand's plans as badly as Jotch's own.

One can't fault Holden's motivation, I'll give him that. He's slow, but motivated.

Flip's start of surprise shook the entire couch when Holden mentioned Avi Cormick, the Anointed. "Avi Cormick? The Butcherer? You met with her again? Holden, you idiot. What did you tell her?"

"I gave her the description of a woman. Apparently this person bought a gun off of a child. It matched the description of an Inspector's gun from the Seventh." Holden rubbed his neck and sighed. "Probably shouldn't have told her that."

Flip finished his tea and hurled the cup at Holden.

The officer, impressively, caught the flying dish. It seemed to be a practiced part of their relationship.

"You have one lead, *one,* on the Rebels, and you hand it to the woman who probably killed your friends?" Scorn dominated the Grip's tone.

"You think Avi killed—"

"Why else would she be so involved?" Flip looked to Jotch for support.

Jotch nodded in agreement. "Seems about right."

Flip continued, "The M.O.D. had a secret project. Everyone who got close to it and tried to raise an alarm died. You think that wasn't the work of an Anointed?"

Holden's face twisted in realization."Oh, Almighty."

Flip stood and went to Holden. He rested a massive hand on the officer's shoulder. "Holden, since I met you, you've been a mess. The minute we met, you basically moved in with me for a month. You're lost. You latch on to anything you think will replace what you lost. And now it's bit you in the ass."

Jotch blinked at the frankness of the observation. He wished Recki had been here to— wait.

How could I forget?

"Holden, some men came to your house last night!" Jotch blurted out. He felt small as the men's joint gazes reached him.

"What?" Holden said, standing.

"Sorry! With everything happening I forgot. They circled your home for a good while, calling your name."

Holden looked at the man, flummoxed by his stupidity. "Why didn't you tell me before we left?" He pulled his pistol from its thigh holster, checking the rounds before replacing it.

"I was hiding in your closet at the time. I couldn't do anything about it then. Some time after that, you came home and beat me senseless." Jotch rubbed his head to emphasize the point.

"And after we agreed to work together?" Holden asked, still incredulous.

Jotch offered weakly, "Well, then, I was *recovering* from the beating." A detail occurred to him. "Lacking context, I suppose I thought they might have been drinking buddies. I'm quite sure they were officers."

Holden and Flip exchanged looks.

Flip was the first to speak. "The Fifteenth?"

A look of fear appeared on Holden's face. "They know I stay with Recki sometimes. I gotta go. Flip, watch Jotch."

The behemoth looked at Jotch and said, "No problem. But he can't stay more than a night."

"Fine by me," Holden said, leaving out the front door.

Hearing the latch come into place, Jotch looked about the room. "Don't suppose you play chess?"

To his surprise, Flip brought out a board.

13

WITH TROUBLE COMES
TROUBLE

Recki crammed the last of her emergency kit into her backpack and looked around her home. She was unsure what the immediate future held, but it felt as if the wind was at her back. Her whole life, she had never had much faith in the Almighty. She had signed on as an officer in hopes of —well, earning a decent living— but also helping protect the people. Years of experience had robbed her of that illusion. In the expensive districts, the precincts played at protecting those who needed it least. Down here, where children went hungry and unbathed, corrupt officers bullied their way through the ranks. She had gone numb to it. Keeping her job to eat had kept her coming in. Now Holden had accidentally bought her a way out by finding people who were called to a truth Recki could follow. Her heart filled with something she had not felt in years. Purpose.

A fat pile Imperial Will turns out to be. Will of God? Will of bureaucrats. She amused herself by pretending to gag.

She clasped the buckles of her pack and slung it over her back. The papers were as hidden as they could be at the very bottom.

Now, if I were a rebel, where would I be?

There was a soft knocking at her door.

Recki froze. She didn't have many friends, and none who would come unexpectedly to her home.

A second, louder knock now.

I wouldn't be there.

Recki made her way to the back door. She turned the latch as quietly as she could and peeked out. From her limited view, all seemed clear.

One of the porch boards to the left squeaked.

On instinct, she ducked.

An officer's club smashed into the doorframe, through where her head had been.

Recki fell backward and drew her sidearm. She tried to shrug off the pack, but the straps were too tight.

Shit, shit, shit.

A uniformed officer stepped into the doorway,

blocking the light. A Fifteenth Precinct badge glinted on his chest.

Recki fired a haphazard warning shot at the doorway.

Someone screamed from out in the street as the uniformed man fell back out into the yard.

"Do you know who you are fucking with?" she screamed. "Give me one good reason, and I won't miss again!"

The front door burst inward from a kick, showering her in splinters. Three officers spilled into the kitchen.

Recki kicked her kitchen table at them, and ran for her bedroom. She barely managed to lock the door before the weight of a body slammed into it.

Seconds, Recki, seconds.

She managed to get the pack off. The rifle latched to the side was illegal for civilians to own. She slid it off the pack as her bedroom door rattled violently.

An odd, giddy excitement rose in Recki's stomach.

Never gotten to kill officers before. Least I know they deserve it. You owe me again, Holden.

"Where is he?" a voice shouted. "Give us Holden and we'll let you be." There was fear in the words. They hadn't expected a fight.

Recki chambered a round and slapped the breach shut. In one smooth motion, she leveled the gun and fired. The high caliber round obliterated the door and met flesh.

A holler of pain came to her ears as she loaded another round, leveled and fired again.

"Crazy cunt!" a man screamed.

There was now a hole large enough for Recki to see through. One officer was dragging another out of the way.

Too late.

Recki aimed at the carrier and put a bullet in his head. A cascade of blood painted her wall.

A pistol appeared at the split in the door, firing blindly.

Recki dropped behind her bed.

Five shots; a moment of silence; the sound of the ruined bedroom door being kicked open.

Too close now.

Recki dropped the rifle and pulled her pistol. She rose and aimed at a muscular man, diving across the bed toward her.

He slapped her arm to the side and tackled her waist.

She was slammed into the wall before they both collapsed to the floor. Her ribs creaked.

The man threw a blind fist toward her. She

deflected the best she could with her left, then jabbed her right elbow into the attacker's face. He clutched his face at the blow, letting her go. A second man was nearly on her, boot pulled back for a kick.

Pathetic.

Recki rolled, taking the kick to the back, and crawled under the bed. Someone tried to grab her ankle; she crushed his fingers with her boot. She kicked her way to the other side as a woman with a rifle barreled into the room.

Well, shit.

Recki went for her only remaining option: from a low crouch, she leapt for her pack, then out her bedside window.

Landing on glass and grass, Recki was more shocked than injured. Still struggling to bring in air, she pulled two shards from her side.

Tattoos will need touching up.

Saying a prayer of thanks, she rolled to her feet. Her first full breath in what felt like a minute came to her.

Her back door opened and two officers stepped out. She couldn't outrun them with the pack.

Well, they don't look like they've kept up with their training.

The thought was little solace. A fight would still be two-on-one, with a third coming.

They stopped a few paces short of Recki.

"You fucking killed Thompson!" the fatter of the two said. "I'll gut you." The other glared at her with unchecked rage.

"The score is at least two." Recki gestured back inside. "Bet the other bleeds out."

The fatter man snarled and came at her.

Recki dodged a wild swing and brought her knee to his groin.

The man collapsed to the ground with a dog-like whimper.

The second man came in throwing punches. She blocked them deftly. Boxing had always been her favorite form of combat.

She ducked a blow thrown too wide and landed a heavy gut punch. But the man didn't double over.

Going back on the defensive, Recki noticed the man looking over her shoulder. Instinctively, she ducked.

Thanks for the warning.

A rifle passed above her, swung like a club.

Rolling, she put her back against the wall. The man and woman jumped her together. Fists, feet, and elbows rained down on her head and body. Her arms could only block the first few blows, then gave out. She fell, rolling into a protective ball. A boot kicked her in the jaw.

"Drag her inside!" the man she had kneed in the groin said, finally hobbling to his feet. "We'll find out where he is one way or another."

She was thrown to the kitchen floor. Several more kicks made sure she stayed there. Recki was hurt, but not as terribly as they thought.

Glancing about, she saw the wounded man appeared to have bled out as she predicted, leaving three assailants.

A boot forced her onto her back. Her own rifle was stuck in her face.

The female officer breathed hard as she said, "We'll kill ya quick if you just tell us now. Where's Holden?"

"You're an idiot," Recki barked.

The woman lowered the rifle to her gut and pulled the trigger. Only the click of the hammer sounded.

"Didn't load it," Recki laughed, blood on her teeth. "Fifteenth's filled with inbred morons."

The woman raised the gun above her head to swing down on Recki. As she did, a crack split the air.

Everyone flinched as fresh blood rained onto Recki's face.

Recki lifted her head to see Krolf, the medicine man, standing in her destroyed doorway.

Another shot split the air and the fatter man fell dead.

Finally, the rifle dropped from above as her assailant accepted her death. Another bullet ripped the woman's chest open.

Recki caught the falling gun and pulled a round from her belt.

Krolf's wobbling arm raised the pistol a third time and leveled it at the last officer. "Don't move."

"I'm an officer of the law! You will—"

Recki snapped her weapon closed and took aim. A final crack silenced him forever as his head erupted.

Laughter. Recki heard someone cackling.

Oh, it's me.

Recki got to her knees and laughed hysterically.

The healer eyed her as if she might be mad. "One of the boys came running. Said he saw men circling your home. I should have gotten the police, but—"

"No," she said through tears of laughter. "You're my hero, Krolf."

"Almighty, Recki. Cops?" The old man looked down at his pistol. "I'll be executed for this."

Recki finally suppressed her spasms of mirth and got to her feet. "No, you won't. Tell them I shot them. All you saw was me running for it."

Putting her pack on was painful. She dreaded how she would feel once the adrenaline left her. "I don't think I'll see you again, Krolf. Thank you for taking care of Holden." With that, she kissed him on the cheek, leaving a smear of blood. Then she snatched his gun and darted out the door.

As she wiped the last of the blood from her own face, she nearly crashed into Holden rounding the corner.

"Recki!" he breathed. "God, what happened to you?"

"Gods, Holden. If we're going to be traitors, we might want to break Imp—"

"Not now!" he barked. "What happened?"

"Well, the Fifteenth wanted to annihilate you. I killed three. Krolf got two." The look of confusion on Holden's face nearly made her cackle again. "I got what we need; let's get that Writer and go someplace safe." As they jogged through the alleys, Holden used his sleeve to wipe away the blood Recki had missed on her face and neck.

"Gods," Holden said. "Are you okay? Are you sure?"

Recki wasn't okay, her stomach and ribs burned, but she nodded.

Realizing she was leaving her home behind, Recki grabbed Holden's arm and made him stop. She kissed him, still feeling a deep thrill, enjoying his breath, before saying, "We have to start being careful, Holden."

He hesitated before muttering, "Of course. We'll look over each others' backs and—"

She shook her head, pain building in her neck. "Look at us, blood-stained, running through alleys. We can't keep rushing about. If we're going to survive, slow and calculated is our best shot."

Holden took a deep breath, trying to calm his mind. "Okay, what do you suggest?"

Recki found herself wanting to stick her tongue in the dummy's mouth. "Quick tumble in the alley probably isn't smart, so get Flip and Jotch. Then, find a rat-hole inn and plan. Bonus is, you'll feel right at home. Seriously, your place is disgusting."

His sudden hug shocked her, and hurt. "You just came with me. I broke from the Empire and you're right with me." He released her. "Why?"

Recki looked to her friend. "Cause you're a good man and you were wronged. Plus, an Anointed knows your name and face. You're going to die. I just wanna see how."

They shared a smile, which faded as they contemplated the truth of the statement.

"You don't think she'll hunt us personally?" Holden said.

"Let's not think about it," Recki said, peeking from the alley into the street where Flip lived. "All we need to focus on now is getting that Writer to safety."

"Agreed."

APPROACHING THE HOUSE, Holden kept one hand on his gun. Recki's words rang true: they had been so reckless, allowing adrenaline to push them from one move to the next. If they wanted to live, they needed to slow down and think. Easier said than done, especially when a murderous demigod might already be on their trail.

Almighty— Gods, I'm a traitor.

The house seemed just as they had left it, but both still peeked in a window before heading to the front door. To Holden's surprise, Jotch and Flip were sitting across from each other at a chess board, chatting happily. Holden actually felt a pang of jealousy. That had been his and Flip's evening tradition for much of their time together.

He walked from the window.

"Why did you stop seeing him?" Recki said in a low voice. "You two were good together."

Holden knew the answer, but he had never let

himself consciously admit it. "Khlid introduced us, right before—" He took a beat. "I can't see Flip without thinking about what happened."

"Oh." Recki walked past him to the door.

In truth, Holden missed Flip dearly, but now hardly seemed like the time to bring it up.

FLIP and Jotch stood at the sound of the door opening. When the two beaten officers entered, Flip asked Recki what happened and she explained at length. Guilt rolled through Holden. The Fifteenth had come to hurt him, very likely to kill him, and Recki had been caught up in it.

He wasn't sure if the killing had been required on her part, but when dealing with attackers, he didn't blame her for going to whatever length necessary.

Acknowledging the feeling in his gut, Holden also had to admit that Recki was always fast to the trigger. He had never seen her use her sidearm, but it was well known she had a body count far higher than most officers. Now that body count included some of those officers.

"Then you can't stay here." Flip stood. "They'll come looking for you, Holden. We weren't very discreet when we were, uh, dating? I'll help anyway I can, but sleeping here isn't an option."

"Fair enough." Recki said examining her rifle. Holden could tell she was wanting to clean it.

Jotch looked at them all nervously. "So where do we go? My family is obviously being watched."

Holden scratched at his chin. "Time to change appearances the best we can and hole up in the worst inn we can find."

"Yup," Recki said, getting to her feet.

Flip lent them old civilian clothes. Recki took a jacket left behind by a friend of Flip's. It was a bit tight on her, but the hood would be useful. Flip found Holden a change of clothes he had left behind the last time he had been there.The exchange was uncomfortable.

Jotch plucked at the fine-yet-flashy material of his shirt. "I have a suspicion this will stand out where we're going."

"At least they aren't Minister's robes." Flip's eyes conveyed disapproval. "You really didn't pack a change?"

"Oh, yes. Let me just bring a day bag into the Ministry of Truth. That won't bring any unwanted questions." Jotch crossed his arms. "Or maybe I should have swung by my home after stealing top secret documents from them!"

"You could have left a bag in a hidden spot outside." Recki was hiding a smile. "Y'know, retrieve it later."

Jotch opened his mouth, then closed it, lowering his lecturing finger.

Holden clapped his back. "New to the whole crime thing?"

"A bit."

They left Flip to clean up the evidence of their visit. The three made their way through the worst parts of the Eleventh District, areas where people were least likely to cooperate with law enforcement. There were no fine neighborhoods in the Eleventh, but Flip's was probably the nicest.

Slowly moving through side streets, avoiding areas Recki and Holden knew were highly patrolled, the party arrived at the Lower Eleventh's market. Pubs and inns surrounded dozens of booths hawking their wares. In rapid succession, Holden was offered colorful stones, fried meat whose provenance he could not identify, and knives he doubted could puncture wool.

Just as the smallest inn in the darkest corner of the market came into view, its red door swung open. A dozen members of the Red Hand emerged into the market in full battle attire. Rifles were slung over armor thick enough to stop anything short of a close-range rifle round. Maroon interlaced with gold signified this battalion had been stationed within the Ministries' districts. The fact they were here meant the military was already on the move looking for Holden and Jotch. To Holden's horror, a Grip in matching uniform lumbered last into the street.

Jotch stopped in his tracks. Recki and Holden each grabbed one of his fleshy arms to keep him moving as smoothly as they could. Correcting course just enough to avoid running into the soldiers, the three headed for a pub next door.

Holden kept the soldiers in his peripheral vision. They were scanning the market, breaking into groups of three. For a nauseating moment, one of the Red looked directly at Holden and paused.

Holden's free hand tightened on the pistol under his jacket.

The man's eyes moved on.

Did he dismiss us? Or is he covering the fact that he recognized me?

They entered the pub and let the door close behind them. A crowded scene welcomed them. Men and women laughed and drank as a band played in the corner; low brass instruments backing a lead on drums.

Recki subtly locked the door. "Back door. Now."

She took the rear as Holden pushed Jotch

through the room. No one seemed to pay them close attention.

That's right. Just three travelers looking to use the toilet.

They walked past the toilets and through a door into a back alley.

Looking back into the pub, Holden heard a pounding on the front door.

"Go!" he yelled as Recki passed him. "Go, go, go!"

The party sprinted into the trash-laden alley.

Holden wasn't sure how far they had to travel before they were safe, but it was well over an hour before Jotch finally said, "I can't!" Breathing hard, the Minister slumped against a stone wall by a small stream.

Holden crouched to give the man a once over. He was dehydrated and exhausted, but nothing worse.

They were in a slim dug-out stone waterway less than three meters wide and just over one deep. The waterways allowed for rapid travel without being seen if you knew the city well enough, and could ignore the stench. The putrid water flowing by carried waste from all over the city out into the main river.

Recki pulled a waterskin from her pack and

handed it to Holden. He took a long drink before passing it to Jotch.

Noticing Recki's expression, Holden said, "You're in pain. Lemme look you over."

She nodded, removing the pack. Unlacing her shirt, she allowed Holden to poke and prod the bruises covering her torso. Her face was only scraped in a few places.

The worst of Recki's trauma seemed to be mental. Her hands shook hard.

"You didn't do anything wrong," Holden assured her.

"No shit," she responded.

At the same time, Jotch regained his breath long enough to observe, "Well, duh. They broke into her home. She didn't even kill em all. Sounds like the old guy with the gun was also a hero today."

Holden and Recki exchanged looks.

"Hero?" Recki asked.

Jotch blushed. "I mean, yeah. You lot are saving me. You're leaving your lives behind and taking on an Empire. You're heroes."

A laugh from Recki surprised Holden. She said, "You're adorable, Mr. Minister."

The portly man's red face deepened as he turned to the water.

Holden finished looking her over. "A few cracks

and dings, maybe a mild concussion, but you'll be okay.".

As Recki got to her feet, Holden took the pack from her. "My turn."

She reluctantly let it go.

"So," Jotch said. "It looks like they are searching *every* inn more than once. I shouldn't be surprised." He looked at them as if they had all the answers. "What's the plan?"

Holden met Recki's eyes. "To be careful."

The Minister looked between them. "Umm... that's not a plan."

14

THE DEVIL'S KNOCKING

Flip finished sweeping his front porch and went back inside. The dishes in the sink were the only remaining evidence anyone had been by. After he put those away, he collapsed on the couch and processed the last few hours.

Holden, you dumb bastard.

Flip had really begun to fall for the idiot before he vanished. Seeing him again filled him with anger and hurt, but the greater situation at play made all of that meaningless.

He was terrified Recki or Holden might be killed in all this. Flip wasn't a loyalist —he doubted most Grips were— but today was the first time he had dabbled in treason. It seemed like a safe bet the same was true for Recki. Holden had that effect on people.

The man's drive was contagious. Stopping was not an option.

Part of the attraction, I guess. Just wish he wasn't so muleheaded.

Flip wasn't sure if one trait could exist without the other.

Rising, Flip did one last scan to make sure all evidence was gone. He had tossed their clothes into the community bin. They wouldn't be found any time soon. Someone had to be highly motivated to dig through that filth.

A knock sounded at the door.

His heart kicked up its pace. The knock wasn't particularly harsh, but it had been firm enough to echo through the house. Suddenly, Flip found his efforts to disguise his guests pathetic. What if they brought dogs? He had done nothing to conceal anyone's scent.

The knock sounded again. "Mr. Vrencho, I would like a word." It was a female voice; smooth as honey and disarming.

Opening the door, Flip was greeted by a raven-haired young woman with gray eyes. Her face was all sharp, delicate angles. She wore a well-fitted military uniform cut for combat. His eyes landed on the badge she flashed from beneath her uniform. The symbol of the Anointed shined up at him.

Oh... Almighty, no.

She was completely alone. That thought brought him no comfort. "Can I help you?"

"Yes. My name is Avi Cormick." The woman stepped into his home, nearly pushing him back. "May I come in?"

Flip recovered enough to manage a "Yes." As was tradition with the Anointed, he bowed his head and placed a hand to his chest. Grips were required to do less than most, but respect was still owed.

"Enough of that." The woman waved a dismissive hand and began to openly look around. She went to his kettle and placed a hand on the base. "You make a morning brew, I see."

"Always do, when it's nice enough to sit out and enjoy the sun." The words were true, at least. "Would you like a cup?"

Avi looked him in the eyes. "I'd love one. You're such a charm."

She looked about ten years younger than him — no older than, say, twenty-three cycles— but the manner with which she addressed him belied his estimate.

Flip set about making her a cup of his finest tea, pushing the kettle back onto a low fire beneath the mantle. As he did so, she continued her open examination of his home.

She disappeared into his bedroom for well over a minute before returning, a framed sketch of his cousins held lazily in her hand. "A beautiful family. Siblings?"

"Cousins. Cream?"

"No. Thank you." She kept the photo in her lap as she sat on his couch and looked at the chessboard. "In the middle of a game?"

"Do you play?" As the kettle whistled, he grabbed two cups. He wanted to stop her search of his home. He was a private person and hated strangers touching his things. A game of chess would allow him to keep her contained.

"I used to play much more often. You were in the middle of a game here?" she repeated, not bothering to be subtle about it.

"Oh, yes." Flip handed the demigod her cup and sat in the chair across from her. "Neighbor comes by and we exchange a few moves over drinks."

The Anointed downed the nearly boiling cup in a single pull. A puff of steam came from her mouth as she said, "Lovely tradition. Wonderful to hear of strong community ties, even in this... neighborhood."

Flip suppressed the many responses he would have enjoyed giving to that remark, and settled for, "Care to play?"

Avi's gray eyes lit up. "I would love to. Few are willing to give me a serious challenge these days."

Flip began to reset the board.

She continued, "I think they're afraid I'll kill them if they win. How foolish is that? Over a game?" Her voice carried something sharp.

"Sounds ridiculous to me." Flip tried not to swallow. The board reset, he ran a hand through his short cropped hair. "May I ask what brings an Anointed to my door?"

Flip: Pawn d4

Avi: Pawn f5

"We learned that you had a romantic relationship with an officer Holden Sanders. Is that true?"

Flip: Pawn c4

"Yes." Flip sipped his drink. "We stopped seeing each other, though."

Avi: Knight f6

"I see. May I ask why?"

Flip: Knight c3

"You'd have to ask him." Flip thought about where his nearest gun was: unloaded on his bedside table. "He just stopped coming by and wouldn't answer his door."

Avi: Pawn e6

Flip: Knight f3

Avi: Pawn d5

Avi stood to fill her cup with hot water directly from the kettle. She chose to sip this time, clearly enjoying the taste. "Ah, bad of Holden. Everyone deserves closure. Are you seeing anyone now?"

Flip: Pawn e3

The question gave him pause. "No. Not at the moment."

She returned to her seat and examined the board. "Unfortunately, I am in the same situation." The Anointed gave him a friendly look. "It's a bit difficult to date when you're different from most. I bet you understand."

He averted his green eyes. "Why send an Anointed?"

Avi: Pawn c6

"Well, if I was to find Holden here, a Grip would be protecting him. A couple of city soldiers might not be able to contain the situation."

Adjusting uncomfortably, Flip focused on the game. It was too early to judge her play, but he felt confident.

I have no fear of beating you.

Flip: Bishop d3

Avi: Bishop d6

Flip: Castle

Avi: Castle

Flip: Knight e2

Avi leaned forward and forced him to meet her gaze. "So, judging by those eyes, a Grip with plenty of experience. With those scars on your arms and look in your eyes, I'd say at least a few campaigns under your belt?"

She was prodding him. Flip felt as if he was going under a surgeon's blade.

"Yes," he replied. "I fought in the wars in the West. I swear I still find sand behind my ears. Can't imagine the Endless Ocean is actually bigger than the Deadlands."

Avi: Knight bd7

"I've seen them; rolling waves of sand as far as the eye can see." Avi's eyes scanned the board. "We've tried to send scouting parties out past the Deadlands. None have returned. More dangerous than the actual Endless Ocean it seems. Truth is, despite our best efforts, we actually don't know which is bigger."

"Really? Endless Ocean has the reputation of, well—"

"Mr. Vrencho, don't buy into children's tales. All oceans end."

Flip: Knight g5

"Oh, you're fun to play." Avi picked up her bishop. "I fought all over the continent. There are few countries I haven't bled in."

"I'm sorry to hear that."

Avi: Bishop xh2

That was dumb— oh.

"I'm not." She stared at him, unblinking.

"Are all Anointed like you?"

Her gaze did not waver. "How do you mean?"

"Well..." Flip readjusted. "Poems are written about the rest. The people know how Barrin brings fire. All that is said of you, is you survive. There are no songs of Avi, only rumors."

She gave no answer, as something deep within her eyes began to burn.

"Service to the Empire," Flip barked.

"Service to the Empire," she echoed.

Flip: King h1

Avi: Knight g4

Flip: Pawn f4

Avi: Queen e8

"Do you have regrets about your service, Mr. Vrencho?"

He met her eyes again. There was something dead in her. Flip could see it plain as day. "None."

Flip: Pawn g3

Avi: Queen h5

Flip: King g2

Avi: Bishop g1

Flip: Knight xg1

"How about you, Ms. Cormick?" Flip brought the captured bishop off the board.

Avi: Queen h2 check

"Oh, a few." She leaned back and looked him over. "Lives I shouldn't have taken."

Flip: King f3

"Could you push that pawn for me?" She gestured to the middle of the board.

He obliged.

Avi: Pawn e5

Flip: Pawn dxe5

"So," She looked about his home, "ever killed someone here?"

His eyes snapped off the board. "No. Never."

Avi smiled. "Of course. That chair does look so small under you. Kept up with the Grip exercise regime, I assume?"

Avi: Knight dxe5

Flip: Pawn xe5

"Yes, ma'am." The board had completely shifted. Flip was unsure if he could recover from his blunder. His competitive hackles rose.

Avi: Knight xe5 check

How did I miss that?

"So you said you play often?" Flip rubbed at his chin.

"Not as much as I used to. Nothing worse than playing people who don't give it their all. No?"

Flip: King f4

"Absolutely." He'd seen a path to victory clearly in front of him. Now, he was back against the ropes, scanning for any out.

Avi: Knight g6 check

Flip: King f3

Avi: Pawn f4

"So many are unable to see beyond what is expected." The Anointed rubbed her eyes. A growing annoyance was plain on her face. "It makes people so predictable, no?"

Flip: Pawn exf4

"I've never been able to predict what people will do, unfortunately."

Avi sighed. "A sign of someone who trusts too much." Flip heard an edge of mirth enter her voice.

He continued staring at the board. "What's the point if we can't trust each other?"

"An optimist, I see. Open door policy with the neighbors then?"

"Gods, no." His face twisted at the idea of people entering his space as they pleased. "I think there is much evil in this world. I just don't think it comes from the individual."

Avi, smiling, went to move a piece; but her hand

paused. She refocused on Flip and said, "Then where does it come from?"

Flip paused. He knew the answer. But telling an agent of the Empire that evil comes from false authority would be a life-ending mistake. "I believe evil comes from the old ways. It needs to be purged from us through the Almighty." The propaganda tasted vile on his tongue. "I'm sorry, Anointed. Did I offend?"

As fast as the change had appeared it was gone.

She smiled. "Not at all, Mr. Vrencho. I hope to be back for a game in the future."

Avi: Bishop g4

Flip: King gx4

The conversation felt more tactical to Flip than the game itself. He was having trouble seeing more than a couple moves ahead.

Avi lifted her knight, placing it smartly on e5. "Check. I hope I delivered a more interesting game than Holden."

He looked up to the woman across from him. Just how blind Flip had been was suddenly unveiled to him. Her vicious grin glued him to his seat. It was over.

Flip: Pawn fxe5

"As I said, the game you saw was against a neighbor."

Avi: Pawn h5 mate

Damn this woman.

"A neighbor who, at the idea of them swinging by, causes your face to twist like a child with a sour candy? You really must watch for obvious bait, Mr. Vrencho." She stood and took in his home one last time. "Out of respect, I won't have you interrogated over Holden. Torturing a Grip is always a messy affair. You can just burn yourself out with that damn Grohalind; then we have to evacuate the whole building, maybe even a city block. Horrid poison. Just tell me, how long ago was Holden here?"

Flip's mouth had gone completely dry. "They weren't—"

"They?" Avi stopped and turned to him. "So he's already with the Minister, then. This will be easier than I thought. Thank you for your service, Flip."

As she walked out his front door, Avi Cormick smiled. "Nice to know Holden is telling people about me. I guess I made an impact after all."

Flip slumped in his chair, heart heavy and eyes wide. He had been so easily played.

"So, what if we head for the Imperial District?" Jotch felt he had carefully weighed the odds. It was the best move.

Recki and Holden both looked at Jotch as if he had asked whether they should all drown themselves. Recki responded, "Well, because, Jotch, that's where you fled from; it has the highest density of people working directly for the M.O.D. in the Empire; an Anointed seems to be living there, and... anything else, Holden?"

"No, I think you got it covered," Holden answered.

Jotch let out an exasperated breath. "Well, we look a bit different now; it's probably where they'll ease up the search first *because* I fled from there; and what are the odds of us running into the Anointed?"

"You're wearing a hat," Recki retorted. "And they won't call off the search anywhere for weeks. The whole hide-right-under-their-noses thing doesn't actually succeed very often, Minister."

Holden added on, "In my experience, fugitives that stay fugitive the longest are the ones that get far away. Once they're outside the city, the Empire has to rely on bounty hunters. Then recapturing someone can take months or years."

"This whole being-ganged-up-on thing?" Jotch

pointed between the two former officers. "Not my favorite."

They still sat by the running water. All had agreed they couldn't afford another misstep, nor to risk stillness while they planned their next move. As time ticked by, tension mounted.

"Well, I have a backup plan." Jotch paced by the water, nearly stepping out from under the bridge they were hiding.

"Oh, so this has all fallen in with your *backup* plan?" Holden scoffed. Recki elbowed him in the ribs.

Rolling his eyes, Jotch said, "Okay, fine. I have a new spur-of-the-moment idea."

Jotch turned, noticing Holden rubbing his ribs with a grimace. Recki wore an amused smirk.

"We want the Rebels, right? They might help you rescue Khlid, and they can get me out of the city in exchange for the information I give them." Jotch stopped pacing. "Our only hurdle is contacting them."

"I fail to see how this is a plan." Recki only sounded patient—motivating the Minister to get to his point faster, so they did not lose more valuable time. "We know the issue."

"That's the plan, see?" Holden said, sitting down. "Just keep saying it and *poof*, Rebels will appear. The most secretive organization in existence—they're like witches. Say their name three times and—" he made a lazy spell-casting motion.

"*Anyway*," Jotch continued, "I'm sure they're looking for *us* now. We've caused a great kerfuffle. Perfect targets for a Rebellion to want to pick up. So how can we make ourselves visible to them—"

"...but *not* visible to the thousand soldiers patrolling every street for us right now?" Holden sardonically finished Jotch's thought.

"I'd guess thousands," Recki added. "The Red Hand has a thousand in the city alone. Add in the regular M.O.D. forces and it could be ten. This city is far more militarized than it appears on the surface."

Jotch rubbed his neck. "Lucky for us, they have nearly a million people to look through, if we count the surrounding counties. They might assume we made it out and call off the search within the city limits."

"So where will the Rebels be looking for us that the military won't?" Holden laid all the way down on his back. Jotch couldn't place why, but it annoyed him. Holden had been annoying him ever since they left Flip's home.

Recki sat cross-legged next to Jotch, her chin in

her hands. "Wrong question. What will they leave for us to find?"

Jotch froze. "You're a genius. They'll be leaving us signs. They don't need to look for us, they'll leave a trail." Jotch raised his arms in triumph. "It's the only logical way to make contact!"

Holden didn't sound convinced. "Lower your voice. How would they leave a sign the military wouldn't recognize?"

"They know Khlid, Sam and Chapman, right?" Recki asked, her eyes staring at the invisible puzzle. "Would they have told them something you'd recognize, Holden?"

Jotch kicked a pebble into the water. "Another question: where would they leave this hypothetical trail? Probably multiple starting points converging on one location. A place they could wait for us, but abandon at the first sign of trouble."

Holden got to his feet with a grunt. "Assumptions on assumptions. That this is their strategy. That Khlid, Sam, and Chap would cooperate with—would even *know* the Rebels. That the military wouldn't find it first. Is this the best we can do?"

"What do you suggest?" Recki cocked her head.

"Get caught." Holden had expected the incredulous looks they now gave him. "Hole up in a building and make a stand. Put up a hell of a fight. Then, if we can hold out long enough, the Rebels catch wind of it and come to help."

"That is extremely stupid." Jotch didn't even try to hide the condescension in his tone. "You think *we're* making assumptions? You're assuming we're worth rescuing once we're in a direct conflict. The rebels survive by remaining in the shadows, not open combat in the streets."

At first, the former officer looked about to retort, but after a second of thought he closed his mouth. "So we hunt for a ghost trail, then."

Recki got to her feet and took her rifle back from Holden. "The place to start looking is obvious: The Seventh."

15

ONE PATH FORWARD

Feeling her stomach, Khlid wondered if she could still be considered a human. The flesh on her abdomen —could "flesh" even describe anymore the metallic cords of muscle she found there?— still followed the familiar contours of her stomach and back. Even the faint indentation of her belly button remained.

But as for *what* she was now made of, her transformation was total. The armor-like carapace had recently grown to the edges of her face, the black worms pulsing at the border, constructing away.

Khlid flexed her remade left hand. The fingers were smooth now, no longer a jagged claw. The armor was delicate in its curves, yet powerful. The beautiful, interlacing layers were impenetrable, yet mimicked her physiology so miraculously as to never

inhibit her mobility. She wondered how far below
the surface her new skin extended.

Resting her still near-human right hand against
the new steel wall of her cell, Khlid relished the
intense sensation. The way her mind now processed
the feeling was exquisite: less of a sensation than an
understanding. It was as if she could feel the funda-
mental makeup of whatever she encountered. The
steel was new and pure. Her body told her that it was
stronger than her armor, though not by much.

She closed her eyes and took a deep breath.

If I keep getting stronger....

The image of Sam's severed head flashed before
her eyes. Khlid cried out and forced her eyes open.

*You'll never be strong enough to bring him back.
You failed to protect Sam. Your husband is dead. You
were never a good enough wife—*

Khlid forced the voice out and blinked away
tears. As it always did, a cold anger burned away her
grief and steadied her mind.

Walking to the front of her cell, which was
recently reinforced with a layer of gridiron, she
dragged her hand along the wall. The scraping
sounds from the ends of her fingers caused her mind
to unconsciously dampen her hearing. It happened
without thought. Sounds she wanted to hear were

amplified, while everything else could be separated out, dismissed.

Her hands flexed around two of the vertical bars. They were nearly eight centimeters; far too thick for her to destroy, at least for now.

Keys jingled in the massive door. The lock was retracted and the door thrown open. Light flooded her space.

Lunch... no, dinner. Must be dinner.

Two massive men, Grips, escorted a servant in. They took their positions on either side of the door as the small man approached Khlid. He was older, pale-skinned, and clearly terrified of her. The tray shook slightly as he kneeled to slide it through the gap under the cell door.

"It's okay." Her voice caused the man to start and fall back. The Grips tensed, but made no move.

"I won't hurt you. I know... I know I don't look the same anymore. Or even human. But I am." She looked at her new hand. "Just a weapon on the surface."

The graying man looked in her eyes for the first time. "Do you— I mean... does it hurt?"

She smiled. "Not anymore. Do you want to feel?"

Khlid extended her slim, armored hand out of

the cell, palm facing downward. The same gesture that would allow a nervous dog to take one's scent.

The man glanced back to the Grips. They seemed to be paying no mind. Khlid knew their game. Today, she would play it.

"Can you still feel?" Cautiously he raised his own hand, his eyes fixated on the interwoven pattern.

"Yes." She shrugged slightly. "It's different, though. Go on. It's okay, really. It's strange to me too."

The man caressed her hand. "It's beautiful. Like the finest armor ever made."

"Does it appear so? I can't see it all."

"Yes." He traced one of the flowing lines on her wrist. "Truly, this is —"

She seized him.

The man's eyes bulged.

Khlid pulled his arm hard enough to wrench shoulder from socket. His skull cracked on the metal bars. Blood sprayed over her. She let him fall backwards before pulling again. The second impact caused the cracked skull to explode. A lump of warm matter, a bit of brain, perhaps, landed on her lip. Khlid made a third pull with all her might. The man's arm came away, severed at the shoulder.

A metallic taste filled her mouth.

Khlid was flung across the room. The impact of the Grips' attack was strong enough to slam her into the steel wall. The clang of her body on the bars was comical to her ears. She was released, and slipped down the wall, laughing as she landed on her side.

There was no pain, no cracks in her armor, only an awareness of what had hit her. The Grohalind was legendary. A force of nature that could unleash physical attacks with a thought. Grips could exert raw force equal to their own mass. The best Grips could use the mass of other objects to exert greater force, though Khlid had heard that talent was rare. The poison emitted by the Grohalind wasn't dangerous in small doses, but continual exposure resulted in what many considered the worst possible way to die. It was why Grips, despite their relatively high tolerance to the poison, had to retire after rather short careers.

As Khlid climbed to her feet, one of the Grips dragged away the servant's corpse. Khlid lunged at him, but a Groahlind impact swept her legs out from under her. Her chin bounced off the ground.

Khlid growled as the force continued to push her back. A set of glowing green eyes watched her carefully.

Her cage was locked once more.

They left her pacing, blood rushing in her veins.

She threw the servant's arm from her cell in frustration.

After several minutes, the visitor Khlid knew would come pushed open the door.

Avi openly examined the gore on the bars, staying just out of reach. "Stunning. Truly stunning, Khlid."

"I want you to enjoy this moment." Khlid caught the woman's eyes. She pressed herself into the cold bars. "Enjoy every breath you draw. You'll soon look back on these moments fondly. When I get out, there will be nowhere you can run. They'll write stories about me like I was a demon. The bane of the Anointed. The monster that desecrated God's angels."

A look Khlid hadn't seen before flashed across Avi's face.

"I feel it inside me, you know? Whatever you put in me is growing. It's hungry, Avi." Khlid licked the carnage from her lips. "I'll keep it that way just for you."

"Watch yourself, Inspector," Avi said. "Holden's life depends on what yo—"

"Do it!" Khlid cut in, tearing at the bars. "Kill him! Give me more of a reason to hunt you!"

The Anointed turned for the door.

Khlid began to beat on the bars. She was shriek-ing, spittle flying from her lips.

As soon as she was sure Avi was gone, Khlid stopped her show and collapsed against the bars.

Sam, I'm still here. I know I am.

She imagined Sam in the cell with her, looking her over, revolted by what he saw. Her husband would never abandon her, but this? She looked down over her new form, her foot regrown, covered in the same sleek, layered designs.

I am still me.

Avi Cormick reached her office and slammed the door behind her. For the first time since her rising to Anointed, fear filled her heart. It was raw, and uncontrolled. A scream built up in her core. Her hands wanted to shake, but she gripped her desk and held them still.

What is that thing becoming?

For months, Avi had followed her orders from the M.O.D. and learned all she could about various subjects' response to the Drip; from the first vagabonds who practically exploded as soon as they were injected, then onto the first few minor successes—subjects who survived for a few hours before succumbing to death. Blood samples were always taken from the dead and sent back to the Ministry Of Science. What happened to them there, not even she knew.

The M.O.D. had begun using the still-unfinished Drip in some remarkably successful interrogation sessions. As the victim's bodies began to decay, they would plead for an antidote that did not exist.

Inspector Chapman was the first true outlier: in a matter of minutes, his powerful body had ruptured, transforming into something far greater than the others; a true weapon, horrible in its beauty. Killing him had been difficult in more ways than one. A waste of progress.

Khlid, though. The woman was ascending to something never before seen. Her skin was sleek and powerful. Those *steel bars* had—

No. I can destroy her if I want to. I am the protector of Capital City. The Almighty has Anointed me above all others.

Her mind believed the words, but the tension in her spine refused to depart.

Khlid's eyes burned red with rage now. Avi had seen nothing like it on countless battlefields.

A knock at the door caused her to whirl around. Trying to calm her heart, she called, "Come."

Two men entered her office: a soldier of the

M.O.D. and an officer of the Eleventh Precinct. The officer dropped to his knees upon seeing her.

"Officer Tyth, yes?"

The man curled tighter into his bow. "Yes, Anointed."

"Straighten your back, officer." Avi walked closer to him. The man stank of cigarettes and the Lower District. "You were with Officer Holden when he learned of the missing sidearm, yes?"

Tyth straightened most of the way but kept his head bowed, eyes to the floor. "Yes, Anointed."

Avi put one finger below his chin and forced the man's head up. "I said stand straight. Why did you not report the discovery?"

He trembled under her glare. "I am sorry, Anointed."

She took a deep breath. "Tell me everything that happened that day."

As the man recited the day to her, Avi's mind kept flying back to Khlid's promises from her cell. Disposing of her would be treason. She needed to be studied for the future of the species. Her development was the greatest achievement humanity had—

"Say that again."

Tyth jerked at her sudden demand. "Uhh... the boy who found the gun? He said the woman was shorter, with golden skin. Short curly hair. Friendly smile and pretty."

Holden, you continue to impress me.

He had lied about how the child had described the woman.

She let Tyth finish recounting the day's events. Sensing her displeasure, the idiot actually started describing the places he thought Holden might go to hide. As if she had been waiting all week for this lout's detective skills.

"Thank you for your cooperation." Avi approached the man again.

Annoyingly, he dipped again into a bow. "Of cour—"

Avi brought her hands together through the officer's skull with a single clap. Blood burst over her. She opened her mouth letting the fluid hit her tongue. It was as easy as popping a tomato.

Still, some frustration heated her blood. Holden and this Minister, Jotch, had avoided them for hours. Thousands of men were unable to find two fugitives in the city. The incompetence was—

"Lieutenant," she barked. "I want every soldier, officer, and guard in the city called on. All other duties are to be put on hold. Tell the citizens I have just arrived in the city to aid with the hunt. Let them know that if they find the traitors, they will receive an Anointed's personal blessing."

He put a fist to his heart as she let the other man's corpse fall to the floor. "And arrest the entire Eleventh. Let the M.O.T. know they are all traitors, found to have aided in the Officer's escape."

As THE SKY crept ever closer to night, and a burning red dominated the horizon, Holden laid eyes on the Seventh. He had not seen it since he left the city with Samuel to investigate a case in the country. A case that had annoyed him at the time. Now he looked back on it fondly, remembering Samuel's professional demeanor while working with the stubborn farmers.

The remains of the building were a charred skeleton. Several large pillars held up a lone wall, now transformed into a memorial for the dead. The rest was destroyed. Clean-up crews had hauled away much of the rubble. Ash and soot shaded the once-bright building.

Even as Holden watched from the street, a gust of wind made the haggard brick wall sway dangerously.

Barriers surrounding the building were patrolled

by half a dozen soldiers, their blue-and-gold uniforms signifying they were from the city's garrison.

Holden only felt hollow. He had expected it to hurt, seeing the place he had spent most of his career destroyed. The pain of knowing his friends died here had made him avoid this place for months; but now, no tears came. He was empty.

"So," Recki whispered next to him, holding his forearm, "where would *you* leave a marker for us to find?"

Jotch aggressively scanned the surroundings, trying to contribute.

"Somewhere far away from those rifles, but close enough to be seen," Holden answered. "Problem is, I'm the only one who might know what to look for; and the only one likely to be recognized."

Recki looked up at him. "Do they know I'm with you?"

"Hm. Don't know. It depends on what Krolf said, I guess."

"Yeah." Jotch seemed to be trying to imitate the two of them. He leaned across Holden, scanning the guards before retreating and murmuring to no one in particular, "Dangerous position. Stealth is tricky, you know."

Holden and Recki exchanged an amused look.

"Jotch," Recki said, putting a hand on the man's shoulder. "keep Holden out of trouble for me."

"Hmm?" Jotch looked startled at the request. Recki rounded the corner.

The Minister began to lean out into the street in an attempt to watch her progress, but Holden pulled him back. "Not very subtle."

"Oh, sorry." Jotch left the peeking to Holden. "Are they arresting her?"

"No, Jotch. She's still nearly a block away."

As Recki got close to the precinct's corpse, two guards broke off to challenge her. A large, dark man kept further back while a woman similar to Recki chatted with her. Holden would have sold his boots to hear what was being said. His heart raced as they looked to be tossing casual pleasantries.

"She's very good," Jotch said, leaning over Holden to peek. "They don't recognize her. You can relax, Holden."

Holden didn't look away. "I'll relax when we're out of the city with Khlid."

"That could be days yet. Will you be at your best if you are unable to rest?" The point Jotch was making was solid enough, but it irritated Holden to no end.

"Hush," was all he said in response.

After what was probably moments, but felt to

Holden like half an hour, Recki let out a chuckle along with the guard and walked off. Recki returned with a slight smile, walking the opposite way down the alley. Holden and Jotch fell into position behind her.

"Get anything?" Holden asked.

Jotch said, "Are you okay?"

They both gave Jotch a look. Recki turned to Holden. "You said Chapman had tattoos on his arms, right?" Recki traced a finger over her forearms. "In the Yu'ib style?"

"Yeah?" The three of them ducked behind a shop that was not receiving much business in the early afternoon.

Recki pointed back down the street. "On one of the storefronts down there by the post office, there's some graffiti. It just looked like random street scribbles at first, but I'm sure it's Yu'ib style wood carving. My tattoo artist does similar work. He has sketches exactly like that hanging."

"We were right?!" Jotch exclaimed, nearly yelling.

Holden slapped a hand over the man's mouth, raising a threatening finger. Recki peeked back into the street, then gave an all-clear sign.

"Sorry," Jotch said demurely.

"So they want us to go into the post office?"

Recki shook her head. "They want us in the sewers. It wasn't by the door. It was directly over the drain."

Jotch wrinkled his nose. "Really?"

"I don't like this." Recki pulled the pack from her back. "They've got to be leaving signs everywhere you two have the slightest connection. I wouldn't be surprised if we missed them at your home. It won't go unnoticed forever and they know that. The trail is a huge risk for them and us."

"So they do want us," said Jotch, his voice failing to contain his glee or his volume.

"Jotch, I will cut you." Recki quietly muttered.

Holden wanted to kiss her. Finally, her own irritation towards the Minister was shining through.

Her words seemed to blister the man. He shrunk back and wiped at his face, covering some emotion. "Sorry" was all he managed after a long moment.

"Let's go." Recki walked toward the darker end of the alley. "There should be a manhole cover over here."

Embarrassingly, Holden struggled to get the heavy plate off.

Recki opened her mouth, a snide comment ready to fly.

"Don't!" Holden said as Jotch lent a hand. "Now is not the time."

"I mean..." Recki began to lower herself into the stinking hole. "Nothing really needs to be said."

As Holden helped Jotch into the sewer, Recki removed two Gro-stones from her pack. They were common trinkets, made by Grips and sold at their immense temples, which were more on the scale of cities, really. Imbued with small amounts of the Grohalind, when allowed to touch each other, the metallic pebbles would give off a soft, green glow. Supposedly the Grohalind poison contained within was not enough to make a person sick, although a great quantity of them might yet do so.

Holden had always been fascinated by how slowly the light moved. The idea of light moving at different speeds seemed ridiculous. Whether from candles, opening a curtain to the sun, or the new electric bulbs, light appeared as soon as it was summoned. But not so with Gro-stones.

A soft glow emanated to life in Recki's hands as she touched just the edges. The green glow slowly spread within the sewer, its lazy tendrils pushing the shadows back. After a few seconds, a three-foot radius became illuminated around Recki. She decided more was needed and allowed more of the stones to touch. The light expanded outward until it reached the manhole from which they had entered the sewer.

"I've never seen Glo-stones in person," Jotch whispered. "Fascinating."

Holden was surprised, but the little man was rather odd, after all. He guessed reading by the Grohalind's light wasn't very practical.

They made their way through the filthy tunnels. Wet fluid squished under Holdens boots. The smell caused Jotch to gag several times

A small, round mocko darted by with a squeal, curled tail bobbing. The Minister threw himself against the stained walls to avoid the fist-sized rodent.

"Harmless, Jotch," Holden said. "They don't even have teeth. They suckle on—"

"It's filthy! Disease, human waste, Almighty knows what that thing is covered in." The Minister took a deep breath and gagged again. "Oh, gods."

"Will you two shut up?" Recki held her light high and scanned the walls. "We're below the post office."

Holden scanned the walls. Nothing obvious jumped out at him as Recki moved on further. He looked behind him and saw Jotch standing on his tiptoes to try and peek out of the storm drain.

"Hey," Holden whispered.

Jotch dropped back down.

"Unless you want to scare some kids, keep it

low." Holden gestured for the man to follow. "Can you take the pack, at least?"

"Fresh air." Jotch pulled his shirt over his nose. "Fine."

"There." Recki pointed to a brick by her ankle. Engravings in the Yu'ib fashion pointed South.

"I'll be damned."

16

A TASTE OF METAL

The next few hours were a sweaty march through miles of sewer. Holden thought the falling sun would have cooled the catacombs, but their ability to maintain the heat of the day was both impressive and miserable.

He was about to instruct Recki and Jotch to leave the sewers so they could all find a place to hydrate and clean up, when Recki led them into a massive underground space. Well over a dozen tunnels converged, spilling into a pool that dominated the center floor. A steady current flowed into the darkness beyond their vision.

"Well," Recki said, sliding the Gro-stones completely together. Her green light slithered further ahead. "If they have a flair for the dramatic, they should —"

The sound of a gunhammer being pulled back was followed by the lighting of torches before them. Recki's faint green light was washed away as a dozen soldiers, the torchbearers, stepped forward. All wore Imperial uniforms.

"Under the authority of the Almighty and the M.O.D.," a sly, feminine voice sounded, "you are under arrest."

Jotch's hands went up.

Recki went for her pistol, but froze as four rifles were trained on her.

Holden received another four.

"That was easy." The Imperial drawl was thick in the officer's accent. A white-and-gold badge on her broad chest proclaimed her rank: Capital City Lieutenant. "I believe we've all earned a promotion here today."

A couple of her men chuckled. The sound of laughter from the tunnel behind them betrayed that a handful more soldiers had been tailing them.

The three of them had been lured like children to candy. The hope of salvation had been too sweet.

"To your knees, or die," the lieutenant drawled. "I don't care which."

Jotch dropped first. Holden met Recki's eyes. It was apparent she hadn't considered this, either. They had been so thrilled at the idea of finding a hidden map left by the Rebels, they walked into an unsophisticated trap.

Holden put his hands behind his head and began to lower to his knees. It wasn't until he was all the way down that Recki followed his lead. Her eyes blazed with fury. He knew all too well how she hated being outmaneuvered.

We're done. The trap was so obvious. How could we be this stupid?

Holden's head fell as eight men came around the pool to restrain the failed fugitives. Three kicked him down into the filth of the floor. Recki received similar treatment, crying in pain at the abuse to her already-injured body.

"Leave her alone!" Jotch cried out, trying to resist the two soldiers atop him.

Idiot, Holden thought. He would only make it worse.

Two soldiers beat Holden. It lasted less than a minute, but every blow stung.

One of the soldiers standing to the side hauled Holden to his knees. He placed a restraining cord over Holden's left wrist and tightened it.

Holden wanted to throw up. The defeat was unbearable. Jotch continued to protest as Recki was corded as well.

We're fools. I should have just lived with the lies. What did we even expect—

A whisper sounded in Holden's ear. "When you taste metal, fight like hell."

The cord slipped onto his right wrist, but was left slack.

Yes!

Hope erupted within Holden's chest; the situation was still dire, but help seemed to have come.

The Rebels were here, but they had to fight roughly a dozen trained city soldiers.

Looking to his left, Holden saw Recki being dragged to her feet just like him. Jotch was roughly shoved down. A soldier put a hand on the Minister's shoulder, and, to Holden's surprise, the small man bit it.

"Little shit!" the soldier yelled, kicking Jotch to the ground and grinding his boot into his head. He pulled back a foot and landed a blow on Jotch's gut.

Two figures stepped into the room from the furthest tunnels: Grips in full armor. They wore M.O.D. badges and the soldiers parted before them.

The officer shrunk away from them as they approached. 'We— uh—we've secured the fugitives. We appreciate the M.O.D. sending aid, but it—"

Holden tasted metal. Green eyes glowed within the armored helmets.

The soldier who had whispered to Holden pressed a pistol into his hand. "Ready?"

A Grip's gauntleted fist pointed toward the female officer. A vibration shook the air.

With one small scream, he hurled the woman through the air, slamming her into the stone of the far wall. Blood fanned out where her head made impact. Soldiers stared in shock; an M.O.D. official had just been murdered by what appeared to be a member of the city garrison.

"What—" the soldier standing near Holden began. The rebel who had passed Holden the gun silenced the soldier with a bullet to the head.

The shot was nearly deafening in the cavern. Holden had to clutch his ears before recovering enough to regain his wits.

Across the pool, the soldiers regained themselves enough to raise their weapons. Both Grips braced themselves as, suddenly, every weapon was torn from panicked imperial hands. Soldiers cried out as their fingers were broken by the unseen force.

The Grips walked towards the city soldiers.

Simultaneously, Recki kicked off of the stone wall behind her, sending herself and the two men holding her to the floor.

More shots, from the men coming from the tunnels, added to the chaos.

It was clear that about half of the Imperial ranks were Rebels in disguise. Holden didn't know who to shoot. The scrawny Rebel still with him tried to protect him with his body, but Holden pushed him off.

Recki!

Two of the men were still trying to restrain her as a third fumbled with their rifle. But before he could raise the weapon, a bullet tore through his head. It was impossible to tell where it had come from.

Holden rushed past the falling man and tackled one of Recki's assailants to the ground. Recki would have to handle the other.

Wrapping the loose end of the cord onto his fist, Holden forced it around the soldier's neck. Nails tore into his hands as Holden tried to pin the soldier with his legs.

From the corner of his eye, Holden saw Jotch, who had a pistol to his temple. An Imperial was using Jotch as a shield as he backed away from the chaos.

Pain erupted in Holden's hand. The soldier Holden was choking had cut Holden's knuckles with a knife. Holden used his right leg to try to restrain the flailing arm, but suffered a gash on his thigh in the attempt.

Bile and spittle frothed from the choking man's lips.

Holden only needed a few more seconds.

A splash. Recki was in the pool. She sputtered to the surface.

A pistol was aimed down at her.

"No!" Holden's shriek filled the cavern.

A flash from the barrel.

Recki sank into the water.

Holden released the rope in his hands. A gasp of breath came from beneath him.

The soldier who had just shot Recki trained his sights on Holden as he charged, still screaming.

A flash. Yet no pain came to Holden. He collided with the Imperial and sent him crashing into the stone wall. He slammed his head into the man's nose. Blood. His fist connected with teeth.

Holden felt the pistol being pressed into his stomach. The soldier tried to fire but Holden was too fast. He slapped the gun away. His hands wrapped around the blood smeared throat.

He bashed the man's head into the wall again. And again. And again. And again.

Only when bone cracked did he drop the dead man.

Recki.

Holden spun. The man he had been choking was

vomiting on the floor. Holden picked up the dropped pistol and executed him as he ran by.

Jumping into the pool, Holden waded through a thick layer of grime. Frantically, he searched the dark slush. Horrid fluids filled his cuts, fell on his lips, stung his eyes.

"Recki!" he screamed.

A Grip's raised hand launched a screaming woman well above Holden and onto the stones across the pool. She landed with a vicious snap.

Holden didn't care.

"Reck—"

A limb. Holden seized what felt like an arm. Pulling a mass from the water, Recki's face came to the surface. She was terribly pale.

"Recki, I've got you. I've got you." Holden walked back to the edge of the pool. The chest-deep water made her hard to carry. "Don't worry. You'll be okay."

Placing her on the edge of the platform, Holden lifted himself out of the muck. People were screaming at each other. Jotch yelled Holden's name, with fear in his voice.

Holden ignored it all. His hands ran over Recki's face. Her eyes twitched.

"Recki! Look at me, Reck."

You've got to stay with me. Please, Recki. Please.

He rolled her into recovery position. He beat on her back until water flowed from her mouth. Holden placed her on her back and began pumping her chest; ignoring the blood accumulating around her stomach.

A breath. Raggedly, Recki pulled in air and coughed up water. Pain pulsed over her face. She clutched her stomach and rolled onto her side. Vomit spewed from her mouth— much of it black sludge.

"Yes!" Relief flooded his body. "Recki. I'm here. We're okay."

She was so pale. Far too pale.

"Let me see." Holden pulled her hands away. Her stomach had a gaping wound. He applied pressure. Blood poured between his fingers. "Just a bullethole, Recki. You've had worse."

His panicked mind tried to believe the words. He couldn't lose her. She was better than him. He loved her so dearly.

"Recki, I need you to talk to me." His eyes scanned her body for more injuries. Blood seeped from some unseen cut beneath her trouser leg.

"Fuck." The word from her was so faint, but Holden's heart leapt.

She was shaking. To his horror, blood was mixed into the vomit.

No. No. No. No!

"Look at me!" Holden yelled.

Her eyes tried to focus on him as she convulsed.

"Holden!" Jotch's voice was panicked.

"Look at me, Reck."

Her eyes drifted away.

Someone crouched next to Holden. He didn't bother to see who.

"She might be too far gone." The figure held up Recki's head.

Applying pressure to Recki's stomach wound, Holden wanted to lash out. He wanted to strike the dark-haired woman, golden-skinned who had appeared beside him, but a faint, animal hope that she might save his friend rooted him to the spot.

"Even if she makes it, that filth will cause her problems." The woman emptied a vial into Recki's mouth. "Let's hope he was right about this shit."

Holden finally looked directly at the woman. Short, dark curls danced over a pretty, stout face with wide brown eyes.

"Holden, for the love of the Almighty, help!" Jotch's voice cracked several times during his plea.

Finally looking over, Holden saw the last Imperial soldier, holding a pistol to Jotch's head, a terrified grimace plastered to his face as two Grips and five Rebels surrounded him.

"Just let me go," the soldier chattered, clearly in shock. "I'll release the Minister after a few blocks."

One of the Grips raised both of their hands in a soothing gesture. "Easy."

"Just let me g—"

The man's head exploded in two different directions. It was as if two invisible hands had torn him in two.

Gore coated Jotch as he fell to the floor, screaming.

The shorter of the two Grips looked at the other. "You really have gotten good at that tie-down maneuver. Just one connection to each wall?"

"Takes a tremendous toll. Pushes me near to igniting if I hold it too long," the larger grumbled with a cough. His voice was an avalanche compared to the other's landslide. "But you can't beat it for efficiency."

Flip never talked of doing something like that.

Holden looked back to Recki. Her blood loss had slowed substantially. Short, sharp breath came from her, though her eyes still wandered.

"What did you give her?" Holden asked frantically. He caressed Recki's face, pushing her hair away.

The Rebel woman was examining Recki, looking for additional injuries. "Something I took from

Chapman's place before it was raided. We don't have much left. She better be worth it."

"Chapman?" The name shouldn't have been a surprise, he supposed. "You worked with him?"

"Yes. His work is why we're all here." The woman stood and snapped her fingers. In response, a man and a woman, dropping the last of the dead into the water, came over. "Take her to Carrie. She'll do what she can."

The two other Rebels picked up Recki's small form as carefully as they could. Holden walked alongside as they made for a tunnel. At its mouth, the shorter Grip barred Holden's way.

Holden turned to the curly-haired woman. "Please. She's—"

"Holden, whether you are with her or not will not change the outcome." The leader of the gathered Rebels turned to Jotch, still whimpering in terror as he wiped the blood from his face. "*His* fate, on the other hand, depends on you completely."

17

CLEAN-UP

Holden and Jotch were led by the small party through the sewers. The woman gave her name as Pirka. Whether or not that was true, Holden didn't care. The Grip kept an oversized hand on Jotch's shoulder as they made their way through the darkness.

Where they were in the city was impossible to guess.

"How did you know?" he asked.

Jotch's question went unanswered for several seconds before the Grip finally said, "'bout the trap?"

"Yeah."

"Any harm in telling him, Pirka?"

Pirka glanced over her shoulder and shrugged.

"Well —I'm Crom, by the way, nice to meet you — we have people in the city garrison. But unless you're an idiot, you know that by now. The entire city military is scrambling to find you. Caused a lot of clashing with officers. Some precincts aren't too happy to see soldiers patrolling the streets in their jurisdictions. *That* means more cops are talking than usual. Because of *that*, tracking what's going on has been relatively easy, ya see. Only thing that wasn't easy was finding you."

"So you heard of the trap from some officers?" Holden felt a momentary twinge of pride; perhaps some officers were putting up some kind of resistance to the M.O.D.'s power grab.

"Yes and no." Crom had a presence that was strangely disarming for his size. It reminded Holden of some of the quieter nights with Flip. "We heard they were trying all kinds of crazy shit to find you; those pissed-off cops couldn't wait to spill all about it. Once we knew they were getting creative, we suggested the idea of a trail to one of the officers we've turned. Once we heard they'd taken the bait, we seeded that party with our people. A few more lurking in the tunnels to pick off the rest."

"For now." Pirka's voice was far less eager to charm. "We have to get out of sight immediately. The crackdown for this will be monumental."

"Yeah. We gotta make sure this bugger is worth it." Crom squeezed Jotch's shoulder. "Couple of my friends just put their lives on the line back there for you, Minister. Our ears heard of your little theft. Did you really just walk out with classified files tucked in your pants?"

"Well," Jotch coughed. "I think we all have our own approach to these things. You seem to be on top of everything though, which is nice. I don't think you lost anyone. At least from what I saw."

Pirka stopped and slowly turned on Jotch. Her tone was deadly. "We have lost everything, Minister. Our entire plan of action. Careful incursions, information bought, agents turned, rumors spread, safe passage out secured. But now the city is in lockdown. Why? Because some Writer wanted to play at treason."

"I...uhh," Jotch swallowed. "I have valuable information about what happened to the Seventh."

Pirka continued walking. "We know what happened to the Seventh. Your value comes from your job, Minister."

They exited the sewers at one of the major runoffs into the Imperial harbor. The early evening air felt extraordinary on Holden's skin. A small ladder built into the concrete led directly down to the docks. Before they stepped into the light, the Grip shed his armor and stowed it awkwardly in a bulging pack. Once that was done, aside from his

size, glowing green eyes, and massive red beard,
Crom looked somewhere in the neighborhood of
inconspicuous. If you were half blind and the sun
was in your eyes.

Fortunately, they only had to walk three slips
over to a wide trading vessel. Seaworthy, but not
equipped with any luxuries, the ship was wide, and
meant for cargo, not speed. A few small cannons
poked out from either side. Jotch's legs wobbled as
they ascended the ramp. "I just don't like water."

Crom helped Jotch aboard with a hearty shove.

The sails were packed away — the ship looked to
Jotch as though it couldn't have more than six small
sails. Pirka gave an order to begin readying the ship
for travel. A small bell was rung and sailors appeared
from below decks.

"Wait." Holden walked towards Pirka. Two of
the sailors drew pistols at him. It was at that moment
Holden realized his own weapon was missing. He
raised his hands, confused and annoyed. "What's
happening?"

Pirka looked him up and down. "First, you'll be
forced to bathe and change. We have clothes that
should fit you. Once the lockdown is lifted, we're
headed far away. You'll be kept below for several
days, probably in a barrel in case we are searched."

Holden's jaw dropped. "What? We can't leave. This is—"

He realized he was about to say home. It sounded so stupid in his mind.

Why in the fuck would I want to stay here?

A different concern took over. "What about Khlid?"

Pirka looked at him with open confusion. "The Inspector? What about her?"

"We have to save her!"

Several sailors, Crom, and Pirka all looked at him as if he were insane.

"Holden..." Crom raised his hands in a calming way. "She's dead."

"No, she's not." Holden couldn't believe they didn't know.

"Holden is correct," Jotch threw in. "She's infected with something. They're studying her at the M.O.S. right now. They called her a success." For once, Holden appreciated the little man. "Whatever has been done to her is important."

Pirka's eyes had widened with every word. "Crom, get them cleaned off, then bring them below."

The next hour went by in a blur. Holden and Jotch were given heavy cloaks to hide under and were taken to an inn. There, they bathed together under Crom's guard.

As the adrenaline died down, pain and exhaustion warred within Holden. Jotch looked much the same, letting the shower wall hold him up as Crom pumped them both water.

Once dry, Holden donned the plain clothes he had been provided. Still, without any weapons, he felt naked. Jotch was given clothes a size too large for him.

"Used enough soap for four men," Crom intoned.

Holden massaged his sore legs. "We were filthy enough for ten. I'm still worried about infection."

Crom just nodded and led them back to the boat. The docks were mostly empty. A few skeleton crews moved about, drinks in hand.

What purpose would they find at the docks when the city was in lockdown?

After being ushered below decks, Holden and Jotch were put in a small room with two barely-large-enough cots and locked in with no light but that from a small window near the ceiling.

Before leaving, Crom said, "Looks like Pirka's having a chat. Stay here and rest. I'll grab ya in a bit. Hungry?"

The two shook their heads.

"Right." The hulking redhead closed the door, leaving the fugitives alone.

"Do you think Recki is okay?" Jotch sat on one of the cots and rubbed at his legs and back. "People survive gut shots, right?"

Holden tried to ease the pain in his own bruised back. "Don't know."

"Well, what of their plan?" Jotch asked uncomfortably. "We want to leave the city, right?"

"*You* sure do." Holden threw off his towel. Despite how tense he felt, his body told him he would be able to sleep. He'd take even a few minutes' worth. "Rest. We don't know when the chance will come again."

"How can you sleep?" Jotch scoffed. "With everything—"

In an instant, Holden loomed over the Minister. He leaned in as close as he could. In the small cabin, Jotch had nowhere to go.

"Shut up. You don't speak to me again. I'm not your friend. I'm not your partner." Holden grabbed the man's face. His voice was ice. "This is your fault. *All* of it."

The Minister shrunk away as best he could.

Holden fell into his bunk. He curled into a ball, compensating for the lack of a blanket. He was terrified for Recki. She had been so pale. He hoped Flip was safe. His entire life, what little he had made of it, was gone once again. If Jotch had never come into his home, everything would have—

You quit your job to go hunt him, you stupid dog. Even if he hadn't come straight to your house, you still would have thrown it all away. You throw everything away—

Holden slammed his fist into the wall with a bellow.

Jotch was on his feet now, breathing hard.

Then Holden did something he had not done since he first learned of the massacre of the Seventh. He broke. The numbness he had felt since that time washed away; the unrelenting stress of the last months of his life crashed down in an overwhelming wave. He screamed, fell to the bed, and allowed it all to rip him to pieces.

HOLDEN HAD no idea how much time had passed. He became aware of Jotch sitting next to him on the cot, tears on his own face. "I know, Holden. I shut down after my brother was killed. I didn't even go to the funeral. How could I when I knew it was a lie?"

Jotch lay his head back against the wall. Holden brought his knees up to his chest.

"I keep expecting to get better," Jotch continued.

"But I see something that reminds me of him and.... I really loved my brother, Holden. He was such a good man."

"I'm sorry." Holden wiped tears from his own face. "Since it happened... I— I'm just so angry. I'm so afraid. I want to kill them all. I want to get in bed and never wake up."

Their eyes met.

"I tried to kill myself, Jotch. I put my pistol in my mouth and pulled the trigger. It didn't fire. The round was faulty." Holden chuckled. "Can you believe it? Hours of working up to it and—" he play-acted the motion of firing a pistol against his temple.

"You can't do that, Holden."

Holden nodded. "I know, life is—"

"Not until they're all dead. Everyone who is responsible for your family's death. That's what they were to you, right? Family? You can't die until those who gave the orders know pain and misery. That's why I found you, Holden. I knew you would feel it too. That itch. The need. I can't do it. I know you can."

All Holden could manage was a blink. The portly man stared back at him with an intensity Holden had never seen from him.

"I'm no killer, but you, Holden, you are. I saw your record." Jotch looked to a noise from outside their room. "Get your revenge, however possible. What else do you have left?"

The door opened, and Crom looked down at them. "Uhh, everyone okay?"

"No." Jotch got to his feet and extended Holden a hand. "But we just finished a good chat though, right, Holden?"

Holden got to his feet, not looking away from the Minister's now calm eyes. "Yeah."

"Right, then." Crom gestured out to the hall. "After you."

They walked down the length of the ship to a room roughly three times the size of Holden and Jotch's. Pirka and three others sat at a circular table. She gestured for them to take the two vacant seats.

"The two of you have either given us our greatest opportunity, or destroyed what so many have sacrificed for," Pirka spoke in a calm, unforgiving tone. "We wanted you, Jotch, for what you might know of the inner workings of the M.O.T. As long as you continue to give us information willingly, you will remain unharmed. If we so much as smell a lie..."

A man with graying hair on Pirka's right placed a knife on the table.

"...we will begin taking pieces of you. Am I understood?"

Jotch stared at the knife. "So we're not friends, then?"

Holden barked out a laugh.

Pirka's lips parted into a slashing grin as she said, "We could become great friends."

"Is Recki alive?" Holden could not hold in the question any longer. "Please, I have a right to know."

Pirka looked up to Crom. "The last we heard, stable, but not well. She's fighting infection now."

"You mentioned Chapman when you gave her medicine. You knew him?" Jotch looked between them with a curious expression. Holden continued, "Was Chapman responsible for what happened to the Seventh? Were you?"

The tension in the air grew. Hands went below the table to rest on what Holden assumed were pistols.

"I've no stomach for any more violence today. My bandage is already soaking through." Holden raised his hands. "I just want the truth. Please. They were my family."

Pirka seemed not to breathe for a long moment. "Chapman did what he did on my orders. We tried to force the truth into the light."

Holden's chest felt tight. "What was the truth?"

"We wanted to expose the M.O.D. for trying to use this "Drip," as they call it, to punish the royal class. We wanted to get ahead of their plan, and drive a wedge between the police and the military to destabilize the city. If the M.O.D. had the police on their side, the royals wouldn't dare retaliate. But with an internecine war on two fronts? That leaves room for games."

"Games." Holden felt so cold. "This was for martial advantage? The M.O.D. butchered a handful of people to send a message, so you send the entire Seventh into the meat grinder to shift the balance of power?"

"They weren't supposed to die!" Pirka's voice rose. It was the first strong emotion Holden had seen from her. "This is the price, boy. Blood and fire. When your enemy deals in lies and corruption, the only option left is chaos."

"So you signed their death warrants for a cause they—"

Pirka stood, slamming her fists on the table. "You're not the only one who has lost everything! There is no respite. There are no victories. There is only sacrifice."

"So why the fuck are you fighting?" Holden tried to stand, but Crom's heavy hand held him in his seat. "Why do you keep sacrificing?"

"Because my son is dead, Holden." Pirka's sudden calm was disturbing; unnatural. No one moved as a tear rolled down Pirka's face. "When my service was up, I came home and only got two years —." She choked and looked around the room. Looking for what, Holden was unsure. "My son was sent away for reeducation. He didn't return."

Holden couldn't look her in the eyes. Her cold tears, falling in her otherwise calm face, bespoke a never-ending grief.

"Some of us have no choice. Whether we fight for truth, revenge, or the old gods; no one is here because they want to be." Pirka took a rattling breath. "We are here because lies are a sickness. A plague infecting our peoples. Across the Empire the ease of deception weakens once great nations. Why fight? Imperial food, shelter, and medicine are so easy. We just have to agree to never question. The old ways were savage, right? Forget who we were, sell our children's futures, and follow *it*. The Almighty."

"We can discuss your reasons for rebellion if we all live through what is to come." Holden looked at everyone in the room in turn. "We have to save Khlid. Do you have a plan?"

Pirka sat carefully back in her chair. "It would seem Khlid has been infected with the Drip and is their greatest success yet. From what we know of it, it seems she's the only success they've had."

"What does that mean?" Holden put his elbows on the table. "Is she going to die?"

Pirka looked at the other rebel leaders around her. "If she hasn't yet, I would assume no. But all we can do is assume."

"So she's extremely valuable," Jotch said, copying Holden's engaged posture. "Their one success. If she's the key to whatever the Empire is attempting, getting hold of her could prevent it. Whatever 'it' is."

Doesn't matter, Holden thought to himself. *With or without them, I'm getting her out.*

"We've learned all we can about the Drip over the last two months. And what we've learned is unpleasant," Pirka said. She rubbed her neck, trying to relieve tension. "It changes a person in extreme ways, Reduces them to... something else."

Holden leaned forward. "So what exactly do we have here? Just some sophisticated poison? Why?"

"No, Holden, it's more than that; and our intelligence suggests they aren't done refining it. It's meant to turn people. Make them into..." Pirka raised her arms, palms to the ceiling. "As for the why, it seems not even the highest up at the M.O.S. know."

Jotch leaned forward. "And Khlid is the first survivor? She's alive and has become something new."

The man who placed the knife on the table

picked it up and sheathed it, saying, "Or it means that she's just *dying*, rather than dead."

Pirka grunted in agreement.

"Doesn't matter." Jotch rubbed at his own neck. "Getting her out of their hands one way or the other is now—"

"Crom, on your way here, did you tell the Minister he was in charge?" Pirka looked at the giant man.

"Nope."

"I didn't think so."

Jotch shrunk back in his seat.

"Yes, we have to get to her," Pirka continued. "Inspector Khlid could be the key to solving this horrid puzzle." Her annoyance melted away as she continued. "We just need to finalize a plan."

Holden leaned back in his seat, more weary than he had ever felt. "And that is?"

"We were planning on leaving." Pirka ran a hand through her curls. "A few were to be left behind in key positions to continue sowing doubt... but we've already made contact."

"Contact?" Holden and Jotch said in unison.

Pirka looked to her comrades for confirmation before continuing. "Before the last kingdoms fell, a desperate attempt was made to save their royal families. Ships were launched into the Endless Oceans.

At the time, these were thought to be suicide missions; and indeed, the ships' crews resorted to atrocities to survive. I will spare you those details... but, as it turns out, the Endless Oceans do not live up to their name. A few of these ships found their way to foreign shores."

Jotch's jaw fell open.

"After all this time, we have finally been offered an escape. Princess Koya, the second daughter of the Yu'ib Royal Family, lives. In exchange for the secrets of the Empire we will bring her, the New World will grant us sanctuary. She is our leader and our savior." Pirka's eyes turned to Jotch. "You, dear Minister, will be of immense value once we arrive. Khlid, if she is safe to transport, would be even greater."

Jotch looked puzzled. "Why me?"

"You know how the lies are spread. How the souls of nations are eroded away with honeyed lies. Before any soldiers crossed borders, the fallen kingdoms were battling the words of your Ministry worming its way into their people. You will make sure that does not happen again across the sea."

Holden stood. Crom's hand didn't stop him this time. "So we have months, maybe a year, to prepare —with a people we don't know— before the Empire crosses the Endless Oceans?"

"The signs are everywhere," Pirka replied.

"Recruitment is up in the outlying villages. Steel production is the highest it's ever been. Grips are being forced to preserve their burns. It all points to war."

"More blood," Jotch said hollowly. "The wars will never stop."

"The New World has no rifles or steel. Only rudimentary explosives and iron." Pirka's eyes drifted. "We're their one hope at putting up some semblance of a fight. This ship is loaded with as much knowledge as we could possibly fit. The barrels below hold no spice or wine. They're filled with books and schematics."

Holden found himself trying to stare into the cargo hold below him. "That's what the Rebellion has been doing all this time? Gathering knowledge?"

Pirka nodded. The tension in the woman's shoulders suddenly made much more sense to Holden.

It all clicked.

"Plans have changed. Only a few will leave on the boats you have," said Holden.

Pirka's silence was his confirmation.

"You spent years securing ships to ferry your people; now they will have to fight and die, to possibly grab Khlid."

Jotch looked around, confused. "What changed?"

Holden's heart broke for the woman before him. "The Rebellion will make a stand in the city," he said. "They will give us the distraction we need to get Khlid onto this ship. There can be no survivors."

Pirka's voice held a dark pride. "My people will fight to the last."

18

THE CAPITAL BURNS

Holden lay in his bunk, amazing himself by not immediately falling asleep. It wasn't the morning sun seeping through the window that kept him awake, but a drumbeat of anxiety just behind his eyes.

He had to be the first to Khlid. If there was anything left of her inside, he would be the one person she could trust. He and a small crew would take the sewers underneath the Ministry of Science and, after the battle began, break her out.

Rebels moved every resource they had at their disposal into position. Spies embedded near people of power would turn into assassins. Soldiers would prepare to kill squadmates they had trained with. The Rebels numbered less than eight hundred, but all were well placed to wreak havoc. Now, the city would burn. Thousands would die tomorrow, all for Khlid — and a faint hope that getting her out of the city would gain the Rebels a tide-turning human weapon. All future hope now rested with her.

Jotch shook in his cot. Holden guessed it wasn't from the night air. *Not that these blankets are very thick.*

Holden rolled onto his side and closed his eyes.

If Pirka kept her promise, Recki would be on the boat before the ship set sail.

Holden's last conscious thought was of his failure to protect his friend.

"OUR TIME HAS COME, HOLDEN."

The sun cast an orange glow in the small wooden room. Pirka stood over him, close enough not to wake Jotch with her words.

"We have to move."

Holden sat up and rubbed his eyes. His body ached from head to toe. His head still throbbed. "What time is it? Any hiccups?"

"Almost two, and not yet," Pirka said, opening the door. "When the plan is to create chaos, little can go wrong. This is desperate, but the less we have left to lose, the more effective we can be."

Gods, I slept till two.

Minutes later, Holden walked out into the afternoon air above deck. Crom stood near the ramp, his Grip armor glowing in the sunlight. He stared at his pocket watch intently, counting down the seconds.

As Holden approached, he put the piece away. "Top of the hour. Now people die."

Pirka walked up to Holden and handed him his pistol. She held a rifle of her own. "I say two minutes until alarms start."

"Nah, they'll need at least five." Crom stretched his arms, reaching higher than Holden could possibly jump.

They were counting on the bustle of the city at this hour to maximize the impact of the attack. The streets would be packed, and panicked crowds would become one of the threats the M.O.D. would have to manage.

Pirka lit a cigarette. Holden cadged one.

Men and women moved in the docks below, making a happy hubbub, unaware of the battle to come.

Holden flicked away embers. They played in the breeze. His mind followed them, trying to process everything that had transpired over the last few days.

Pirka, adjusting her green coat, caught his eye.

"So... lost nation across the sea." Holden pointed down river, out into the apparently misnamed

Endless Ocean. "Sounds like some of those children's stories."

Pirka quirked a sharp grin before burying it. "Sounds exactly like one I know. A rather popular story of a fleet finding a country overflowing with food and wondrous new magics with no poisons to suffer."

Crom grunted before saying, "So I'd still have my hazel eyes?"

Pirka turned to the hulking man fighting a clasp on his layered armor. "I thought Grips had green eyes from birth?"

"No." Crom finally snapped the piece in place. "Turn the first time we let it into us. I was seven, but most of us are even younger. Course, they take us off to the temple once that happens, so most people only ever see the green."

"Huh." Pirka looked back to Holden. "Regardless, I doubt we'll find three foot tall winged angels on the other side of this voyage."

Holden pulled his eyes away from staring at Crom's muscles, still somehow notable under all that armor. "You don't strike me as the type to know many kids stor— I am so sorry."

How he had blanked on the fact the woman before him lost a child he would never know.

That quick grin hit Pirka's lips, but her eyes remained still. "It's okay, Holden."

After a beat Pirka continued, "A lot of parents get into swapping old family stories. It's one place the empire hasn't managed to squash that kind 'old talk'."

"What do you mean?" Holden realized his head was cocked, so he straightened it. "People can discuss what they please."

Pirka eyed him thoroughly before saying, "You're correct in that no laws stop us from passing on these stories."

"Then wha—"

The ring of a bell sounded.

The people milling below froze.

"Let's move." Crom stepped onto the ramp, Pirka and Holden directly behind him.

The three of them reached the sewers, where five armed Rebels awaited them. Each was dressed casually, ready to disappear into a crowd at a moment's notice.

Holden tossed his cigarette into the water.

In the distance, something exploded.

Khlid, be ready.

Alarm bells brought Khlid to her feet. She walked to a small hole she had drilled into the wall with her clawed hand and peered out into the city. From her cell high up in the M.O.S., she saw smoke rising across the city. Her lips parted in surprise as flames erupted almost simultaneously at multiple locations. An explosion in a nearby building shook the walls around her.

Gods, what—

The door to her cell opened. As the last locks were retracted, she reached the bars.

Four soldiers entered the room, each wearing the blood-uniform of the Red Hand.

"Back against the wall!" one of them bellowed, leveling a rifle at her.

"Yeah, not going to do that," Khlid answered, her clawed hand wrapping around the bars.

"Final warning!" Three more rifles were pointed at her.

"Come on, you won't shoot—"

Something slammed into her belly, causing her to fall on her ass, more out of shock than the impact. The sound of a shot rang in her ears. Khlid looked down and saw a dent in her armored skin, surrounded by the shattered scraps of a bullet.

It hadn't hurt.

She grinned. "Oh, something big is happening, isn't it?"

Three more shots pushed her back, yet her grin never wavered.

The four soldiers loaded new cartridges, leveling their rifles again.

Khlid stepped back and raised her arms. "Fine, then. Am I being moved?"

A man bearing the lowest rank pulled out comically thick metal restraints and approached the bars. The leader called out, "Put those on."

The steel shackles were laid on the bars with steady hands.

Khlid picked them up as the soldier backed away. "Nah."

Gunshots slammed into Khlid once again. She stumbled as one impacted her head. It had torn away a patch of what little skin still existed on her face. Yet it seemed the armor coated her bones beneath. The skin began to knit itself back together.

Khlid chuckled, joy igniting in her chest. "You've done it. You've made me a god killer."

Rifles were reloaded and aimed at her again. With a mild effort, Khlid withstood their shots without falling.

For the first time, she let herself truly feel the

power that had been building within. Her bones had been eaten away, replaced with something greater. Her muscles moved faster than conscious thought. She saw light in new ways, darkness no longer a barrier. Her bladed left hand was sharper than any razor. She could predict how others would move even before they did.

Whether or not she was still herself was something she couldn't know, but Khlid now fit her purpose: to kill the Anointed. Every last one.

Khlid wrapped her hands around the metal bars, and with a smile, she found they weren't so strong after all.

Avi Cormick's head snapped up as a distant rumble shook the Ministry.

Why would—

An alarm from a nearby Ministry building rang out.

A rifle's shot cut through the air.

In one smooth motion, Avi leapt over her desk and exploded through her office door. As splinters rained, she saw a uniformed woman lying dead in a pool of blood outside the lift. A man stood over her, pistol in hand.

Recognition shocked her mind. The woman was

the head of the city garrison. The man was her bodyguard.

Avi shrieked as she leapt at the traitor. Jackson had walked beside them for years. Her heart broke as she tore his head from his body.

Why Jackson?

She dropped to one knee and checked Bella's pulse. Dead.

This couldn't have been the cause for the alarm bells. Something larger was happening.

The lift next to her let out a soft chime. The doors opened, revealing a man wearing a vest filled with raw explosive powder.

"I was supposed to find you." The man's voice trembled as his hand rose.

Avi's eyes widened as the shaking hand lit a match.

Pain consumed her body.

"CHARGES SET." The Rebel appeared from the shadows ahead, dragging an ignition line.

They hunkered in the sewer —*gods, please for the last time*— directly below the M.O.S. The charges were set to blow a hole into the floor of the building. Distant explosions continued to vibrate the walls.

Crom had told Holden the Rebellion had placed suicide bombers at key points to slow the Imperial counterattack. Their dedication floored Holden. Only days ago, these people had had hope of salvation in a new land. Now, each and every one was willing to sacrifice their life to secure that salvation for the surviving Rebels.

Holden had asked Pirka if any had refused orders. Her only response had been, "None of us fight for ourselves. We fight for our legacy, and for other's futures."

They may be radicals, but they are radicals I can walk with.

The woman holding the ignition line looked to Pirka. She gave a curt nod.

Five fingers went up. Four. Three. Two. One.

The roar of the explosion echoed through Holden's whole being.

They should have been further away. All collapsed into the muck of the sewer. Crom held his head, blinking wildly. Pirka was the first to her feet, shouting orders.

Holden got to his knees as the riflemen sprinted on. He, Pirka and Crom stumbled after them. Shots rang out up ahead, audible even above the ringing in Holden's ears.

Holden pulled himself up through the new hole

in the floor and into the Ministry of Science. Smoke choked his lungs as he stumbled for cover behind a reception desk. His eyes barely noticed the gigantic white and green hall covered in dust and debris.

Two of the Rebels took cover next to him. The other three stood behind pillars and exchanged fire with Imperial guards, mixed in among the civilians fleeing in panic.

Screams tore at Holden's ears.

The Rebels with him aimed over the desk and added to the fire. Expert marksmen, nearly all their shots found their targets. Experienced hands swapped out cartridges with lightning speed.

Crom stepped from the smoke, taking his time to evaluate the situation. His hand rose as his eyes glowed brighter green.

A metallic taste flooded Holden's mouth.

Where Crom's hand was aimed, heads exploded. Blood rained down on the few remaining, now fleeing for the doors to the city.

Pirka hauled herself from the smoke last. Behind her, the chime of the lift announced more people incoming.

A pistol in each hand, Pirka emptied her weapons. The men and women in black lab coats stood no chance.

"Stop!" Holden screamed. "They're unarmed!"

He was too late. All of them fell, gore spilling from beneath their black coats.

Holden got to his feet and checked the room before asking Pirka, "Why? They were—"

Pirka whirled on him. "The more of them we kill, the slower their research."

Crom nodded.

Holden wanted to vomit.

"You five, protect this exit. If we lose the tunnel, this gets a whole lot harder." Pirka headed toward the lift. "Crom, Holden, come on."

With no other options, Holden followed.

Crom moved the bodies with the Grohalind, their limp forms dragging across the floor.

Holden averted his eyes. It felt so wrong.

As the doors closed, tension filled the small space.

"Holden." Pirka's voice was soft.

"Yeah?"

"They deserved it. I need you to trust me."

He did. With what he now knew the Empire was doing to its citizens, there was almost no violence Holden could imagine that wouldn't feel justified. But none of that settled his stomach.

Floors chimed away.

"You sent two ties from the man to opposite walls and pulled?" Pirka asked Crom. She paid no attention to his answer. She was nervously filling the silence, her eyes glued to the lift doors in front of them.

"Yup." Crom answered. "Finally got ties down just a few weeks back."

Pirka nodded. "If that Anointed shows up, don't hesitate."

"Never do."

An explosion sounded below. The lift came to a stop between floors as the electronic light above went out.

"Fuck, I told them to leave the power lines to the M.O.S.."

Crom stepped up to the door. "In battle, damage cannot be contained. I told you we should have—"

The Grip ripped the doors open to a field of corpses. Dozens of soldiers, all wearing the uniform of the Red Hand, were torn to shreds. Holden's eyes flinched away from a man cut from groin to throat— only to see a woman with a bayonet driven through her face.

He looked to the roof of the lift. "Gods. What happened?"

Pirka pushed past Crom. "Guessing your mentor saw an opportunity in our chaos. We have to find her." She lifted herself into the opening and out into the crimson massacre, climbing past the nearly bisected man.

Crom did the same.

Holden took two long breaths in the elevator. "Gods. Fuck."

His stomach finally gave. Vomit spilled over his boots.

"Holden, I thought you had battlefield experience—"

"Not like this!" he shouted. "Men and women *shot*, not—" He made the mistake of looking at the corpses again. His breath was rapid and shallow.

Crom extended an arm to him. "It horrifies me too, lad. But we have no choice."

Taking one final breath —one tinged with the stench of both his own vomit and the room full of blood— Holden took Crom's hand and let himself be pulled from the lift. His mind blocked out the red carnage surrounding him. As something squished under his boot, Holden looked to Crom for reassurance.

The Grip met his eyes and nodded. "We're okay."

"She didn't take the lifts down. The door to the stairs had blood on the handle." Pirka said, looking at the smeared liquid. She pushed open the door and her gaze followed the steps. "She went up."

"Up?" Holden and Crom asked in confusion.

"Let's go. Follow the trail of blood." Pirka pushed onward.

Crom and Holden followed behind.

"At least our source got the floor number she was being held on right." Crom said, stepping over a twisted corpse.

———

HOLDING the severed head of his secretary, Khlid relished the look of fear on the Minister's face. "Where is she?" she said calmly, as cold as a morning breeze over ice.

As Khlid reached his desk, he backed away into the wall. "I... I don't know. She comes and goes as she—"

Khlid threw the secretary's head. It exploded on the wall next to the man.

Bounding over the desk, Khlid landed with a grace impossible for any but her, or the demigod she now hunted.

She placed her short claws at the Minister's throat. Blood began to seep out where blades touched skin, though she had yet to exert any pressure.

Placing her lips to the fat man's ear, she whispered as if to a lover, "I've learned so much today about what was done to me."

The Minister prayed to the Almighty.

"Your needles and knives jabbed and sliced. Samples of my flesh were torn away again and again." Her free hand stroked his face. "It's only fair I get to conduct experiments of my own, no?"

"Avi's office is at the M.O.D. I don't know if she's there now, but—"

Khlid arched her hand upward, tearing through the man's diaphragm, and seized a lung. He shook around her metal arm until she tore the organ away with a wet squelch.

The man fell to the floor. He flopped around, trying to cover the violation of his body.

A noise outside pricked her ears.

Good. Bring me more.

"WELL, if I was her, I'd go for the head," Crom said, approaching the Head Minister of Science's door.

Pirka kept scanning the hall around them. The stone building was eerily quiet.

Holden went to the opposite side of the office door and nodded at Crom.

As the Grip moved directly in front of the door,

that metallic taste filled Holden's mouth once more. He hoped Grip armor was as good as people said at containing the illness associated with the Grohalind.

Crom gave an enormous physical effort, though he seemed to be pushing nothing but the air around him — yet the doors exploded open, sending him stumbling back.

The three of them entered the office.

It seemed empty at first; that is until Holden saw a man attempting to breathe behind the desk. Blood foamed at his mouth as he clutched a massive wound in his wide gut.

"What the fuck," Holden said aloud. "What have they—"

"Holden?" The voice was familiar, yet somehow also entirely inhuman. No human vocal cords could produce that sharp, grinding undertone.

The three whirled as something dropped from the ceiling: a creature of flesh, bound in something — metal? — its smooth, angled lines melding with human skin at the face with slitted, red eyes — a face Holden found familiar. A head of curly hair hung wildly, complementing the swirling, plate-like patterns that ran down the creature's, hugging it so tightly it was impossible to know whether she was wrapped head-to-toe in the clinging substance, or naked and composed of it.

"Holden!" Pirka tried to put out an arm to stop him, but he shoved past her, dropping his weapon.

She said my name.

Khlid accepted his embrace. Her skin felt hard, yet organic, as she wrapped her arms around him.

"I'm so sorry." Tears ran down Holden's face. "I've got you. I wasn't there, but I've got you now."

Khlid let out a sob, putting her weight into his arms. She was far heavier than he remembered.

"I wasn't there," was all he could manage.

Khlid's new voice sounded as though steel could speak. "I will forever be grateful you weren't, Holdi. All you could have done was die."

Holden released Khlid so he could look her in the eyes. She touched her own face, feeling the tears there. "I can still cry. They haven't taken that from me."

Holden smiled through tears of his own. "You look strong. New workout regimen?"

Pirka stepped up to them.

Khlid's demeanor changed. Shoulders hunched and a clawed hand opened. "Khlid," Holden cautioned her. "This is a friend. We have a way out."

Eyeing Khlid distrustfully, Pirka said, "Well, what we have is a plan. You may be the key to stopping an oncoming war, or at least delaying it. Please, come with us."

Khlid looked at Crom, standing back. The big man raised his hands saying, "Just an escort... uhh, if you're willing."

Eyes narrowing, Khlid looked back to Holden. "Not until I find her."

19

A HICCUP

As a precautionary measure, Flip had gotten halfway into his retired Grip armor when he heard screams outside his front door. The explosions in the distance seemed to be getting louder. Opening the door a fraction, he saw officers of God in the street. People sprinted by as uniforms ordered them indoors.

Smoke from distant fires began to cloud the air.

My God, the city's on fire.

Gunfire popped only a few streets over. Flip's trained ear told him it was more than just pistols.

Now, he saw one of the officers getting trampled by the crowd. He finished donning his armor and marched to the front door.

Catching his reflection in a wall mirror, he noted how the green of his eyes seemed to be enhanced by the black armor. They glowed in the depths of his helmet. Something old in his mind stirred. Something that had slept for years.

Holden and Recki are in this. Almighty, they may have caused it.

He knew they had been planning to rescue Khlid from the Ministry of Science. Whether they were responsible for the chaos out there now, it seemed a smart bet that if they were ever going to rescue Khlid, now would be an excellent time to attempt it.

The energy in the street was unhinged. Men and women screamed. Children cried. The illusion of the infinitely secure Capital City was ripped away. Few officers remained. A sergeant yelled for the few she had left to stay by her side.

Flip got to them, the sea of humanity parting around his massive form. Even when they're insane from fear, instinct told people to avoid a massive man in Grip armor.

"What do you know?" he shouted at the sergeant over the pandemonium.

Seeing the armor, she said, "The city is under attack. The M.O.D. massacred a precinct this morning. Bombs have gone off in countless government locations and targeted officials have been kill— hey, back off!"

A woman grabbed onto her, frantically asking for

help finding her husband. One of the officers clubbed her with a pistol, throwing her into the crowd.

Flip dove for the woman. Someone unseen bounced off of Flip as he roughly pulled her to her feet. Stumbling away, half-carrying the woman, Flip shoved her onto his porch.

"Stay there!" he screamed as he heard nearby shots. He turned to see city garrison soldiers firing into the alleys from which they had just emerged. Something about the size of a fist was tossed from a gutter, landing amidst the garrison men.

An explosion ripped them to pieces. The ball lobbed into their midst was a brutal grenade filled with ball bearings. The shrapnel bounced off Flip's armor.

The panic reached a crescendo as cries of pain overcame all other sounds.

Flip looked to see if the officers would help, but they had fled. Seeing the military torn to pieces crippled what order was left.

Men and women dressed casually, in no type of uniform, emerged from the alleys with rifles; executing the injured city troops.

"No!" he cried.

Heads and rifles snapped in his direction. The woman behind him screamed.

As fast as he could, Flip grabbed her and dove through his front door, shots ringing out behind them. Splinters of wood exploded all around as they fell inside his front hall.

"Stay down and get under my bed!"

Stupid! A Grip in armor would be a target for any Rebel.

Flip crawled to his back door and ripped it open. He ran through his back yard and barreled through his fence, sending boards flying.

A man screamed. A group began to flee in the opposite direction.

Stay alive and get to the M.O.S., Flip told himself, directing his feet toward the Imperial District.

Avi could feel her body rebuilding itself. Gurlges and cracks sounded as her consciousness returned. The pain was beyond anything she thought possible: nerve endings regrowing like spider's webs through the writhing mass of flesh she had been reduced to. Today, her gifts felt like a curse. It would be easier to die than to suffer this horrendous reconstitution. As her throat reformed, a low howl was all she could manage. Blurry vision returned as her eyes regrew.

A soldier in a Red Hand uniform looked down at her, fear in his eyes.

Beyond the pain, a murderous rage boiled at the indignity she had suffered. How dare they resist her? How dare anyone strike at a god of the Empire?

An as-yet skinless leg pulsed into existence beneath her, a ripping sound in her new ears as it did. It was followed by a nascent fist slamming to the floor.

What could almost now be called a head flexed upwards, teeth moving into place like ants in formation.

She croaked one word: "Mask."

"KHLID, WE DON'T HAVE TIME," Holden pleaded. Desperation filled his heart. "Our way out of the city is closing."

Gods, I need to make sure Recki is safe. Please.

She pushed past him.

"Listen, people are dying for you! For a hope!"

Khlid reached the office door.

Pirka came forward, "Would your husband have wanted you to fight today, or live for tomorrow?"

Khlid's head snapped toward the Rebel.

"You can kill more than just one Anointed if you

come with us. We're not going into permanent hiding; we are retrenching in order to continue the fight." Pirka holstered her pistols and approached Khlid. "The greatest war is yet to come. You will be our greatest asset; the scourge we unleash on any Anointed who shows their cursed face outside of this godsforsaken continent. Including the one who killed your husband and Chapman."

Khlid's face, the only still recognizably human part of her, contorted.

Crom couldn't help but add, "Mrs. Whitter, what's been done to you goes beyond torture or murder. Only right now your future should be your own. You can go out those doors alone, or you can trust Holden and come with us. Believe me, though, there will be more fighting with us. I won't stop until I personally see you kill the woman who butchered the Seventh."

Khlid let go of the door's handle. Her eyes darted about as if playing out the possibilities. "How are we getting out?"

Holden let out a long breath.

"We have a ship in the harbor. My people will keep up the fight until we are safely out of the city. Soon, the Navy will be called in. We have to get out before that happens." Pirka's eyes contained a glimmer of hope. "Khlid, please. We need you."

Khlid came uncomfortably close to Pirka, weighing the woman, examining her from head to toe like a predator playing with its victim. Finally, she met Pirka's eyes. "Do you promise I will be the one allowed to kill Avi Cormick?"

Pirka didn't flinch. "I will do whatever is in my power to make that happen."

"Fine," Khlid said, withdrawing from Pirka and letting out a sigh. Then she asked Holden, "Do you have a cigarette?"

20

THE COST OF ESCAPE

Their flight down the stairs winded everyone but Khlid. It seemed her energy was endless. She glided down the dimly-lit steps, her feet barely touching the marble. She kept having to slow down to allow the others to catch up.

They moved with a caution she found tiresome. Then she realized it was the darkness. Only one slim window graced every floor, leading to darkening skies of smoke.

To all but Khlid, this was a black pit.

As Khlid raced down to a floor below them, a sound outside the door made her freeze.

She tossed her cigarette and positioned herself.

Two soldiers burst into the well, throwing the door into her.

She reacted as fast as thought. Her hand closed around the nearest soldier's throat, tearing it away. Ligaments and tendons slid through her fingers.

Holden rounded the flight above as Khlid's free claw pierced the face of the second soldier still stepping into the stairway. Her talons dug into mouth and eyes, silencing her forever in an instant.

As Khlid withdrew her claws with a loud slurp.

Holden looked at the scene in horror.

Khlid met his eyes. A shame she could not yet understand formed in her heart.

Pirka continued down the stairs and stepped over the bodies. "Almost there. Let's move!" As they reached the bottom floor, the sound of gunfire echoed into the well.

"Ready?" Crom asked.

Holden and Pirka nodded as Khlid drew herself into a crouch, readying herself for the battle waiting just outside the door.

Crom shoved it open and Khlid leapt past him.

Since Holden and the Rebels had exploded through the green-and-white lobby, a team of the Red Hand had recovered the floor and taken up positions. Now, they fired from behind makeshift cover at the far end of the room where the remaining rebels ducked in cover.

Several of the Red Hand turned, hearing movement behind them.

Too late.

Claws met flesh. Bones snapped; muscles torn apart by teeth. Khlid killed like an animal.

Armed people in plain clothes tentatively peered out from the shadows.

Khlid looked down at her body. Blood lay thick over her armor. It dripped down the patterned grooves, filling the lines in crimson streams.

I was designed for this.

"It's okay!" Pirka called to the terrified Rebels. "She's what we came for."

Two emerged from behind a desk, their eyes glued to Khlid.

"You okay?" Holden asked, approaching with his hands raised yet again. The kid-glove treatment from her erstwhile apprentice irked her. She nodded curtly.

Light returned to the room. Pirka looked up at the electrical wonders, woven into giant decorative spheres, above them. "That's not good. If they're already working to restore power, our chance to escape is closing."

"Doesn't mean the battle's ended," Crom said, leading the way to the hole they had blown in the floor on their way into the Ministry, only half an hour or so earlier.

Pirka looked to the two soldiers. "Get ammo. Gather their weapons and cover our retreat as long as you can. More will be coming."

The rebels soldiers nodded and searched the dead.

Khlid noticed Holden looking at the two with something close to admiration. Then she saw just how much her apprentice had changed. He was slouched, with unkempt hair. There was a startling lack of muscle under his coat. Even his gait was less confident than Khlid remembered.

He noticed her gaze. "What?"

"Missed you is all." She followed Crom's lead to the hole in the floor.

Holden still had the same childish grin. "You too, boss."

A noise from the tunnel. Shots sounded distantly in the sewer below. Pirka's eyes widened as she stared into the darkness.

The taste of metal came so strongly to Khlid, she actually spat.

Crom grabbed Pirka and Holden, diving away from the tunnel. Khlid watched a wave of green light build below.

"Run!"

Khlid wasn't sure who had yelled it, but all were running from the green flames exploding out of the tunnel.

She caught up to Crom, with the Rebel soldiers right behind.

Barely ahead of the green flames, Crom smashed through the lobby's ruined glass front doors with his armored body, sending them all sprawling into the evening air.

A green flash dominated everything. The world vibrated as a buzzing toxin filled Khlid's existence. Crom still ran with Pirka, covered the best she could by his armor. Holden, seemingly discarded, crawled away from the building. Red marks flared on his pale skin.

Khlid ran to her former student and dragged him further from the still-glowing building. Sounds of panic began to register, not just from the rebels

Lifting her eyes, Khlid saw the city up close for the first time in months.

It was a nightmare.

Buildings burned wherever she looked. Smoke filled the sky; an orange glow dominated the horizon. The sun failed to penetrate the choking cloud over the city. The people were in desperate shape. Soldiers were being trampled by panicked civilians, people frantic to flee as fighting reached their neighborhoods. From their garb, it seemed all types of people from all over the city had come to the Imperial District in hope of protection.

Khlid watched a soldier fire wildly at a crowd that had knocked him down, desperate not to be trampled to death.

No wonder we didn't meet more resistance. The city had gone mad.

Khlid got to her feet.

A Red Hand Grip near the main door raised his gauntlets in a motion of surrender and backed away.

Before stepping into light, Khlid didn't consider the effect her appearance would have on an already terrified mob. As she stood atop the Ministry of Science's steps, visible to all, a wave of terror gripped the panicked crowd.

Where people had been running in every which way, the entire mob now moved in one direction: away from the blood-soaked demon in their midst.

The soldiers who saw her were no less panicked. They were not disciplined like Red Hand. They were City Soldiers, and she, as far as they were concerned, was the Devil.

Only the nearby Grip didn't flee. Oddly, he ignored her and stared at Holden.

Holden went for his pistol before a look of recognition came over him.

Is that Flip?

HOLDEN'S SHOCK FINALLY SUBSIDED. "FLIP?"

Crom lowered his defensive stance at the tone of recognition. "You know him?"

"Yeah."

Holden openly returned the man's stare. "What are you —"

Pirka cut him off. "Are you willing to help us get out of the city?" The Grip nodded.

"Holden, can we trust him?" Pirka asked impatiently.

"With our lives."

"Good." She shoved Crom to his feet. "Move!"

The six of them made it into a cobblestone street with small evacuated shops on either side. Holden noticed Khlid slowing her stride to stay by him.

"What under the gods was that green flash?" Pirka asked, sucking down air between words.

Crom looked about to answer but Holden spoke first. "An Imperial Grip must have detonated themself in the sewer. They were probably ordered to do it to prevent our retreat. If we go in, we'll die of exposure to the Grohalind."

"Can we get in a few blocks over?" Pirka asked.

Flip answered, "it will be toxic for blocks. Everyone in this district is likely to have symptoms. The poison spreads even farther in tunnels like that."

Crom finished with, "The sewers may help contain it. Fewer will die. As for going down there, we have to move fast. In armor, we two will be okay. You lot might have a rough few days ahead."

"Shit," was all Pirka had to say.

As they rushed to the next manhole, Crom gave Holden and Flip a reluctant nod of approval.

Recki, you were absolutely right about cardio. Holden made a mental note to thank her for always bugging him about it.

He glanced over to Flip. *What in the hell are you doing here?* he thought.

They reached another street crowded with people running by. Though this area was not yet in full stampede, most citizens reversed course when they saw Khlid.

Holden couldn't be angry at the terrified people. His former mentor terrified him, too.

It wasn't her appearance. It was how she killed like a machine built for that purpose. Every movement was exact and lethal. The sound of that soldier's throat being torn out still filled his ears.

A small break in the influx of people headed for

the Capitol emerged. Pirka ushered them all forward.

As they reached another maze of alleys, Crom turned to look back. "They'll all be poisoned if they head toward the Ministries, damn it."

Pirka replied, "That's the imperial's problem. More pressing is the fact that we can't move as quickly or directly as we could've in the sewers."

With only partial relief, Crom asked, "How did the military even know to block our escape?"

"Dozens who fled the M.O.S. saw us blow our way in through the floor," Holden answered.

Pirka said, "One suicidal charge was probably all they could manage in this. Which is why we need to *move!*"

Crom looked back at the panicked crowd one last time. "Fuck." Pulling off his helmet, he followed after Pirka.

Flip made sure to stay close to Holden as they made their way toward the docks.

"How did you find us?"

Flip shrugged, pulling off his helmet to breathe easier. "Said you wanted to get Khlid out of Ministry hands. That would require something insane. Insane things started happening. Rather safe bet where you'd be."

"Alright, so you got lucky."

"Yeah, pretty much. Where's Recki?"

The sound of battle nearby prevented Holden from answering.

As they ran into the mouth of an intersecting street, a platoon of Red Hand soldiers met them, arms at the ready. A hooded soldier in their midst fired a flare into the sky.

Khlid snatched Holden and dove with him behind a building pouring smoke into the street.

Seeing Khlid and Holden leaping for cover, Flip and Crom ground to a halt before hurtling out of shadow.

Pirka didn't.

As she intersected the waiting Red Hand, shots filled the air. Though the bullets flew through her, she rushed on toward Holden. Reaching him, she dropped and let out a cough. As she did, he felt warm fluid spill onto him.

Khlid was already on her feet, sprinting back to butcher the Red Hand team.

Holden slowly laid Pirka down. The sounds of soldiers dying reached his ears. As blood darkened her coat at the shoulder, her eyes locked onto his. "Leave me—"

"Shut up," Holden said as he pressed his hands on her wound.

Pirka grunted in pain, grabbing his arm with her good hand. "I'll slow you down."

"I said shut up."

"Holden—"

"Shut up!" Blood soaked between his fingers.

"Look down, Holden."

He did. Two more stains were spreading on her thigh and calf. Blood seeped through, dripping onto the stones.

"Flip! Crom!"

The two Grips had been providing cover to the Rebels firing on Imperials, but by now Khlid had butchered most of them. The sounds of gunfire dying behind them, Flip and Crom jogged to Holden's position.

"Put your hands here." He placed Flip's hands on Pirka's shoulder, then removed his belt. They worked as fast as they could, shaking from adrenaline. The tourniquet slowed the blood loss in Pirka's leg, but it wouldn't be enough. They had a whole district to go, and by now every soldier in the Empire would be hunting for Khlid.

The soldiers Khlid was fighting fled as they realized their bullets had no effect on the silver woman. And yet, Khlid was about to chase them down regardless.

"Are you fucking crazy? Khlid!" His call made

her turn, murder in her eyes. "That flare means more are coming."

"It means *she's* coming!" Khlid said. She kicked a rifle from the floor to her hand, then hurled it like a javelin, faster than Holden's eyes could track. A retreating soldier's head exploded at the impact.

"Fuck. Flip, take Pirka and the soldiers. Go to Dock Thirteen. People there will recognize her. Go!"

Concern flooded his former lover's face. "I can't leave you like—"

Holden grabbed the man by the collar, kissed him hard and shoved him back. "She'll bleed out. Go!"

Flip picked her up, looked back only once, and sprinted toward the docks.

At Crom's nod, the two Rebels followed suit. Their guns would be of no use here.

Crom stood, but Holden pulled him roughly back to the ground. "Something's wrong. Khlid has never been like this before. Be careful!"

Nodding, the Grip got to his feet.

Holden tasted metal.

───────

KHLID LOOKED into the soldier's eyes as he screamed, her hands wrapped around his skull. She squeezed harder. His eyes bulged from his head, blood leaking from the sockets. With a crack, his head exploded under her hands.

Warm liquid poured over Khlid's perfect skin.

She wasn't satisfied. She wanted more. The worms had returned. She could feel them writhing beneath her skin. They craved Anointed blood.

For you, Sam. It's all for you.

"Find me!" she screamed. The metallic grind of her voice cut through the air. "See what you have made!"

There were no more soldiers. So many had escaped justice.

"Khlid?" came a calm voice.

That taste of metal filled her mouth once more. She turned to see the Rebel Grip approaching her, his stance submissive.

"You promised you would come with us. Please. Pirka is hurt. Holden has been exposed to far too much of the Grohalind. We need to move."

Can't he see? Khlid could protect them all. There was no rush. She could purge the whole city—

As soon as she thought it, her own mind recoiled in horror, as if the very idea had been placed in her brain by some malevolent external force

Holden emerged behind the Grip. He looked scared— scared of *her*.

Khlid found she could barely contain the rage building within her. Her claw was pointed threateningly at the Grip.

Then**,** a voice consumed the night. **"Rabbit."**. The voice boiled in Khlid's mind. **"You escaped your cage."**

A white mask seemed to float in the roiling, polluted sky above, staring down at them from a slate roof. Even Khlid's eyes could barely discern the black cloak from the churning smoke.

"You—"

Khlid allowed the Anointed no more words. Stones cracked under her feet as she leapt towards Samuel's killer, clawed hand extended.

The two creations of the Almighty collided.

Khlid rammed her claw vertically into the Anointed's jaw. Blood gushed onto her hand. Screaming with delight, she pulled back and stabbed again and again.

Khlid atop the Anointed, they fell onto a tiled roof.

Rage drove Khlid to land blow after blow. She wanted to obliterate the woman beneath her. The Anointed accepted the attack without resistance.

"Fight me!" Khlid landed a right cross snapping Avi's head to the side.

Still, the Anointed remained still.

Khlid ripped away the vile mask. She froze at what she saw: skin was peeled back from the woman's eyes and mouth. Her teeth had no lips to hide them. The Anointed's skin was nearly transparent, the veins visibly pulsating underneath.

"Creature," Khlid spat.

Avi's grin was a mirror of the rictus mask. "Your husband—"

Khlid grabbed the Anointed by the throat and squeezed. Blood sprayed as her clawed fingers punctured flesh. "Don't speak of him!"

The Anointed's hands rose and calmly wrapped around Khlid's wrists. Slowly, deliberately, she pulled Khlid's arms away.

"Your husband died kneeling to me. Remember that, Rabbit." Spittle and blood frothed from the Anointed's mouth.

Fear stabbed through Khlid's heart. "No!"

No, I'm supposed to be stronger.

Avi casually tossed Khlid aside, sending her rebounding off of the roof. Spinning end over end, Khlid dropped from the roof, crashing painfully to the stone street below.

As she rose to her knees, Avi landed on top of her, slamming her back to the ground. Cracks split through her armored skin.

Khlid struggled to take a breath as Avi kicked her

in the back. She didn't see the blow coming; she felt the armor on her head split. The world spun.

"Weak." Avi's face consumed her field of vision. The gashes Khlid had given her were already knitting shut. "After all of this, you're just another failure."

They shouldn't have, but the words stung.

Khlid aimed a kick at Avi, but the Anointed was already a blur. Dodging forward and stomping down hard, the armor of Khlid's leg shattered like porcelain beneath her foot. Khlid screamed in pain as a white pus began to leak between the cracks in her armor.

A white knife appeared from under Avi's black cloak. She pinned Khlid's chest under a knee. "We'll just try again. Perhaps with a few of your friend—"

The taste of metal returned.

Both women turned to see Crom lift his arms and throw them forward, his green eyes ablaze.

Avi flew through the air and crashed into the wooden door of a building on fire.

"Get up!" Crom shouted.

Holden was picking Khlid up. "Let's go!"

Khlid tried to put pressure on her leg, but collapsed in pain.

"Come on, Whitter," Holden said, his voice trembling. "A dark alley is no place to die."

She rose again, using her apprentice as a crutch.

Defeat beat in her heart. Khlid had spent weeks planning this moment, fantasizing of destroying the Anointed who murdered her Samuel.

It had all just been a dream.

Avi had tossed her about casually, as a child would a ragdoll.

Crom had both his hands extended forward, a look of immense concentration on his face. "Go!"

Holden half-dragged Khlid into the darkness, terror playing on his face.

THE WEIGHT on Avi's back was crushing. It pinned her to a fireplace within the burning building. This Grip seemed to remember its training: when overpowered, immobilize the combatant.

Avi planted both her hands on a chunk of stone debris. Her flesh sizzled. Flames licked her boots as she screamed, pushing against the Grohalind force pinning her to the wall.

The Grip felt her resistance and reacted. With a yank, he whipped her through the air, back into the street.

The rough cobblestones scraped her skin and snagged her cloak, the seams snapping and tearing as she whipped end over end through the street until she crashed through the wall of a nearby structure. Shards of brick and wood rained down, battering her aching form. Flames licked the beams above. Avi could sense the foundations begin to crumble.

The Grip smashed through a charring doorway, his green eyes blazing, one hand extended toward her, another reaching behind him.

He was utilizing the mass of something Avi could not see to hold her in place. Depending on his stamina, he could potentially keep this up for hours.

"Fuck you!" she hissed, pushing up from the ruined stairs.

Those green eyes flared as the weight increased.

As she took a struggling step forward, the Grip levitated off the ground, adding his own weight to the force upon her.

Avi fell to one knee; the floorboards cracked under her. She kicked off what footing she managed to find.

All at once, the Grip released her. She tumbled forward.

Transferring the focus of the Grohalind, he launched himself high into the air, flipping above her.

As he descended, Avi felt the force return. Invisible hands grabbed her face— one at her chin, the other at her temple— and *push*. She felt the bones of her neck explode from the pressure. Her skull cracked loudly.

Any normal person would have been killed instantly.

The Grip landed before her, his arms raised high. He threw them down, yanking her head to the ground with such force, Avi's spine tore to pieces.

"Bye!" The mocking word was followed by an explosion of force at her chest.

After a peaceful moment soaring through the night air, Avi collided with a cart, the shoddy wood shattering with the force.

That hurt.

Bones re-knitted themselves. Avi's spine moved snakelike within her torso, climbing back into place. Sensation returned completely to her limbs as her neck snapped and popped in realignment.

Avi allowed herself three long slow breaths, staring at the smoke pouring into the night sky above.

Splinters fell from her cloak as she rose and patiently walked back toward the Grip. He was on his knees, panting heavily, totally unaware of her. Blood dripped from his nose as he vomited onto the street.

"Well done, wizard."

The man's head shot up. "No. You can't—"

Green light flickered in his eyes as they struggled to focus on her.

She lunged, her knee shattering the bones in his shoulder through the armor. The Grip slid across the street for several paces.

Avi tasted metal again, but she was prepared this time.

A second blow caused the man to career into a barrel.

She approached as the Grip tried to push himself up with shaking limbs.

"What is your name, wizard?"

The man's eyes were frantic as he looked at her. "You broke."

"I can't break." She placed a hand under his chin. The light within his eyes winked out, returning them to a much more human green. "Please, your name."

"Crom Rollik."

"Well done, Mr. Rollik. I will remember you." It would take hours to torture any useful information from the man. By then, Khlid would be out of the city. The soldier deserved a respectable death. His neck snapped with a flick of her wrist. "Well done."

Avi fell to one knee, her body giving out.

THE CITY WAS the darkest Holden had ever seen it. Both moons shone tonight, but their light was completely consumed in the black smoke.

Occasional screams reached his ears. The military had taken back control of the city. Formations of soldiers marched in the streets. Holden had dragged Khlid from dark corner to unlit street, desperately avoiding watchful eyes.

Commotion a block over caught Holden's eye. His heart broke as he saw two Rebels kneeling. An officer's arm dropped and soldiers opened fire on the defeated men. The fight had turned. Once the Empire had even a little time to organize, the chaos had been overcome. Within the hour, Holden guessed the fight would be over.

He kept the two of them moving, giving a wide berth to the distraction of the execution.

To Holden's amazement, Khlid recovered enough to walk on her own. The only sign of the damage was a harsh cracking whenever she one leg extended too far. Khlid didn't appear to be aware of it. She followed Holden, lost in her failure.

The smell of the dock gave Holden a rush of hope. . Ships rested peacefully on still waters. The only occupied ship was theirs. The three-masted vessel was untied and ready to sail.

Holden ran for it, with Khlid keeping pace.

The deck crew sent down the ramp, wasting no time to draw it back up once Holden and Khlid were aboard. Faster than Holden thought possible, they sailed from the dock into the still river.

The Naval crews had mostly been called ashore to help fight fires. Only one patrol boat shone a light their way, but it was too far to do anything but note their departure.

As their ship pulled out into open sea, Holden and Khlid watched the stars above the city begin to shine.

"How many died for me, Holden? Hundreds? Thousands?"

"Not for you." He rested a hand on her shoulder. "For what they did to you. The responsibility is not yours."

He looked her in the eyes, their crimson color bright in the night. "I'm not who I once was," Khlid said. "This mind is new. Virgin to the world. My thoughts— my emotions are not my own."

"You're still in there."

"What makes you say that?"

Holden reached into his pocket and removed a pack of cigarettes. "There are a few tells."

Khlid managed a smile as she took the pack from him. "Holden, I was supposed to beat her. That creature, it killed our—"

A sailor in striped pants approached them. "You're wanted below."

"Is Recki on board? Did Flip and Pirka make it?"

"Aye," the sailor said before heading below decks.

"Make new friends, Holden?"

"Aye," he said in his best impersonation of the sailor, and walked to the steep stairs below.

Flip greeted them at the bottom of the stairs, blood staining his armor. "She's stable. Stubborn woman won't even put her head down, despite being pale as a sheet. She's demanding to see you."

"Thanks, Flip." Holden moved past him in the cramped hall.

"The other Grip, did he make it aboard?"

Holden met his gaze. "He stayed behind so we could escape an Anointed."

Anger flashed in Flip's face. "That fucking creature came to my home."

"You'll get your shot at her," Khlid said.

Flip nodded. "Oh, shit. We are moving? My house..."

Holden squeezed Flip's arm, "Probably burning. You can't go back."

The Grip looked deeply upset for only a moment, before letting out a long breath and heading above.

Pirka and Recki occupied two beds side by side in a cramped medical room at the back of the ship. Holden couldn't help noticing a wooden table covered in blood just opposite Pirka.

As they entered, her head rose from the pillow. "Gods, you did make it. Is Crom above? Tell him to get his ass down here—"

She noted their expressions. "Oh."

"I'm sorry," Holden said, sitting at the edge of her bed. "The Anointed came."

Pirka's head came up again. "The Anointed?"

"Crom delayed her so we could escape."

Khlid stepped forward. "If it weren't for him, she would have killed us all."

"Then he died for something." Grief tinged Pirka's tone. "He was a great man."

"I know how this may sound, but it is possible he escaped," Holden offered.

"Doesn't matter either way. We'll never see him again."

"What a stupid fucking thing to say," Recki said weakly, though with characteristic snark. "If your friend is alive, of course that matters. Gods!"

Holden thought she had been unconscious. He fell on her, careful not to touch her stomach. Holden kissed her cheeks, lips and forehead. "You wonderful bitch."

"Call me a bitch again and I'll stick you." Recki looked past Holden, seeing Khlid for the first time. "Okay, so Holden? Statues are coming to life and they're scary."

Khlid looked down at her own form. Not an inapt description from someone barely conscious.

Holden stood up straight and looked at Pirka, tears rolling down her face. He placed a hand gently on her good shoulder. "We've made it. The ship is sailing downriver toward the ocean."

"The price was high," she took a rattling breath. "I had to take the last of Chapman's medicine. It felt wrong."

A rumble shook the boat.

"What the Hell?" Holden said, touching his pistol.

"Engine," Recki said. "The fuckers managed to snag a powered boat."

"Amazing." Khlid placed a hand on the wall, feeling the vibrations.

As the ship left the river and entered the open sea, they felt stirrings of relief; there would be more troubles to come, gods knew, but they had escaped the Empire's reach for now. Holden knew the worst of this coming war was building on the horizon, but they had something now. Time.

Holden walked with Flip to their shared room.

Suddenly, he found himself holding the Grip for balance. "Sorry, just— uhh..." Holden's knee buckled, his vision churning.

"Holden! Somebody help!"

"No. So sorry." His voice was slurred. Something was terribly wrong. He couldn't figure out who had vomited on the floor below him.

"Holden, it's the Grohalind. You were exposed to too much. Almighty, what did Crom do? Someone help!"

Holden felt Flip's powerful, useless arms holding him, then felt nothing, as he began to convulse.

EPILOGUE

Weeks passed before Avi was able to return to her office at the M.O.D. After waiting for the Grohalind's poison to clear, the Ministry found repairing the buildings an arduous process. Hauling in marble and finding laborers was difficult. The people were rattled, and for days, hardly anyone populated the streets. A form of societal shock froze the city.

The Ministry organized marches to re-instill a sense of security in the people. Rebel corpses were displayed for all to see. Officially, only a few dozen Imperial soldiers, as compared with thousands of Rebels, had been killed.

In reality, five hundred sixty-two Imperial soldiers had died. Nearly as many civilians had been killed. Fewer than seven hundred Rebels had been killed in the conflict. Imperial soldiers had managed to take only two Rebels alive. One hanged himself in his cell with his belt. The other used the metal frame of her bed to slit her wrists.

The humiliation of total defeat stung all who knew the truth.

After weeks, a form of normalcy did return to the city. New construction concealed its wounds. New security measures were implemented. Avi oversaw response training for the city garrison in case of a similar future attack. Her presence in the city was trumpeted to the public. A demigod was watching over the capital city.

Though several precinct captains made public statements about the Ministries' abuses of power, several assassinations soon quieted the rats. Loyal replacements were installed as eyes and ears. The Ministry of Truth had released several stories blaming various captains for the attack. Their lack of oversight within their districts had allowed the rebellion to organize and strike.

At least, that's what the people believed now.

The Empire had been shaken, but stood strong.

Avi was overjoyed to see the highest voluntary enlistment numbers since the wars. It seemed the Rebels had not counted on the patriotism of the people. They felt attacked and they wanted blood.

Stories of Rebel attacks in the countryside and smaller cities were being fabricated now. After their brazen attack at the heart of the Empire, the Ministry of Truth could invent all manner of new Rebel atrocities. The masses would receive them eagerly.

Now Avi sat at her desk, reading espionage reports on the noble houses' doings behind closed doors. After the Burning, as the widespread Rebel attack was now being called, rumors about the Drip had spread amongst the nobles like wildfire. They had already disseminated that, should any more of their caste be struck in this hideous manner, it would not be a strike from the Almighty, but a brutal remonstration from the Ministries themselves.

Eager to quash the next potential uprising, Avi had placed a handful of trusted veteran agents undercover as servants to noble houses of concern. Performing menial labor for those considering treason was an embarrassing assignment to have to give her best lieutenants; but for now she deemed it necessary.

Unfortunately, all these weeks later, the lack of intelligence gathered was infuriating. Somehow, every one of her spies was being uncovered, iced out or fired. Nobles wouldn't dare escalate matters by killing a spy; and why would they, when they had succeeded in neutralizing them nonviolently?

We still have leaks from within.

A knock came at her door. "Come."

A tall man entered. His bright blue eyes and sleek hair complemented a toothy grin. "Avi, so wonderful to see you." The condescension in his voice was barely hidden. She wanted to tear his head off.

"So sorry to hear of what happened here in the city. I hope you didn't lose anyone too close to you." He punctuated the statement with a false look of concern.

"Well, Barrin, the responsibilities of watching over the Capital weigh heavy. I often envy those of us assigned to... lesser cities."

His eyebrow twitched as he dragged fingers across her desk. "Yes, I imagine you do."

"We have become complacent since the campaigns came home. The people have rested enough. It's time we put them back to work for the Almighty."

A darker woman entered her office without knocking. "The man out front is cute. Can I have him?"

At the sight of Rindah, Avi's fake smile for Barrin transformed to an authentic one. "Down, girl," Avi said. She stood and hugged Rindah. "No one in the M.O.D."

"Oh, but it's so much sweeter if I'm not supposed to." Rindah looked to Barrin. "Isn't it wonderful to be back with our own? The people of the lesser nations are so tiresome."

Avi poured herself and Rindah, but not Barrin, a drink. She felt a pang of annoyance at Rindah's remark. The two had met when Rindah had been stationed in Avi's homeland.

She dismissed the thought. She was an Imperial now; an Anointed. "You're home. Be sure to enjoy the Capital while you can."

"Oh, I plan to." Rindah took the drink. "Are the fighting pits still active?"

"Indeed they are."

"Well," Barrin interrupted, "if we could get to what's important? The ships are ready."

Avi looked at Barrin. "Already?"

Rindah nodded enthusiastically. "Every ship is armored and crewed with trained sailors."

Barrin flashed his dimple. "Three hundred steel-plated ships. Supplies have been secured, and new Anointed found to replace us when we leave."

Avi looked at the two Anointed with her and felt a deep connection with them. They had been blessed by the Almighty, brought above mortals to carry out the will of God. Tools of the heavens.

The Rebels had succeeded wildly, Avi had to give them that. The eyes placed within the Noble Class had found a substantial increase in backdoor meetings and plots; several of which were being held by the Empire's most powerful families. The Rebels had left behind the seeds of truth to divide the people from the military. But they had no idea how badly the odds were still stacked against them; how many moves ahead the Empire truly was. This New World already had Imperial agents digging in, planting the seeds of the Almighty among the people across the sea.

Prepare them, Khlid. Tell them what is coming to their shores. It will make no difference. The Almighty will still save this world.

Barrin walked to her desk and poured himself a drink. "The question is, Avi, do we have the soldiers?"

Avi grinned. "The people have been properly motivated to give us more than we could ever need."

Rindah shared her smile. "Then we sail to war."

ACKNOWLEDGMENTS

Thank you to everyone who supported me in this fantastic writing journey. I would not be here today if not for the support of my friends, family, and subscribers.

ABOUT THE AUTHOR

Daniel Greene is a fantasy YouTuber, entertainer, and with the publication of this book, author. He is known for his video reviews of various science fiction/fantasy works. You may also know him by his moniker, The Disheveled Goblin. You can find him posting videos to YouTube and streaming on Twitch. All you have to do is search his name.

twitter.com/DanielBGreene

instagram.com/dgreene101

youtube.com/DanielGreeneReviews

CPSIA information can be obtained
at www.ICGtesting.com
Printed in the USA
LVHW010954081121
702737LV00003B/94